D0373728
ACCEL·WORLD
06
SHRINE MAIDEN OF THE SACRED FIRE
REKI KAWAHARA
ILLUSTRATION BY HIMA
DESIGN BY bee-pee

IVORY TOWER
Burst Linker belonging to the White Legion, "Oscillatory Universe." Participates in the meeting of the Seven Kings as an avatar given the full proxy of the White King.
"Naturally, the agenda today is about the contamination of Silver Crow by the Armor of Catastrophe."
PURPLE THORN
Leader of the Purple Legion, "Aurora Oval." The Purple King; nickname: "Empress Voltage."
GREEN GRANDÉ
Leader of the Green Legion, "Great Wall." The Green King; nickname: "Invulnerable."

## YELLOW RADIO

Leader of the Yellow Legion, "Cosmic Crypt Circus." The Yellow King; nickname: "Radioactive Disturber."

"Good, so then everyone's here. Now then, I'd like to start the meeting of the Seven Kings."

## BLUE KNIGHT

Leader of the Blue Legion, "Leonids." The Blue King, with many nicknames such as "Vanquish" and "Legend Slayer," among others.

## SCARLET RAIN

Leader of the Red Legion, "Prominence." The Red King, nickname: "the Immobile Fortress."

"Please don't worry about this. I changed into my gym clothes before I came, ready for just such an eventuality."
UTAI SHINOMIYA
Elementary school student at Matsunogi Academy, which is affiliated with Umesato Junior High

"It takes a bit of time for my Incarnate technique to activate."
"C. You only have to do it once, but please defend against the enemy's attack.
ARDOR MAIDEN
Burst Linker particularly skilled at long-distance fighting

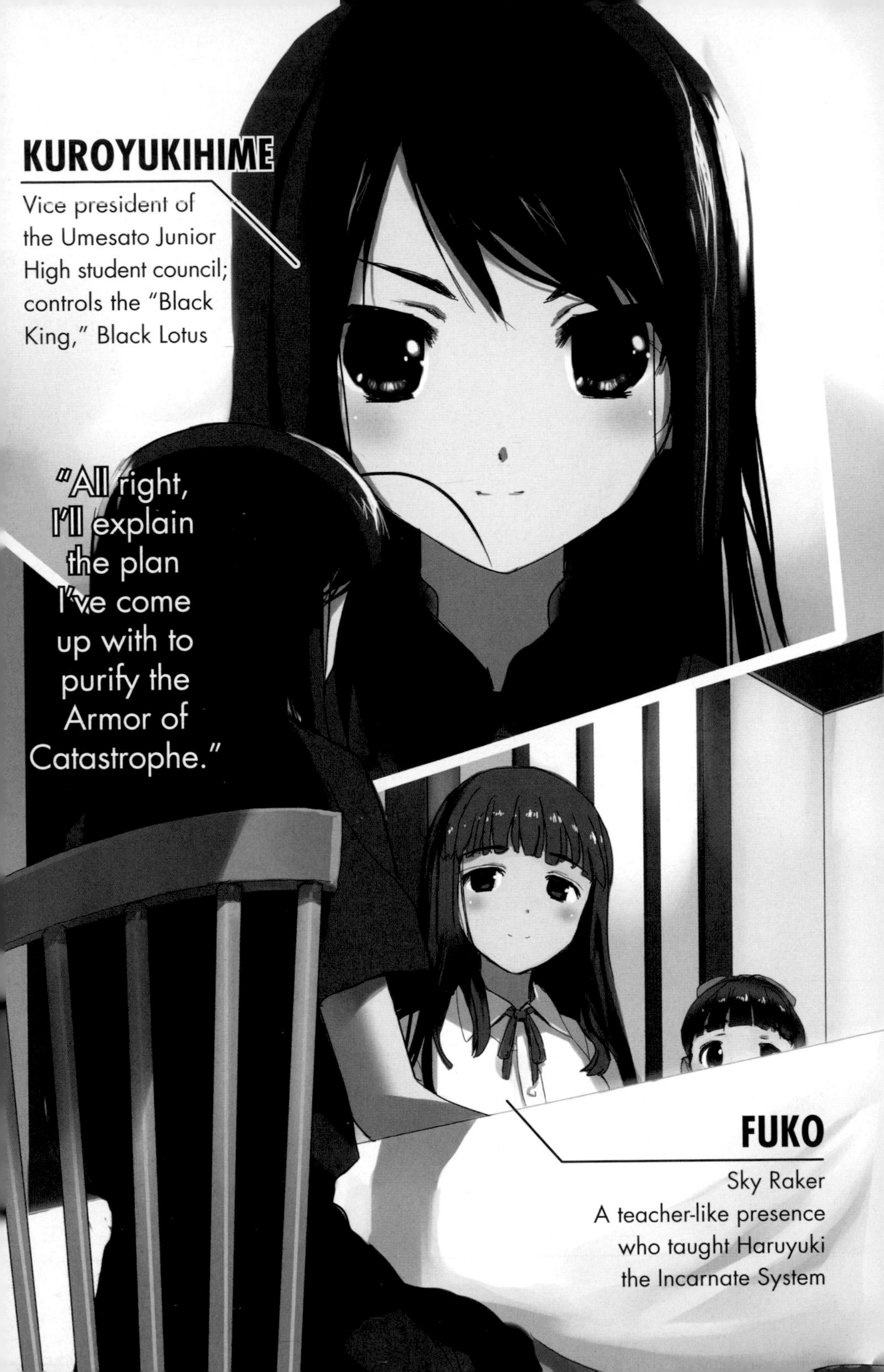
KUROYUKIHIME
Vice president of the Umesato Junior High student council; controls the "Black King," Black Lotus
"All right, I'll explain the plan I've come up with to purify the Armor of Catastrophe."
FUKO
Sky Raker
A teacher-like presence who taught Haruyuki the Incarnate System

HARURUYUKI
Boy in the lowest school caste
"......!!"
TAKUMU
Haruyuki's classmate and good friend
CHIYURI
Haruyuki's childhood friend

# DUEL AVATAR COMPATIBILITY IN BRAIN BURST

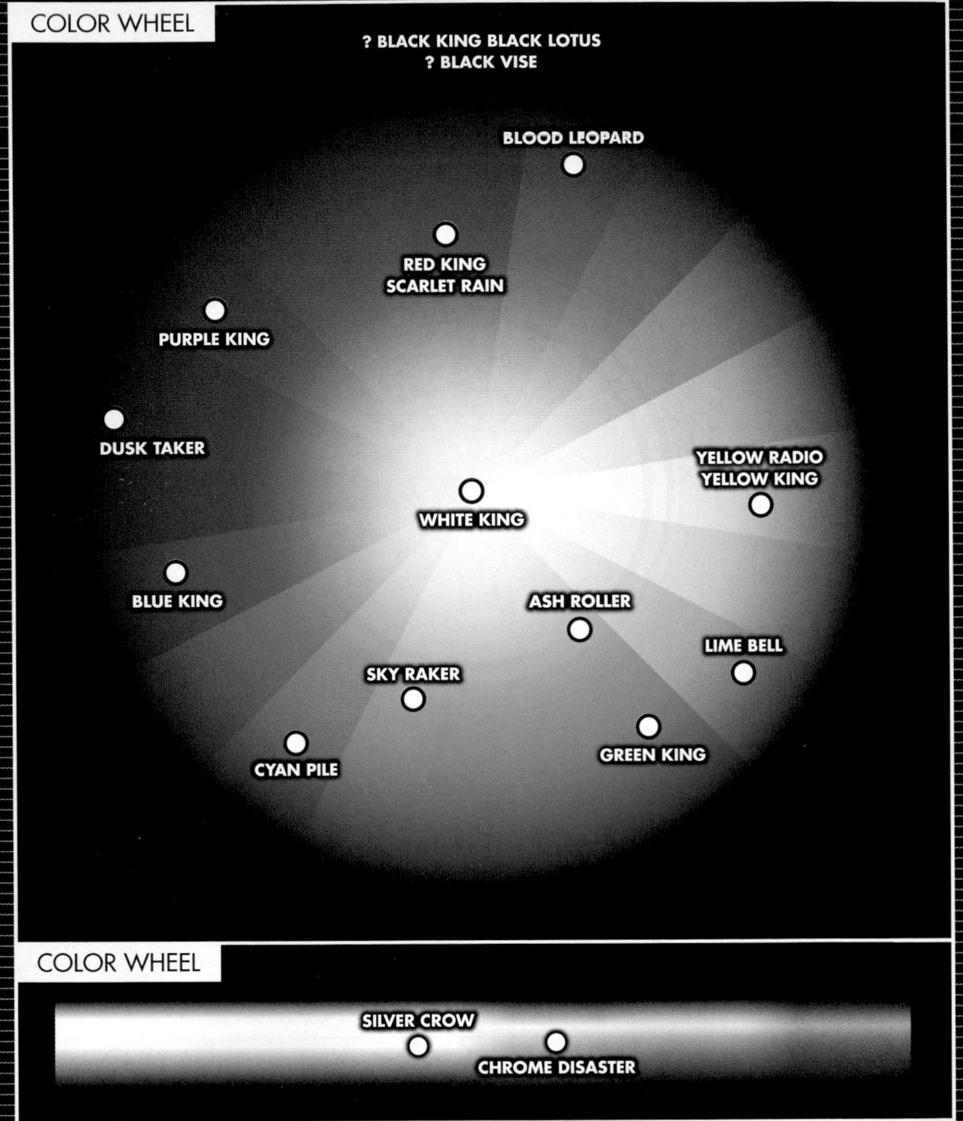


In the English names automatically given to Burst Linkers, a word that references color is always included. These colors allow players a rough grasp of the affinities of each duel avatar. Blue indicates close-range direct attacks; red is long-range direct attacks; and the yellow line of avatars is for mid-range attacks. Meanwhile, secondary colors such as purple and green have characteristics straddling the two color lines that combine to make them.

In addition to the colors on the color wheel, there are the metallic colors: those crowned with the names of metals. From the left of the chart, the colors are: platinum, gold, silver, chrome, bronze, and iron. Rather than attack traits, these colors indicate defensive abilities: The farther left the color on the chart, the greater that defensive ability against special attacks; and the farther right the color on the chart, the greater the defense against physical attacks. For instance, although Haruyuki's avatar, Silver Crow, has resistance to severing, piercing, flame, and poison attacks, he is weak to corrosion and hitting attacks.

# ACCEL·WORLD

## SHRINE MAIDEN OF THE SACRED FIRE

Reki Kawahara

Illustrations: HIMA

Design: bee-pee

NEW YORK

■ Kuroyukihime = Umesato Junior High School student council vice president. Trim and clever girl who has it all. Her background is shrouded in mystery. Her in-school avatar is a spangle butterfly she programmed herself. Her duel avatar is the Black King, Black Lotus (level nine).
■ Haruyuki = Haruyuki Arita. Grade eight at Umesato Junior High School. Bullied, on the pudgy side. He's good at games, but shy. His in-school avatar is a pink pig. His duel avatar is Silver Crow (level five).
■ Chiyuri = Chiyuri Kurashima. Haruyuki's childhood friend. Meddling, energetic girl. Her in-school avatar is a silver cat. Her duel avatar is Lime Bell (level four).
■ Takumu = Takumu Mayuzumi. A boy Haruyuki and Chiyuri have known since childhood. Good at kendo. His duel avatar is Cyan Pile (level five).
■ Fuko = Fuko Kurasaki. Masterful Burst Linker belonging to the old Nega Nebulus. Lived as a recluse due to certain circumstances, but is persuaded by Kuroyukihime and Haruyuki to come back to the battlefront. Taught Haruyuki about the Incarnate System. Her duel avatar is Sky Raker (level eight).

---

■ Neurolinker = A portable Internet terminal that connects with the brain via a wireless quantum connection; it enhances all five senses with images, sounds, and other stimuli.
■ In-school local net = Local area network established within Umesato Junior High School. Used during classes and to check attendance; while on campus, Umesato students are required to be connected to it at all times.
■ Global connection = Connection with the worldwide net. Global connections are forbidden on Umesato Junior High School grounds, where the in-school local net is provided instead.
■ Brain Burst = Neurolinker application sent to Haruyuki by Kuroyukihime.
■ Duel avatar = Player's virtual self operated when fighting in Brain Burst.
■ Legions = Groups composed of many duel avatars with the objective of expanding occupied areas and securing rights. There are seven main Legions, each led by one of the Seven Kings of Pure Color.
■ Normal Duel Field = The field where normal Brain Burst battles (one-on-one) are carried out. Although the specs do possess elements of reality, the system is essentially on the level of an old-school fighting game.
■ Unlimited Neutral Field = Field for high-level players where only duel avatars at level four and up are allowed. The game system is of a wholly different order than that of the Normal Duel Field, and the level of freedom in this field beats out even the next-generation VRMMO.

■ Movement Control System = System in charge of avatar control. Normally, this system handles all avatar movement.
■ Image Control System = System in which the player creates a strong image in their mind to operate the avatar. The mechanism is very different from the normal Movement Control System, and very few players can use it. Key component of the Incarnate System.
■ Incarnate System = Technique allowing players to interfere with Brain Burst's Image Control System to bring about a reality outside of the game's framework. Also referred to as "overwriting" game phenomena.

---

■ Acceleration Research Society = Mysterious Burst Linker group. They do not think of Brain Burst as a simple fighting game and are planning something. Black Vise and Rust Jigsaw are members.
■ Armor of Catastrophe = Enhanced Armament also called Chrome Disaster. Equipped with this, an avatar can use powerful abilities such as Drain, which absorbs the HP of the enemy avatar, and Divination, which calculates enemy attacks in advance to evade them. However, the spirit of the wearer is polluted by Chrome Disaster, which comes to rule the wearer completely.

ACCEL·WORLD

Brain Burst was a full-dive, competitive combat network game.

However, unlike similar games on the market, the servers on the global net did not determine the fight matchups.

The standard for matchups was the location of the real-world body of the player—the Burst Linker. Burst Linkers could not be paired up in a fight unless they were within the same particular section of the real world. In Brain Burst, this section was called an "area."

Area sizes were different in the city center than the other regions in the country. Within the twenty-three wards of Tokyo, a single ward generally had between two and four areas. Suginami Ward, for instance, was divided into three: Suginami areas one through three. For each of these areas, a list—the "matching list"—displayed all Burst Linkers currently present within the area. A player could either choose a duel opponent from this list to challenge or go into Standby mode and wait for an attack.

There was a total of approximately sixty areas in the twenty-three wards of Tokyo. Because nearly all of the roughly one thousand Burst Linkers lived in central Tokyo, there were roughly ten to twenty people registered on the matching list of any single area. Of course, this varied by place and time of day; a list of more than a hundred people around Shinjuku Station or in Akihabara on a weekend afternoon was not at all unusual.

When that many people gathered in one spot, occasionally something unexpected happened: The opponent a player had selected at random from the list would abruptly appear very close nearby in the duel stage—even mere meters away—or one of the duelers might, conversely, enter the stage from near the Gallery.

Brain Burst's VR duel stages were re-created from images captured by the network of high-resolution security cameras set up all over the real world, the so-called social camera network. Which meant that the buildings and roads within a stage—although given a variety of new facades in line with the randomized "affiliation" of the stage—were basically the same as those existing in the real world.

This meant that when two duel avatars appeared close to each other in this terrain, both players were also right in front of each other in the real world. This was relatively unpleasant, even dangerous, because exposing the real face or name of a Burst Linker—outing them "in the real"—was one of the Accelerated World's greatest taboos. Someone could take a Linker's photo and follow them, outing their address and real name, and anyone who had that information could kidnap the Burst Linker or threaten them in the real world with the intent to steal all of their burst points.

And although they were very few, extremists who would run the risk of this kind of violent criminal behavior did actually exist in the Accelerated World. They were known as Physical Knockers, or PKs for short, and although the major Legions insisted that the PKs be neutralized, simply having your name revealed was extremely distressing. Because, almost without exception, any Burst Linker attacked in such a manner lost all their points, and thus, the Brain Burst program itself, together with all related memories, preventing the player from ever returning to the Accelerated World. The likelihood of this happening was small, but the terrifying risk lurked under the surface of the passionate, excited crowds in the busy weekend areas.

Conversely, the possibility of being outed in the real in areas with a low population density of Burst Linkers was infinitely reduced. Of the twenty-three wards, the western part of Setagaya Ward, as well as around Ota and Edogawa Wards in general, were three such "depopulated" areas. For as large as they were, the number of people on the list was always low. Unexpectedly, the place in Tokyo where the danger of a near miss was lowest was thought to be the center of all the areas, Chiyoda Ward.

Chiyoda was the only one of the twenty-three wards not divided up into areas. It was one of the biggest areas, outside of the special, independent area of Akihabara, but more than that, there were essentially no Burst Linkers making the area their home ground. This was because up to 20 percent of Chiyoda Ward was the Imperial Palace, and that was somewhere your average city dweller could not go.

This rule also extended into the Accelerated World. In every stage was an Imperial Palace in a form matching the stage's affiliations, but a barrier stood in the center of the moat, preventing any entry into the palace itself; it was simply a vast prohibited zone in the center of the large city map. If a dueler were so inclined, they could easily assault their opponent with a single long-distance attack and then spend the next thirty minutes running around to win by decision.

Given the difficulty of fighting in this terrain, there weren't swarms of players looking to fight in Chiyoda, especially in comparison with the fighting meccas of Akihabara to the immediate north and Shinjuku to the west. Thus, the Chiyoda Area matching list was always almost entirely empty of names. This was not to say, however, that the area was without value.

Given the area's location in the center of Tokyo, the risk of a real-body near miss was low. This feature gave rise to an unexpected use for the Chiyoda Ward: a place for negotiating, rather than dueling. When powerful enemies wanted to make contact whilst keeping to the barest minimum the possibility of being outed, the vast and desolate Chiyoda Ward served quite well.

For these reasons…

SUNDAY, JUNE 16, 2047. 1:45 PM.

Kuroyukihime, aka Black Lotus, the Black King, and leader of the Legion Nega Nebulus; Fuko Kurasaki, controller of the duel avatar Sky Raker and Legion deputy; and Haruyuki Arita, aka Silver Crow, a junior member who fought alongside them, sat in a small electric vehicle parked in Fujimi Nichome, Chiyoda Ward, Tokyo, waiting for the time negotiations were to start.

No, these negotiations were not to be simple talks between separate Legions.

Because, at two PM, a meeting of all seven Kings of Pure Color would begin. They were coming together for only the second time in the entire eight-year history of the Accelerated World.

# 1

"Is this your car, Master?" Haruyuki asked abruptly from the backseat, unable to completely overcome the nervousness he felt at the upcoming meeting of the Seven Kings.

"Not likely." In the driver's seat, "Master"—aka Fuko—turned her head, surprised. "It's my mother's. There's totally no way I could buy a car on my allowance. I'm still in high school."

"I—I guess so!"

The EV was cutely rounded, the light, cream-yellow interior real leather, and an emblem patterned after a snake and a cross sat in the middle of the steering wheel. It was the mark of an old Italian automaker Haruyuki knew very well. The price was probably well beyond what any young person with a job could afford, much less a university student.

"You just seem really used to driving it, so I thought maybe. So…you paid for your license yourself, I guess?"

"Ha-ha, of course." The answer to his timidly voiced second question came not from Fuko, but rather Kuroyukihime in the passenger seat. "Fuko turned sixteen this year, which means she's a grown-up now. She can get her license and get married, unlike the rest of us."

"Sacchi, don't put it like that…"

*Huh. So she's a grown-up, huh?* Haruyuki shook his head

quickly at this momentarily unsteadying thought and got his head back on track.

They had in fact lowered the age at which you could obtain a regular automobile driver's license from eighteen to sixteen, seven or eight years ago. The reason was ostensibly that the rate of traffic accidents had dropped dramatically with the completion of the social camera network and vehicle control AI being made mandatory, but this, in fact, seemed to not be the whole story.

Japan in the 2040s was on the brink of a total collapse of the nation's social security system due to the unbounded decline in the birth rate and the rapidly aging population. The generation currently working could no longer completely support public expenditures such as medical and caregiving costs, what with public pensions increasing year after year, too. Thus, it appeared the government intended to also increase the number of young people legally allowed to work by lowering the age at which a person could obtain certifications or qualifications, typified by the driver's license. In fact, the Labor Standards Act had also been revised at the same time to allow young people to enter into full-time employment from the age of sixteen.

In other words, in the eyes of the law, Fuko was already more adult than child. And given that she was fifteen that year, Kuroyukihime would be in the same position the following year. Haruyuki's time, too, would come in a mere two years. Obviously, he wasn't actually going to get a job right after finishing junior high, so in practical terms, he would continue to be a child, but even still, he couldn't help but feel a certain uneasiness about the whole thing.

*Just how long can I keep being the me that I am now?*

After this thought popped into his head, Haruyuki laughed wryly to himself. He had for some time now felt the longing to not be the him he had been back then, to run off somewhere far away. And it wasn't like this desire had vanished. He hated the way he looked, and he still couldn't get himself to like junior high.

But if some godlike presence had come along just then and said it could make him a different person in a different place, he would no doubt have refused. This place—the backseat of the car Fuko was driving in the short term, his own corner of the Accelerated World as a Burst Linker in the long term—or, put differently, his place as a player of Brain Burst, boasting as it did a vast scale and incredible detail, a game that gave him endless thrills… He could ask for nothing more, not a single thing.

But even this wouldn't last forever.

Brain Burst was a game. And a game had to end at some point. In fact, the reason Haruyuki and Kuroyukihime fought was precisely in order to reach that ending.

He didn't know at that point what form this ending would take. He had no idea if Kuroyukihime would reach her long-sought level ten, thus ending the entire game of Brain Burst itself, or if the right to play would be mercilessly ripped away with the inevitable arrival of the end of their childhood, or if some other ending entirely awaited them.

Which was exactly why he had to give it everything he had now. He would throw all his energy into playing, into having fun, into protecting. Into this world where he and the people he loved could be together.

Haruyuki clenched his hands into fists as he made this vow in his heart in the somewhat small rear seat. But he soon remembered the situation he was in and let out a deep sigh. If he was honest with himself, he was in no position to be talking tough about protecting anything.

First on the agenda for the meeting of the Seven Kings, less than twenty minutes from that moment, were countermeasures for the Acceleration Research Society, the mysterious and destructive organization that had suddenly appeared in the world of Brain Burst. But the second item was how to deal with the impossibly resurrected Enhanced Armament, the Armor of Catastrophe, Chrome Disaster.

Both of these issues had been, until a mere week earlier, nothing but talk up in the clouds for level-fiver Haruyuki. He had been content to simply gaze on from the sidelines as the kings and those closest to them debated such matters. But he had now been dragged far from the sidelines and forced to stand center stage.

Because the one who had brought back from oblivion the Armor of Catastrophe to become the sixth-generation Chrome Disaster was Silver Crow—Haruyuki himself.

"No need to be nervous, Haruyuki."

He jerked his head up at the gentle words coming from the front seat.

The owner of the voice suddenly pulled the lever to recline the passenger seat and leaned way back. Hurriedly fleeing to the driver's side, Haruyuki watched as the seat fell into a fully flat position. Long black hair flowed down, some of it touching Haruyuki's knees.

Unusually for her, Kuroyukihime was out of uniform today and in a tight-fitting, patterned T-shirt with slim gray jeans. She had layered on top of that a thin, short-sleeved shirt made of punched leather. Black, of course, in contrast with Fuko's more feminine ivory dress with leggings that reached midcalf, but Kuroyukihime's crisp, almost terrifying beauty was not lessened in the slightest.

Now lying down in front of Haruyuki, she stretched out her right hand, grabbed on to the collar of his T-shirt with her fingertips, and yanked him toward her. He pitched forward and a sweet fragrance wafting up to his nose, different from the scent of the car, and the gears in his brain ground almost to a halt.

"You have nothing to be afraid of. It's okay. I won't let those kings lay a hand on you. I'll protect you."

As she murmured the words so close to his face, he felt even dizzier, but he forced himself to put his brain into gear again. "Th-thank you," he replied. "But…all the other kings naturally want to take action against Silver Crow, right? Which means… the Judgment Blow from the Legion Master."

"I suppose they do."

"Won't...won't it be bad for you if you refuse? Like, I mean, in terms of your standing or whatever?"

Haruyuki knew from experience just how cruel a majority wearing the mantle of justice could be. The delinquents who had so ruthlessly bullied him in seventh grade hadn't started doing so out of some irrational violent impulse. They had first approached him under the guise of friendship, and the instant Haruyuki refused their invitation and tried to put some distance between them, they bared their fangs in the name of friendship betrayed.

And this time, in theory, the odds were likely not with Kuroyukihime, but with the kings. The Armor of Catastrophe was a curse to which too many had been sacrificed since the dawn of the Accelerated World, and Haruyuki knew only too well that it needed to disappear. He had actually been working on annihilating it himself for a while now. But if that proved impossible, then the Armor would have to be dealt with, together with the Burst Linker who owned it. If Kuroyukihime rejected this "just" opinion, what kind of mental and physical pressure would the kings put on her? That was Haruyuki's concern. But...

"Ha-ha-ha! After all this time? What are you talking about?" He blinked rapidly at the light laughter that came flying his way. Then Kuroyukihime's smile took on a daring edge. "I'm already their enemy," she intoned quietly. "I won't have anything to do with their idiotic nonaggression pact, either. And if they have any complaints, the kings could just come at me themselves in a duel. Although that is exactly what I want."

"...Kuroyukihime..."

*Seriously. She's just so strong, so cool...so awesome.*

Of course, Haruyuki didn't have the ability to take the deep emotions in his heart and put them into words; all he could do was stare wholeheartedly at the obsidian eyes twinkling so near his own face.

The sharp glint in her eyes softened, and as she met his gaze, she smiled gently, softly. Her lips moved slightly, and her barely audible

whisper rippled in the air between them. "Now that I'm thinking about it, you've been the one protecting me right from the start, hmm?" Fingers stretched out effortlessly to caress his cheek.

"That's...," Haruyuki somehow managed to reply hoarsely, heart pounding. "That's not true at all. I'm the one who's—"

But Kuroyukihime ran her index finger along his cheek, shutting down any arguments. "I'm your 'parent.' I have the *right* to protect you. Which is why you should simply lean on me now. You don't have to say anything."

"...Kuroyukihime." His eyes still locked with hers and, chest suddenly full, her name was as much as Haruyuki could manage.

The swordmaster returned a gentle nod and, fingertips still on his cheek, she softly repeated, "I promise. I will protect you."

"...Okay. Okay...I trust *yngerk*!"

A mess of noise drowned out the end of his sentence, as he was crushed by the driver's seat back dropping onto him abruptly.

A hand reached over the edge of the seat to yank on Haruyuki's left ear, followed by Fuko's face popping out, cheeks puffed out. "Look, Sacchi!" she said indignantly.

"Corvus! Getting carried away all by yourselves in someone else's car is not okay!"

It was almost 2:30 PM by the time the front seats had been returned to their original positions and Haruyuki had pushed himself deep into the backseat. Outside, the mid-June sky was slightly cloudy, a bit grumpy, but they could see pops of pale blue here and there. A sudden thunderstorm seemed unlikely, so there was no need to worry about Neurolinker connection problems.

Kuroyukihime cleared her throat lightly. "This meeting is not going to be in Battle Royale mode," she said, sounding much more nervous. "Not everyone connected is going to be a duel opponent. Instead, the duel is between our host, the Blue King, and a close associate, with the rest of us automatically diving as the Gallery. Which means we don't need to consider the risk of anyone attacking us."

"Um…Even attacks via the Incarnate System?"

"Yes," Fuko replied. "Even if someone were to try and use Incarnate, it's impossible for the Gallery to attack or be attacked in a general duel field. Members of the Gallery come into the stage without HP gauges. The reason both participants and spectators got hurt by Rust Jigsaw's Incarnate in the Hermes' Cord race last week was because of the Special Field status. Everyone had HP gauges, but the values were locked."

"Oh, that's right…I just…Somehow, it's like…," Haruyuki muttered unintelligibly.

"Somehow," Kuroyukihime interrupted quietly, "it's as if an opening was deliberately left for someone to use Incarnate to destroy the race. Is that it?"

He hurriedly shook his head. "Huh? N-no, I wouldn't go that far." Because if he did, he would be forced to accept what inevitably followed from that thought: that the developer of Brain Burst approved of Rust Jigsaw's destructive behavior.

But there was no way. That couldn't be true. The exact motives of the unknown developer were still a mystery, but Haruyuki had come to feel a nebulous sort of respect for him or her as a gamer. A person who could build and maintain this sort of fun, exciting, and totally compulsive game—no, *world*—would never help anyone who played as dirty as the Acceleration Research Society.

"Haruyuki." Kuroyukihime's gentle voice called him out of his thoughts when he began to forcefully grind his teeth. "Listen. Remember this at least: The main actor in the Accelerated World is each and every Burst Linker. This means you as well. The choice of how you'll commit to this world is left entirely to you. Whatever the intentions of the developer."

"…Right!" He nodded fervently, while the clock in the edge of his field of view announced that they had ten seconds to go.

"Good answer. All right, then, everyone: Open a global connection."

At their Legion Master's instruction, all three pushed their Neurolinker link buttons. The global net connection display flashed, followed by the connection status, and then about two seconds after these icons disappeared—

*Skreeeeee!!* The sound of acceleration filled Haruyuki's senses. The flaming text A REGISTERED DUEL IS BEGINNING! burned brilliantly in the center of his vision.

# 2

A sky filled with a curious yellow-green light. Ground covered in blue-black tiles. Clusters of buildings adorned with fanged protrusions, and a thick fog flowing down, out, and around these.

"A Demon City stage? Well, I suppose it's a good match for today's agenda," the Black King, Black Lotus, said, each step of her sharply pointed tiptoes ringing out on the tiles.

After staring momentarily at the fluid, ferocious figure of the Legion Master he so loved and respected, he let his eyes rest on the sky-blue avatar standing next to her inconspicuously. Simple and graceful, she had thick, blue-tinted hair that flowed like wings down the back of her slender, feminine body. The smooth lines of her legs and arms showed no sign of any equipped weaponry.

But Haruyuki knew. He knew that those thin legs themselves, planted firmly on the ground at that moment and keeping the avatar upright, were proof of the miracle that had happened with her—Sky Raker.

If Black Lotus was the swordmaster and Haruyuki's "parent," then Raker would have to be his teacher, his Master. She had retreated from the accelerated duels that were the world's battlefront to live for a long time as a recluse at the top of the old Tokyo Tower, a place forgotten by everyone else.

Because two and a half years earlier, she had, of her own volition, cut off both legs at the knee, and with them, the better part of her fighting power. However, after meeting Haruyuki, who had also temporarily lost his own power—the ability to fly—and initiating him into the ways of the Incarnate System, she gradually regained her passion for the duel until finally, in the Hermes' Cord race the week before, she was able to overcome the psychic trauma that had bound her and recover both legs.

After being taken over by Chrome Disaster even just that one time, Haruyuki knew in his bones how very difficult it was to get out from under the influence of negative imagination. Most likely, if Chiyuri—Lime Bell—hadn't helped him with her special attack—her transcendental ability to turn back time for the target avatar—Haruyuki would have been swallowed up by the armor and his own self-hatred and indiscriminately attacked the hundreds of people in the Gallery.

In only a few minutes, the negative will of the Armor had penetrated his marrow, so much so that he had been on the verge of never finding his way back. And yet Sky Raker had somehow managed to cut the chains of fear and despair that had held her for two and a half years of real time. If that wasn't a miracle, then what was? Struck by deep emotion, he stared hard at Raker's legs.

"Honestly, Corvus. Do you like my beautiful legs that much?" she said in a voice filled with mirth.

Haruyuki hurriedly waved his hands somewhat frantically in front of his face. "N-no—I mean, of course, they're incredibly beautiful, but that's not what I was—"

"Oh ho! So you have a leg fetish? Sorry I don't have calves or ankles." Kuroyukihime spoke now, her violet-blue eyes glittering dangerously.

"Th-that's—!" Haruyuki turned his head and excused himself again. "I love your legs, too—I mean, it's not like I have a fetish or anything like that, okay?!" He felt like he would just sink further into this swamp if he said anything more, so he pointed southeast and shouted, "A-a-anyway, look! The guide cursor's pointing that way! Let's hurry! Let's get going!"

Just as Haruyuki noted, the two gray triangles in the center of their fields of view were still, pointing in the same direction. Beyond them lay the two members of the Blue Legion executive who were hosting that day's meeting. Two HP gauges were also lined up above the cursors, with a countdown between them. The timer would have started at 1,800 seconds but had already dropped to 1,750.

"Mmm. Now that you mention it, we did say to ensure that we met within a hundred seconds. That does it, then. Shall we run?"

All three nodded and took off as one south along the roads of the Demon City.

In exchange for not having the right to destroy the terrain or objects, members of the Gallery in a general duel were given maximum mobility and jumping power. Haruyuki and his Legion Masters ran up the wall of a building blocking their way and then charged forward in a straight line from rooftop to rooftop.

After they had been running for about twenty seconds, the heavy fog blanketing the road ahead abruptly broke.

"Whoa!" Haruyuki unconsciously cried out at the sight spreading out before their eyes. "I-it's huge..."

The palace.

An enormous building soared up as if to pierce the sky a little to the southeast of the cursor. Made up of steel spires shining with a blue light and bizarre sculptures, the palace stood in the center of the demonic stage with a sense of presence that overwhelmed all else; it was almost even divine. The building was surrounded by high castle walls and a wide moat, with nothing remotely resembling an entrance to be seen.

Although he had caught glimpses of the palace rising up in the distant eastern sky from countless duels in Suginami and Shinjuku, this was the first time he had ever been so close to it, and he gaped as he took in the majesty of the colossal castle.

"In the real world, *that* is the Imperial Palace," Kuroyukihime murmured, immediately to his right. "The only place you can never enter, in the Accelerated World as well, no matter what you try."

"E-even if you're flying?"

"Yes." The answer to his question came from Fuko running to his left. "There are invisible barriers set above and below the castle walls, so you can't get in even if you try to fly over or dig under. Apparently, in the early days, people tried all sorts of things, but..."

"Mm-hmm. There were any number of rumors, too, that there was a super-amazing Enhanced Armament hidden inside, things like that. But in the end, not one person was able to penetrate those walls. In the Normal Duel Field, at least."

Sensing something in Kuroyukihime's phrasing, Haruyuki asked in response, "Huh? What do you mean?"

However, before she could give him an answer, Fuko said sharply, "I see it. On top of that hill!"

He turned his gaze in the direction she pointed. And indeed, there, on the top of a small hill ahead of them, he could see two—no, three small human figures. The place probably corresponded with the East Gardens of the Imperial Palace in the real world. Unlike the palace, this area was open to the general public; Haruyuki himself had been there a long time ago, on a social studies field trip in elementary school.

Slowing slightly, he approached cautiously. Although they were participating as the Gallery and there was no possibility of being attacked, he couldn't keep himself from shaking at just the thought that he was about to finally have a close-up encounter with the Seven Kings of Pure Color, the rulers of the Accelerated World.

They crossed the bridge over the wide moat, slipped through a magnificent gate, and climbed the stairs set into the slope of the hill. The utterly impenetrable Demon Castle stood to their immediate right, but Haruyuki didn't even glance at it, instead training his gaze exclusively on the top of the hill. The stairs finally came to an end, and an expansive space covered in paving stones opened up before his eyes.

In the real world, this would have been the lawn of the remains of the inner citadel of Edo Castle. But not a single plant grew here; there was only a stand of steel pillars, forming a large circle. For some reason, however, a single pillar on the other side was noticeably shorter, only fifty or so centimeters tall.

And on it sat a duel avatar.

*Blue.* A deep, somehow transparent blue that threatened to suck any viewers in. It was not the color of the sky, nor of the sea. The avatar's entire body was a pure blue, so pure that a real object that color would have been hard, if not impossible, to find.

The armor shape marked it as a perfect knight type, but without a shred of the ominousness of the Armor of Catastrophe; a gallant figure, the hero of legends. Dragon-like horns stretched out on both sides of the visored helmet, while a two-handed longsword hung from the left hip.

The blue avatar, who had adopted a relaxed pose—both arms crossed, left leg on right knee—was not that large. Standing, he was most likely the same height as Takumu while in Cyan Pile. However, his entire being emanated an overwhelming force, a meteorite hurtling toward the earth through space, and Haruyuki stopped when they were still more than twenty meters away from him.

"Th that's...," he said in a hoarse voice, and Raker next to him nodded slightly.

"Yes. That's the leader of Leonids, the Legion ruling the areas of Shinjuku and Bunkyo. The level niner also known as 'Vanquish,' 'Legend Slayer,' and many other nicknames, the Blue King, Blue Knight."

"Blue...Knight..."

It was an extremely simple name, the sort that would get attached to some small-fry monster in any other game, but hearing it in the Accelerated World, there was something about the name that made Haruyuki conversely feel the absolute uniqueness of it.

A shiver ran up his spine at the fathomless air of intimidation before he finally remembered that the knight was not actually his duel opponent. In terms of position, they were both simply members of the Gallery. That Haruyuki would feel this kind of force from an observer with absolutely no actual fighting power, without an HP gauge even…Just thinking about the hypothetical possibility of getting stuck in a one-on-one duel was terrifying.

At that moment, he heard a slight ringing sound and the ice in his heart receded slightly. It was the sound of Kuroyukihime taking a single step forward. The Black King, Black Lotus, moved forward several steps as if to say the fierce air of the Blue King was nothing more than a gentle breeze to her, and then waved the sword of her right hand lightly.

"You're the host today, so I'll let you save face and say my greetings first. You look suffocating as always, Knight."

At Kuroyukihime's words, Haruyuki shrieked in his head, *You're practically sticking your tongue out and challenging him to a fight!* When Raker laughed softly next to him, he got ready to flee with a frantic back dash, but fortunately, the blue warrior was faster than he was.

"Now, look, that's no greeting, Lotus," he said in the clear and cool voice of a young boy. "I haven't seen you in two and a half years, and you're just as crabby as ever." His armor clanged as he shrugged his shoulders. At the same time, the bloodlust he had been radiating vanished as if it had never been at all.

From his tone, the Blue King appeared to be much more affable than Haruyuki had been expecting. The Blue Legion attacked Black territory without fail every week, so he had assumed that the King himself would certainly be burning to censure Kuroyukihime, but unexpectedly, this appeared not to be the case.

Just as Haruyuki relaxed his shoulders, two very similar human forms silently slid out of the heavy fog to linger on either side of the Blue King.

*Traditional warriors!* was his immediate thought. Complete sets of Japanese armor covered the slender, tall figures, layers of rectangular metal panels. The avatar on the left was a deep ultramarine, and on the right, a fairly bright blue green. Rather than full *kabuto* helmets, they had armored *hachigane* headbands tied around their foreheads, and their bound hair hung long. From the size and shape of their bodies, both were female types.

The two female warriors advanced several meters with a strange way of walking that was more like gliding, placed a hand on the grip of the sword dangling from each left hip, and spoke quietly at the same time.

"You who sneers before our Vanquish does not deserve the title of king!"

"The traitor should be grateful she's even allowed in this place!"

And then, again, a bloodlust to make the air tremble jetted in the direction of the Nega Nebulus delegation, and Haruyuki squeaked.

As the Black King's follower, he likely should have fought back, tossing off a similarly cool line right then and there, but he felt like they would send his head flying the moment he uttered a single word, and he was unable to even open his mouth. There was no doubt that these were the Blue King's aides, the ones who had generated the field—in other words, the duelers—and thus they alone had the right to remove any obstructive members of the Gallery, as long as they both agreed on which members those might be.

However, in the next moment, Sky Raker replied in a voice filled with laughter. "Goodness, I don't see you for a while and you manage to find your big-girl pants, hmm, ladies?" Moving to stand next to Kuroyukihime, her high heels clacking, she stretched out the palm of her right hand to the warriors and waggled her fingertips. "I'm ready to hang both of you from the top of the government building again anytime, you know?"

*Eeeeeeee!* Haruyuki screamed silently once more. *Did you really just say that?!* he shouted in his heart before accepting that

Sky Raker was just the sort of person to say that much at the *very* least.

A blazing anger flared up in the almond-shaped eye lenses of the armored warriors, and they grabbed the hilts of their swords simultaneously.

"You—!"

The shout, two voices in perfectly synchrony, was interrupted from behind by the wry laugh of the Blue King. "Let's stop right there, Cobalt, Manga."

"...Fine." The pair quickly bowed deeply and took a step back at the same time.

Haruyuki breathed a sigh of relief before once again staring at the two HP gauges lined up in the top of his field of view. Underneath the left-hand gauge shone the avatar name Cobalt Blade, while under the right was Manganese Blade. Given the amount of overlap in name and appearance, they must have been fairly similar in the real world as well. If, for instance, they were twin sisters, the Blue King really had to be an incredible person in many ways to be able to inspire both to follow him like this as his closest aides. This and other random thoughts wandered through his brain, while Kuroyukihime opened her mouth again, shrugging lightly.

"So then, Knight. Maybe you could get me a chair so you're not the only one sitting?"

"Whoops. Excuse me." With a wave of his hand, the Blue King signaled his two aides.

They dropped into fighting stances immediately to brace themselves and set hands on the hilts of their swords once more. Haruyuki didn't even have the time to jump and shrink back before two beams of pale light sliced a broad circle around the stage, accompanied by the clear, high-pitched *clang* of metal.

Reopening his eyes, Haruyuki saw a blurry mess of motion in the warriors' hands, swords glittering for an instant before being returned to their sheaths; the whole scene wouldn't have taken up even three frames of a film.

This show was immediately followed by a thin break in the white, thickly flowing fog, and then the massive pillars soaring up on either side of the warriors began to fall soundlessly in groups of two, as if chasing that fog. The six columns crashed into the earth, setting off successive waves of sound rumbling the earth, and shattered into countless blue-black metallic chunks. All that remained were stumps with mirror-smooth cross sections.

"N-no way…," Haruyuki could only mutter, stunned.

He was sure that the affiliation of this general duel field was Demon City. And the first characteristic of the Demon City was abnormally hard-terrain objects. Back when he had been training in the Incarnate System, he had only been able to dig a few centimeters into the wall of a Demon City building, and he had needed a full week of intense training just to be able to do that much. And yet Cobalt Blade and Manganese Blade had, with a flash of their swords, simultaneously cut down three pillars each. Haruyuki had no doubt that if he had been standing in place of one of those pillars, his head and torso would have been severed from each other in a single blow.

So that was the actual power of the most elite Leonid Linkers. Which meant the king's power would be even greater.

*I—we, we're trying to fight people like this…*

The incredibly deep horror made his avatar shudder all over when he felt an unexpected pat on his back.

Sky Raker, the dazzling avatar bearing no weaponry of any kind brought her mouth to Haruyuki's ear. "Chopping down immobile pillars is a parlor trick, Corvus. You look so freaked out right now, and you know you'll be punished for it later. ♥"

She left him as he snapped to attention and the Black King, together with her sworn friend, began to walk calmly toward the pillar stump closest to them. Kuroyukihime alone sat down, while Raker took up a place standing behind her. Haruyuki, fearing the punishment of his teacher Raker more than the blades of the warrior avatars, could only hurry after them and stand next to her, arms crossed and chest thrust out.

The warriors also retreated behind their master, and the hush that instantly fell over the stage was broken by Kuroyukihime.

"Now then, greetings to the inviting king are finished, so how about you all show your faces already?" she said, slightly exasperated. "One hundred seconds have long since passed, you know."

Indeed, the counter was already cutting into 1,600 seconds. But what did she mean by "show your faces"? There were still only the six members of the Blue and Black Legions there…

This thought in mind, Haruyuki was about to search the stage with his eyes, but before he could, a voice that held both innocent childishness and immoveable strength rang out from somewhere, followed by a gentle footfall.

"Dang. What's with that tone, Lotus? And here I was being respectful."

He lifted his face with a gasp to see a single silhouette appear about three meters to the right on an adjacent stump. A dark red avatar, erect, with a form reminiscent of a carnivorous beast. He didn't have to see the triangular pointed ears or the long tail to know that this was a senior member of the Red Legion, Prominence, nicknamed "Bloody Kitty": Blood Leopard.

And seated on her left arm was a small crimson avatar, the owner of the voice. Two antennae stretching out like pigtails. Round, cute eye lenses. Curved, smooth armor on her limbs. Her coloring coupled with her tiny size made her almost like a single ruby. But this adorable little girl was the leader of Prominence, ruler of the Nerima and Nakano areas, the Red King, Scarlet Rain.

She didn't have equipped the massive firepower containers from which her nickname "Immobile Fortress" came. Staring at her cute profile, Haruyuki opened his mouth to call to them: *Rain, Pard!* But the two red avatars emitted an aura that was just as fierce as that of the Blue King, and he clamped his mouth shut again.

It was different from the overlay of the Incarnate System; it was an invisible, pure fighting spirit. Although this was the Accelerated World, where all things were set in digital code, this phenomenon of "feeling auras" was no illusion. In terms of the logic, a rather occult explanation could be offered—that the aura was perhaps the weight of the battle history information within a duel avatar, coded as an exertion of physical pressure on another person—but in fact, it was simply that the truly strong overwhelmed the lower ranks with their presence alone, in just the way these two red avatars were making Haruyuki cower.

The Red King, real name Yuniko Kozuki aka Niko; Blood Leopard, aka Pard; and Haruyuki were all friends; they had all exposed their true identities to one another in the real. And Prominence and Nega Nebulus had concluded a ceasefire treaty of unlimited term after fighting together in the past. That said, however, their faces clearly communicated that their relationship was nowhere near the sort where they could be familiar with each other and hang out no matter the time or place. Haruyuki felt that this was the right course, although it did make him a little sad. But everyone who possessed Brain Burst was there to fight and grow stronger.

No.

In truth, there was one other reason why it was hard for Haruyuki to face Niko.

As Legion Master, Niko was supposed to have annihilated Chrome Disaster, thought to be parasitizing Silver Crow at that moment, with a Judgment Blow to her own "parent," the Armament's previous owner. So, in a certain sense, Niko's motivation for seeking the death penalty for Haruyuki was greater than that of any of the other kings coming together in that spot.

He forcibly stopped himself from pushing his thoughts further in this direction and turned to face forward again. At the same time, Blood Leopard's low voice reached his ears.

"Just me and the king from Promi. Greetings omitted."

Jumping down from her lieutenant's arm, Niko sat herself on the steel stool and Leopard stepped back to her rear, hands on her hips.

With that, three of the seven kings were together. The Blue King sat on the centermost of the seven amputated pillars, which were arranged in a semicircle. The Black King faced him on the right end, and to her right was the Red King.

Haruyuki braced himself for who would come next and from where.

"Heh. Heh-heh-heh..." Rather than footsteps, a throaty, high-pitched voice echoed from the distant side of the fog.

He had definitely heard this laugh, filled with obvious scorn and ridicule, somewhere else, but he couldn't tell which direction it was coming from. He whirled his head to look around, but each time, the source seemed to cut around behind him.

"Heh-heh...King, hmm? I do believe *king* is supposed to be short for the Seven Kings of Pure Color, if my memory's correct? But isn't the coloring of the little one sitting there a tad too cheap to be red, hmm?" The words flung from the fog were clearly meant to mock Scarlet Rain.

Niko was the only second-generation king among the rulers of the seven major Legions. The previous Red King, Red Rider, had had his head cut off two and a half years earlier in a single strike by the Black King, and had been forced to leave the Accelerated World forever due to the sudden-death rule that applied to fights between level niners. Niko had revived Prominence when it was on the verge of collapse and named herself its new master. Her avatar was indeed a slightly bright scarlet rather than a pure red, but that was absolutely no reason to treat her like an impostor. Because—

"C-color's got nothing to do with it! Rain climbed to level nine under her own power, and there's no other requirement for being a king!"

—is why.

And here, Haruyuki finally realized that he was the one who had shouted the thought rolling around in his brain. Raker giggled next to him, and Niko herself, seated not far from him, appeared to be smiling wryly.

“The crow over there took the words from my mouth, so I’ll just add one thing. If you wanna talk cheap, your banana color’d give me a good run for my money. But we don’t have time for this. Just come out already,” the Red King said, and snapped the fingers of her right hand to point at the middle pillar in line with her, three removed.

Hurriedly directing his gaze that way, Haruyuki realized that a tiny paper doll was standing on a stump he had simply assumed was empty. Cocking his head about five centimeters to one side, he finally understood. It was an observer dummy avatar, just like the one Kuroyukihime had used to gather information in the Accelerated World when she was in hiding from the kings’ assassins. The voice’s owner had taken advantage of the fact that they were connecting to the field as the Gallery to change his avatar into something extremely inconspicuous.

As soon as Haruyuki came to this realization, white smoke puffed up from the paper doll’s center. The smoke was carried away by the slight wind in the stage, leaving a slim, clown-type duel avatar with a brilliant—or garish—yellow appearance standing in the center of the pillar. Hat with large, curved horns jutting out on either side. A face mask with thin eyes and mouth cut into the form of a smile. Long, gangly limbs stretching out from rounded, bulbous shoulders and hips.

“Heh-heh!” The clown allowed another burst of laughter to slip out as he ran a finger as thin as a wire along his chin. “Banana color, what a terrible thing to say! I personally like to offer up the example of uranium, you see? But, well, I suppose there’s no helping it. Everyone knows that the monkey and her child love bananas, now, don’t they? Heh-heh.”

The clown before them bobbing his head and continuing to laugh was the very person who had once laid a trap for Kuroyukihime and Niko: the Yellow King, head of the Legion Cosmic Crypt Circus, which ruled the three areas of Taito, Arakawa, and Adachi, along with Akihabara—Yellow Radio.

Given the king’s chatty style and flamboyant gestures,

Haruyuki didn't feel the same oppressive aura in him as he did with the other kings. However, having witnessed the close combat between Yellow Radio and Kuroyukihime at close range, he knew only too well that this was not an opponent to take lightly. Despite the fact that Radio was an unblemished yellow—meaning that he was a purely midrange-attack type—he had crossed swords with Black Lotus without retreating even a single step.

The Yellow King had apparently come without any aides in tow. Controlling his laughter, he brought his right hand to his chest and bowed in exaggerated curtsy before moving smoothly from the bow into a seated position on the pillar.

*So that's four.*

"So who's not here yet? Let's see," Haruyuki muttered, just as his ears caught the sound of haughty footsteps.

*Rrk, rrk!* Intense vibrations shook the stage from the right behind him. He whirled around just as a large avatar split the fog and stepped forward.

It was big, but not quite a giant. In terms of mere size, it probably wasn't even as big as the main Blue Legion member, Frost Horn, much less Niko with her Enhanced Armament deployed. But Haruyuki had never before faced an avatar possessing this kind of overwhelming solemnity. Mask, shoulders, lower body—all were covered in armor reminiscent of thick boards. But the hips were thin and tense, erasing any suggestion of sluggishness. His right hand was empty, but an equally large and solid shield was equipped in his left. All the armor was a vibrant green, deeper than emerald.

"The Green King," Haruyuki said quietly. He had only seen this avatar once for a few seconds, and in a replay video of a past fight, no less.

Next to him, Raker nodded. "Yes," she added in a whisper. "That's Green Grandé, the leader of the Legion 'Great Wall.' Their territory is large, stretching from Shibuya to Ota. His nickname is 'Invulnerable.'"

"Right, his HP gauge has never once gone into the yellow...,"

Haruyuki murmured with an unconscious sigh. His own gauge frequently ended up bright red in same-level duels, even when he won.

In front of him, Kuroyukihime puffed her nose lightly in indignation. "To begin with, he's actually not been in that many duels. Apparently, he earned the points he needed to make it to level nine almost entirely by hunting Enemies solo. Although that is still a significant enterprise."

"Aaah." Haruyuki let out another admiring sigh. Even the smallest of the strangely shaped Enemies loping through the Unlimited Neutral Field had serious fighting power, and on top of a player having to nearly kill themselves to defeat one, very few points were actually earned in that victory. Haruyuki loved grinding in a regular RPG, but even he was happier begging off Enemy hunting unless he started seriously losing in the general PVP duels.

Completely unaware of the respectful gazes from a distance, the "level-up artisan," the Green King, approached the pillar between Niko and the Blue King with a sure step and set himself down heavily. Like the Yellow King, he had come without any other Legion members. He said nothing, and so the silence remained unbroken, but no one seemed to find this the least bit strange. He had apparently established himself as the quiet type.

Facing forward once more, Haruyuki took a deep breath. With the passing of time here, he felt like he had gotten used to the intense auras of these strongest residents of the Accelerated World, the kings. In fact, at some point, his trembling knees had anchored themselves, and the cold numbness of his hands had vanished.

*Right. There's no need to freak out. I mean, I'm the Black King's subordinate—no, her "child." I have every right to stand tall like Raker,* he told himself and went to thrust his chest out and do just that.

"Ngh?!" He felt something like a cold hand clutching his heart and cringed with maximum fear.

*What…is this? Bloodlust…? No, not that. It's more decisive… the will to remove. A silent declaration…that I will be judged and banished from the Accelerated World.*

*Tak. Tak.* High-pitched footsteps echoed from nowhere.

Stiffening up, he pricked his ears intently. The north. The footfalls drew nearer, walking toward the semicircle of seated kings. He turned his gaze that way, tensed neck creaking.

A single silhouette on the other side of the dense fog. Seeing it only at the shadow level, he intuitively felt it was a girl-shaped avatar from the long hair parts and the skirt-shaped armor swinging. The waist was constricted impossibly thin; the legs were like needles.

*Tak. Tak. Tak.* The footsteps, swords piercing the earth, perhaps sounded so sharp because of pin heels twice as high as the ones Sky Raker had. The instant those feet stepped into the ring of the pillars, the deep fog hanging over the area was largely blown away, as if the ferocity of the auras there was too much to endure.

If there was one word to describe the avatar that was finally revealed then, it was not *king*; nothing other than *queen* would do. What had looked like hair was armor in the form of a long veil stretching out from the circlet on her forehead. Her face mask was pointed and beautiful, and her shoulder and chest parts were also feminine and yet intimidating. Partitioned armor in the shape of a long skirt stretched down from a high position on her waist, exposing her long, slender legs in gaps that went almost up to her hips.

There was no doubt that this duel avatar was the most deserving of the word *bewitching* of all the avatars Haruyuki had ever seen. However, her beauty was not the inviting kind; various parts of her body, including the tiara on her head, were edged with thorny adornments, spiked ends glittering. In her right hand, she carried a bishop's staff about a meter and a half or so long. At its tip was a rose vine with remarkably long needles. All her armor was a mysterious purple that shimmered hypnotically each time it caught the light.

“And so she appears,” Sky Raker murmured, almost inaudibly, while narrowing her eye lenses and staring at the approaching queen. “Of all the kings gathering here today, she is probably the most antagonistic toward us. Leader of the Legion Aurora Oval, ruling over the area from Ginza to the bay, nicknamed Empress Voltage: the Purple King, Purple Thorn. And the staff she’s carrying in her right hand is one of the Seven Arcs, the Tempest.”

“A-arcs?” Haruyuki parroted back.

“The strongest class of Enhanced Armaments in the Accelerated World,” Raker added in hurried explanation. “It’s assumed there are seven in total. The ones that have been confirmed as of present, other than that staff, are the Impulse, the large sword the Blue King has; the Strife, the large shield the Green King has; and then the last one is…” Here, Haruyuki could feel Raker momentarily falter for some reason, but he no longer had the opportunity to ask her about it.

The Purple King, moving forward leisurely through the center of the ring of pillars, stopped when she was closest to Kuroyukihime, who was sitting on the farthest right of the shorn columns. The queen stabbed the bottom end of her staff into the earth loudly, her thin veil swinging and her mask turning slightly toward the Black King. Her angled eye lenses housed a cold amethyst light.

The instant he felt the pressure the girl-shaped avatar had been radiating in no particular direction grow even stronger, and then focus on the three members of Nega Nebulus, Haruyuki very nearly fainted for real. If it had been a clear anger or hatred, he could’ve actually handled it. In the eight months since Haruyuki had become a Burst Linker, he had been in countless fights where he had come up against all kinds of anger.

But emanating from the Purple King was not any simple emotion; it was absolute rejection, a rejection so unyielding anyone who came up against it would instantly realize that there was no room for mutual understanding there. Haruyuki instinctively felt that this opponent would never stop fighting them, no matter

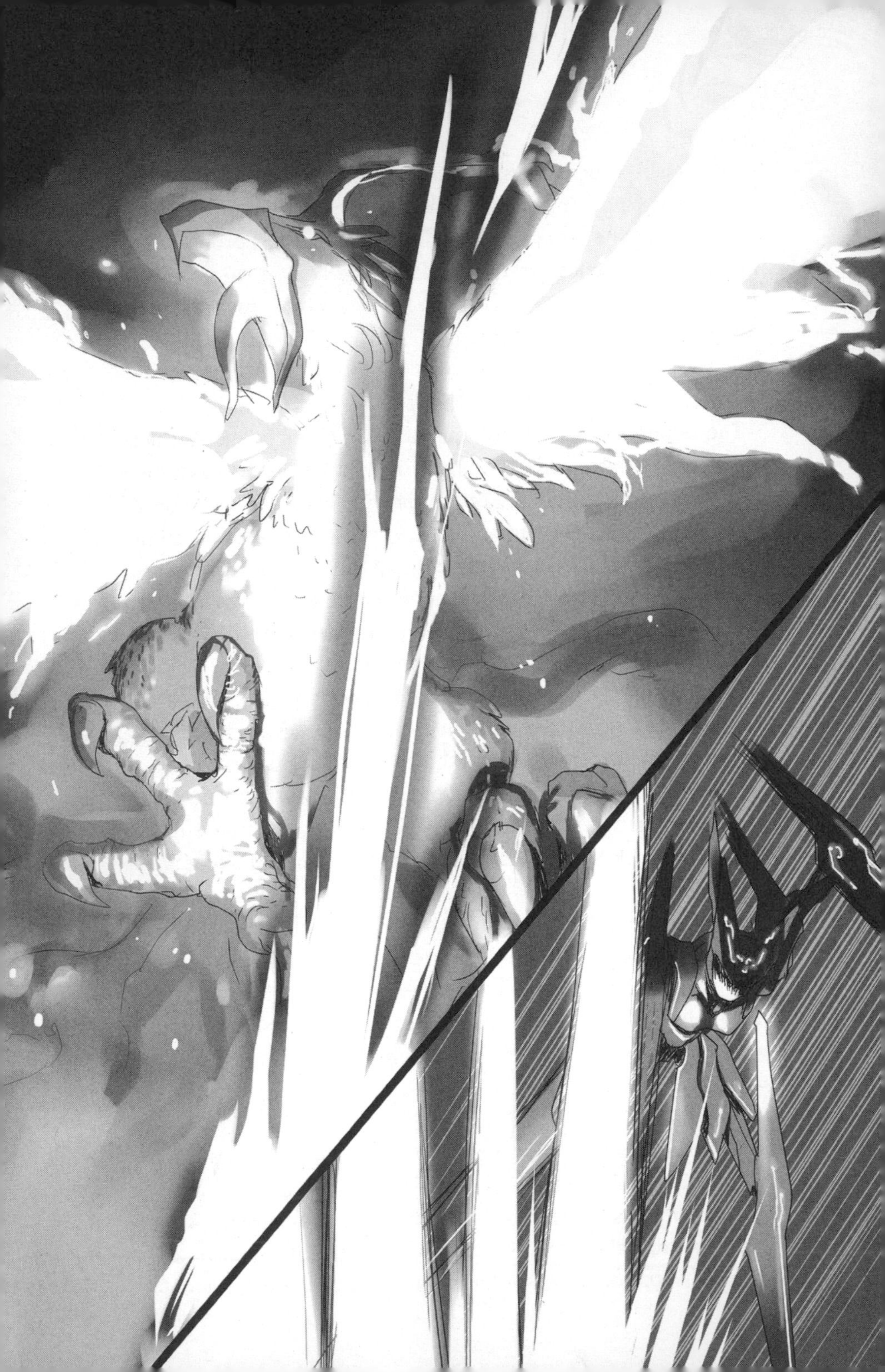

how the situation might change in the future. Right up until the bitter demise of the Accelerated World.

"It's been a long time, Lotus," the Purple King, Purple Thorn, said quietly after looking down at Black Lotus for two seconds. "I never thought the day would come when I would be speaking to you again like this."

There was nothing thorny about her tone; it was smooth like ice. Haruyuki swallowed even harder with the nervous certainty that this voice only had to break to reveal the countless sharp edges it contained. But he had heard the Purple King speak somewhere before, that sweet girlishness mixed in with her grave majesty, and after thinking about it, he remembered soon enough: He had definitely heard this girl speak once before. Not directly, of course. The Purple King had been in the replay video he had seen in the Unlimited Neutral Field. The sound came back to life in his ears from the depths of his memory.

*"Rider, you think I'm just gonna let that go?!"*

*"Hey! Come on!"*

The shout of a girl, indignant and yet still innocent.

In the video, at this moment, the Black King had wrapped both of her arms around the neck of the first Red King, Red Rider. And so the Purple King, who had been close to the Red King, had raised a voice that would have gone perfectly with an angry face. However, immediately after that, the swords of Black Lotus's arms had closed like a pair of enormous scissors, cutting off Red Rider's head.

Burst Linkers who reached level nine were bound by the rule of sudden death: The moment they were defeated by another level-nine player, they lost all of their burst points. Which meant that, in that instant, the Red King was chased from the Accelerated World forever. Recorded at the end of the replay video was Purple Thorn's piercing scream.

The story Haruyuki had heard was that immediately after this act, Kuroyukihime leapt into mortal combat with the remaining five kings, and while the thirty-minute duel time ended with her unable to defeat even one, she was not defeated herself. For the following two years, she refrained from connecting to the global net, sheltering in the obscurity of the Umesato local net until opportunity knocked in the form of Cyan Pile's assault and the birth of Silver Crow in the fall of the previous year.

This intense and heavy history palpable between them, the two kings locked eyes and radiated their own oppressive auras at each other for another few seconds. Haruyuki couldn't help secretly fearing that Black Lotus would lower her face. In her heart, Kuroyukihime no doubt still regretted that day she had hit Red Rider with a surprise attack. Even if the Red King no longer remembered that he had been a Burst Linker.

However.

The black crystal avatar did not avert her eyes from those of the thorny queen; her sharp face mask did not so much as quiver. "Nor I, Thorn." Kuroyukihime's low, smooth voice finally flowed out into the field and the drifting fog. "I was certain the next time we met, one of us would lose their head."

Taking in these calm words, the Purple King slowly blinked the eyes of her avatar, unmoved. When she spoke again, the chill in her voice seemed to have gotten slightly colder, although it could have just been in his head. "Perhaps one of us will, hmm? For instance, if all of us gathered here were to agree to change modes from Normal Duel to Battle Royale…the possibility's there."

Swallowing hard, Haruyuki desperately tried to keep himself from shouting. "Don't even joke about that! I would totally never agree to do that!"

But Kuroyukihime's reply was calm, with a hint of a laugh. "That would certainly speed things up. If today ended up being the day one of us cleared this game, we wouldn't need to have these sorts of annoying meetings."

Instantly, Haruyuki froze in place once more. Her words sounded like a declaration that she would hunt the other four kings then and there and become level ten; they could mean nothing else. He completely could not believe Sky Raker's courage, that she was able to stand next to him so calmly.

The Purple King cocked her head slightly at the Black King's retort and abruptly stabbed the staff in her right hand into the paving stones. The edged *clang* lingered in the air and Haruyuki's cold blood ran even colder. He heard several sets of footfalls, neatly synchronized, coming from the direction the Purple King had arrived from, before eight Burst Linkers revealed themselves. Their coloring and armor shapes were all over the map, but he could tell at a glance that they were all skilled masters; most likely, the most powerful members of the Purple Legion had dived together.

Purple Thorn grinned here for the first time. "Unthinkable that you believe that to be a joke," she said. "Naturally, I came prepared. So that if and when the time comes to fight you, you won't be able to escape again, hmm?"

The show of force was no bluff. She was serious. This girl had feelings so strong locked up inside of her it would almost be presumptuous to think he could even begin to understand them.

Haruyuki felt a pressure so strong he could hardly breathe and pulled his right leg back the tiniest bit.

But Kuroyukihime still did not lose her composure. Somehow, she even managed to laugh. "Ha-ha-ha! Ha-ha…I see. I underestimated you. But, well, Thorn, if you're seriously looking to take my head, shouldn't you really have your troops lying in wait on the very edges of the area? Learn from Radio over there."

*Huh?* Haruyuki looked over at Yellow Radio, seated on the opposite side. The canary clown simply moved his shoulders slightly without saying anything, but now that Haruyuki actually thought about it, the Yellow King would never have come alone if the possibility of the meeting turning into a battle was even just 0.001 percent.

Reacting to Kuroyukihime's comment was not the Purple King, but rather a female-shaped avatar who broke away from the eight-member entourage. Her armor was a deep reddish purple, reminiscent of wine. The broad-brimmed hat and wide thigh area were almost militaristic, but rather than a gun on either hip, she was equipped with a whip rolled up into a ring.

The female officer-type avatar stopped one step back from the Purple King. "Amusing that you would take your bravado this far, cave king," she uttered, her voice chilled to the extreme. "You may have crawled out from underground to run around or whatever it is you do, but I'll have you remember that the Seven Kings need only become serious, and your pathetic little frontier territory and what have you would be crushed in a single day." Her speech was contemptuous in the extreme, but Haruyuki could only grit his teeth tightly.

Unfortunately, he had to admit that what the avatar said was true. Currently, Nega Nebulus ruled all of Suginami Ward, but more than 70 percent of the challenges they got during the Territory Battles at the end of each week were from small and midsize Legions. Of the six major Legions, one or two teams from Leonids neighboring them to the east would always participate, with occasional sorties from Great Wall to their south. And the average level of the challengers was four or five; a high-level Linker at level seven or greater had never once appeared before them.

Still, for Nega Nebulus, with only five members, maintaining their territory was no mean feat. If the six major Legions mustered all their energy and launched a concentrated attack just once during that battle time, Haruyuki and his friends would have been unable to win more than half of the enormous number of defensive battles, and the black flag would have been wiped from the map of the Accelerated World.

In other words, in a certain sense, it was precisely because the six—no, five—kings, excluding Niko and their ceasefire, had adopted a "wait and see" attitude that Haruyuki and his friends had been able to continue protecting their home area of Suginami.

Unable to put up a real fight in his own heart, much less make any sharp retort to the female officer, Haruyuki's helmet sank downward. But just as his gaze was about to fall on his feet, a crisp, insistent voice rang out to his immediate right, and he lifted his face back up with a gasp.

"Well, for someone who could do no such thing, you certainly do manage to sound quite arrogant, hmm, Aster Vine?" It was Sky Raker. As Kuroyukihime's deputy, she stood firm and proud, not backing down before the other officer's bluster.

The whip user, apparently named Aster Vine, narrowed her eyes sharply under the brim of her hat. "Could do no such thing, you say?" Her voice was even icier. "While you were running and hiding all that time, did your head rust to the point where you can't even assess your own fighting ability?"

"And you. I don't see you for a while and your eyes cloud over so much that you're unable to see reality."

Haruyuki could do nothing but stand frozen and listen to this exchange practically electrify the air around them. No matter how hard he thought about it, he couldn't figure out what Sky Raker meant by this *reality*. The difference between Nega Nebulus and the five kings—excluding Red—in terms of both membership and combined level, was so great that comparison was pointless. What on earth was Raker trying to say…?

The answer to his question came after a pause, in Raker's own words. "If you think the kings are letting Nega Nebulus's territory continue to exist out of the goodness of their hearts, you're either thickheaded or not trusted. If they could crush it, they obviously would have done so long ago. The reason they can't… is because they themselves who name themselves *king* know that this controlling power is not something absolute."

"…What did you say?" Aster Vine squeezed out a creaking voice, while the Purple King maintained an eerie silence. He couldn't read what kind of emotion was in the light shining in her eyes suddenly.

"Pay attention." Raker's cool voice continued to echo in the penetrating cold of the Demon City stage. "They may be the six major Legions, but their combined membership is just over six hundred or so. In contrast, more than a thousand Burst Linkers currently live in the center of Tokyo. And nearly forty percent of the Territories map is made up of gray neutral states, including the Chiyoda Area we're in now."

"...And what does that matter? All the Legions outside the ones ruled by the Seven Kings are ephemeral organizations that would fly off into the sky if you blew on them. Your teensy little home included."

"True, the scale of all of those Legions is modest. But, you see, these four hundred people, including Burst Linkers with no Legion affiliation, have one thing in common. And that is that they want nothing to do with the seven major Legions." Stopping briefly, Sky Raker then continued with an air so intimidating, it was as if she herself had become one of the level niners.

"Understand? The majority of them choose the micro of their own volition. Because of their own animosity toward the kings who have caused such stagnation in the Accelerated World with their nonaggression pact. And those Burst Linkers are paying close attention to the return of Black Lotus and the movements of the Black Legion. They're trying to gauge whether her 'traitorous intentions' are real or fake. What do you think would happen if the Legions of the Seven Kings tried to crush her? You're right: Our flag would indeed disappear from the territory map. But that wouldn't make Black Lotus herself disappear from the Accelerated World, and the Legion itself would go on. And the smaller legions would likely take a step forward from 'paying attention.' If they all came together into one stream, I wonder if you'd still be able to scorn them as 'ephemeral'?"

And here, Haruyuki finally felt that he vaguely understood what Raker was getting at.

At the Hermes' Cord race the week before, the more than five hundred members of the Gallery gathered along the course definitely had not been booing at the appearance of the Black King, once exiled as a traitor. They had, in fact, welcomed her with warm cheers, had they not? There was no doubt that those cheers had been laden with expectation, the hope that the Black King would be the one to break through the stagnation.

And if that energy were brought together as a single force? Wouldn't that be something that even the Seven Kings could not ignore—something they would be forced to recognize as a threat?

Sky Raker waved her right hand lightly at the silent Aster Vine. "Do you understand? That there is a far greater strain on the Accelerated World than you think right now? That underneath the pretense of stagnation, more than a few large currents are beginning to twist and swirl?" Her cool, clear voice rippled into the field and lingered before sinking into silence and at last fading entirely.

The sound of the Purple King's high heels broke the silence as she stepped forward. *Tak.* Turning to face forward once more, she quietly walked away as though she had taken no notice of Raker's comments. With a final fierce glare, Aster Vine turned to follow her. The remaining seven members of the entourage standing at a distance did the same.

The Purple King took as her seat the empty pillar between the Blue and Yellow Kings in the semicircle of seven columns. Her eight Burst Linkers stood in a V formation behind her. The heavy pressure of their majestic presence was clearly the most massive of any of the Legions gathered there.

Haruyuki felt keenly relieved that Aurora Oval's territory was Ginza together with Ariake and therefore far away from Suginami, and then hurriedly pulled himself up straighter. Who knew what kind of punishment he'd get later if these two next to him noticed this weakness? He nodded slightly as if to hide it.

"So…that's six. And the last person is, umm…"

Currently assembled were the powers of Black, Blue, Red, Green, Yellow, and Purple. So that meant the remaining king was—

"No," Kuroyukihime murmured, impossibly quiet, before Haruyuki could give voice to his thought. "She won't come."

"Huh?"

"The remaining king won't show herself here. I have no doubt she'll send a proxy."

He was about to ask how she knew that when he sensed something not quite right in one corner of his vision. He clamped his mouth shut and sent his eyes racing around.

But there was nothing out of the ordinary. The remains of the inner citadel in the East Gardens of the Demon City stage were quiet, white fog trailing through. Half of the round pillars standing there had been cut down, and on the seats those seven pillars had become, the seven representatives of the great Legions ruling the Accelerated World were—

"Huh?" The moment he realized it, Haruyuki jerked backward.

Seven seats had been made. Six kings had shown up so far. So one seat should have been empty. But all of the seats in Haruyuki's field of view at that moment were filled. Had he missed someone's arrival? No, he couldn't have. And even if his extreme nervousness had made him miss something, he couldn't believe Raker and Kuroyukihime would have.

Because the seat that had to be empty was immediately in front of the three members of the Black Legion. It might have been a different matter if the seat had been to one side, but they certainly would have seen someone approaching the pillar opposite them and sitting down. However, at some point, a single Burst Linker had actually done just that, taking the seat the very short distance of ten meters away from them.

Tall, slender body wrapped in a subdued, simple armor with nothing resembling a weapon. The sole distinguishing feature was likely the long, thin, and tapered head. Only a curved parting line was carved into the front; he couldn't see any eyes or mouth. It was sitting so neatly, arms and legs together on the pillar, that it looked more like a decorative object than a duel avatar. The entire body was an almost matte ivory white, reminiscent of porcelain.

The avatar had an incredibly dilute presence. He couldn't sense even a shred of the concentrated pressure emitted from its existence like he could with the other kings. Maybe it was actually an object? Impossible. Had there been a sculpture there this whole time and he just hadn't noticed it…?

Just as Haruyuki was gripped by a sudden confusion, the ivory avatar bowed neatly from the waist, both hands still on its knees. At the same time as its upper body was brought back up, a voice flowed out, with no identifying features other than that it was masculine. "My name is Ivory Tower, member of the Legion Oscillatory Universe. I have come to take part in this meeting as full proxy and representative for the White King. I ask for your cooperation."

It was an extremely businesslike greeting, almost as if they had moved from a duel field in the Accelerated World into a corporate conference room without realizing it.

Although they tried to suppress it, this greeting clearly made the other kings and their aides deeply uneasy. Most likely, none of them had noticed Ivory Tower's appearance, either. The Yellow King, directly beside Ivory Tower, tapped the sharp-tipped toes of one foot on the ground, expressing his actual irritation.

However, the discomfort lasted only a few seconds.

The Blue King, Blue Knight, stood up abruptly in the center, armor clanking. "Good, so then everyone's here," he said in a strong, ringing voice. "First, let me thank all seven Legions for taking part. Good to see you."

"Two of the faces here are different from the meeting of the Seven Kings two and a half years ago, hmm?" Interrupting with unnecessary chatter was, of course, Yellow Radio. He might have been making a sarcastic reference to the fact that the Red King was the second and that the White King had sent a proxy, but not a soul responded. The meeting continued forward with just the hint of a wry smile from the Red King.

"We don't have much time, so let's just get right into it. You all already know the situation, so I'll just summarize briefly. In the middle of the Hermes' Cord race event last week, in front of several hundred members of the Gallery, an incident occurred in which the Incarnate System was activated. The first item on the agenda today is how we should deal with this situation. That said, I can think of only two ways. We either expend every effort to hide the system, as we have been up to now, or we give up and disclose it to all Burst Linkers."

"Disclosure's impossible. Wasn't that it?" Yellow Radio raised his voice once again, skirting around the edge of saying the idea was ridiculous. He spread his long, thin arms and shrugged exaggeratedly. "The Incarnate System's like nuclear energy, yes? If it's not strictly controlled, it could bring about catastrophic disaster to the Accelerated World. That was our shared understanding, hmm?"

The clown cocked his horned hat to one side, and the Purple King to his left immediately raised an objection.

"The point is that control has been shattered, Radio. If you're making an analogy with nuclear, then the current situation is equivalent to the raw materials for nuclear weapons being scattered all over the world. How are we supposed to recover them now?"

"So are you then saying we should kindly hand out manuals for missile production? You realize the great majority of Burst Linkers still don't even know what the Incarnate System is? Wouldn't it be better to simply push the idea that there was a problem with the event's stage design?"

"Excuse me, may I speak?" another voice interjected, just as the Purple King was about to refute the Yellow King once more.

Politely raising a hand was the ivory avatar seated on the left end of the semicircle, the representative of the White King, Ivory Tower. When all eyes turned toward him, he dropped his left hand. "Before we debate what measures to take, shouldn't we find out how something like this happened? Who on earth is this Burst Linker who released the Incarnate in the middle of an event and pulled even the Gallery into the Space Corrosion, and what is their objective?"

Silence ruled the meeting venue.

The name and membership of the problem Burst Linker. Haruyuki already knew these. But he was incredibly reluctant to give voice to them here. Because in talking about that mysterious organization, he would inevitably have to touch on the Burst Linker who called himself its vice president. But the color that crowned that player was the same as a certain swordmaster he loved and respected more than anyone else—a pure black. If the kings knew that, it was obvious they would suspect a connection.

"Rust Jigsaw, a member of the organization Acceleration Research Society. That's the name of the Burst Linker who carried out the Incarnate attack at the event."

"Ngh?!" Haruyuki caught his breath the instant he heard the brilliantly clear voice.

It was Kuroyukihime. Without the slightest fear of suspicion being cast on herself, the Black King proceeded smoothly. "We don't know the full story on the organization, but they called themselves a 'circle' rather than a Legion. The other confirmed members are Dusk Taker, who has already left the Accelerated World, and one more—"

"Hold up, Lotus."

Just as she was on the verge of announcing that third name, a single voice interrupted her sharply.

It belonged to the Red King, Scarlet Rain, occupying the seat to their right. With her arms crossed over her chest, she emitted an air of intimidation out of proportion with her small body, the smallest of anyone there.

*You're throwing us a life raft, huh, Niko?* Haruyuki thought, and the tension ran out of his shoulders.

However…

An aura like the flames of hell flew from the roundly cute eye lenses that glanced at them, and Haruyuki stopped breathing.

"If you don't take care of the other item on the agenda, I can't keep sitting here. We got someone not fit for the threat of Incarnate blah-blah right here. Someone living inside the avatar with a cursed power that was supposed to be completely gone, the darkest side of the ultimate Incarnate."

# 3

"Come on! Back to your seats! Extended homeroom's starting."

Some students grumbled at their homeroom teacher clapping his hands together. "What?! The bell hasn't even rung yet. Stick to the schedule."

"Okay, then, anyone not in their seat the instant the bell rings gets extra homework! Come on, it's going to ring—it's gonna ring, you guys! Three, two, one…"

Haruyuki listened, chins propped up in his hands, to the ringing of the sixth-period bell and the clattering of students scrambling for their seats.

On the other side of the window, a drizzling rain colored the city gray. According to the weather forecast, the end of the rainy season was still two weeks away, but he had the end-of-term examinations to look forward to right after that, so he couldn't really muster up any impatient desire for the rain to stop. Of course, if he could make it through the exams, the brilliance of summer break awaited him, but he would need a lot more training before he could manage to be upbeat enough to sustain any kind of anticipation over such a long time frame. He sighed heavily simply thinking about the classes (especially gym) and homework (especially essays) that would assault him in the week ahead.

At least with homework, he could noodle and dawdle and drag it out and still get it done right before it was due if he made a power play and used a burst point. In those final thirty minutes he gained from acceleration, he could mow down any amount of homework, an ability so incredible that even honors student Takumu was stunned and exasperated. "Why don't you just use that kind of concentration normally?"

But he couldn't use an intense burst of acceleration to similarly clear his schedule of the classes crammed into his days, morning to night. In fact, when he was dragging his exhausted self around the track in gym class, he even had the sense that a deceleration function was actually at work. Maybe there really was. According to the operating principles of Brain Burst, the thought clock was accelerated by an increased heart rate, extending subjective experienced time. So maybe if he trained so that his heart didn't pound so hard when he was running, gym class would feel shorter than it did now. All right. He'd try dropping the Chinese Kenpo training app he had been using and do some chakra-type special power training or something.

These useless thoughts ran through Haruyuki's mind as he looked out the window without really seeing anything while the voice of his homeroom teacher went in one ear and out the other.

"...It's been two months now that you've been in this class. And now's about the time when you start to lose focus. See? On this graph, lateness and lost items, starting in April..."

Normally, the last homeroom was precious time when he worked out his duel plans for after school. What area he'd go to, what kind of techniques he'd try, who he'd fight, or whose Gallery he'd sit in while they fought. For Haruyuki, who loved simulations, this was a fun exercise even if it had no effect on his actual duels. Usually, homeroom was over in the blink of an eye, a pleasant surprise, but today, time's march was ridiculously slow.

The reason was obvious.

Haruyuki had been backed into a corner; he had no room for

plotting out duel plans. The pressure he was under now was even, in a certain sense, greater than when he had his flying ability stolen two months earlier, teetering as he was on the edge of a cliff. Was his time as a Burst Linker almost over?

After the meeting of the Seven Kings ended the day before, Fuko dropped Haruyuki off close to his home. Although he managed to meet her and Kuroyukihime's encouragement with a smile, he did indeed drop his head and count the tiles of the sidewalk as he trudged home along Kannana Street.

Head still hanging, he got into the elevator and rode up to the twenty-third floor. After walking down the silent hallway to his condo, just as he was in front of the door about to touch the UNLOCK button shown in his field of view, Haruyuki noticed a small figure crouching in the corner of the doorway and stopped dead in his tracks.

Bright T-shirt with some logo on it, slim-fit jeans. Faded sneakers on bare feet. Despite the rough appearance, he quickly realized it wasn't a boy. The hair tied up on both sides, red like fire, shone lustrous even in the gloom of the hallway.

"N-Niko?" Haruyuki said her name, dumbfounded, and the small girl slowly raised her face, a daring and yet somehow powerless smile crossing her lips.

"Yer late. We supposedly left the Chiyoda Area at the same time, but here I am, waiting for ten whole minutes."

"S-sorry," he apologized reflexively, and she shrugged sharp shoulders lightly.

"Well, Pard did give me a lift on her bike, so it's no wonder I was faster."

"Th-there's no way I could catch up with her. A-anyway...why are you here?" Haruyuki asked, blinking furiously.

Niko looked away momentarily and snorted lightly. "This is gonna take a while. You wanna hear the whole thing in the hallway?"

"O-oh, sorry." Haruyuki hurried to touch the UNLOCK button

still displayed before him. The door of his deserted-as-always apartment opened, and he politely invited her in, to which Niko responded with a long sigh before putting both hands on her knees and standing up.

After showing his surprise guest to the living room, Haruyuki got two glasses of orange juice in the kitchen and returned, only to cock his head anew.

The younger girl seated on the sofa, looking out at the clouds on the other side of the windows, was indeed someone he had met many times before, Niko aka Yuniko Kozuki—ruler of the Legion Prominence, the Red King, Scarlet Rain herself. But why? He had not only exchanged anonymous mail addresses with her, but also call numbers, so she had any number of ways to get ahold of him. And more than that, sitting with her knees clutched to her chest, in the corner of the entryway of someone she had business with, was the polar opposite of what he expected from Niko.

As he set the juice down on the glass table, Haruyuki stole another peek at the small face in profile. He could see no sign of the usual sparkling energy in her lightly freckled cheeks. On the contrary, he felt like he could see an unease of sorts in them. It was hard to believe this was the very Red King who had spoken so sternly at the meeting earlier. Her sharp voice came back to life in the back of his head.

*We got someone not fit for the threat of Incarnate blah-blah right here.*

"Sorry. For saying it like that, I mean," Niko muttered before him the instant he recalled the intense heat of her recrimination, her crimson flames, almost as if reading his mind.

"Huh? O-oh, no, it's—" Having sunken into the sofa, he sat up again and hurriedly shook his head back and forth. "I—I was surprised at first, but Kuroyukihime and Raker explained it later, so...They said you brought up the subject of my—I mean, the Armor of Catastrophe parasitizing me then because we couldn't let any of the other kings, especially the Yellow King, take the lead on this." He rushed to get the words out, and Niko blinked a couple times before a wry smile bled into her large eyes, which looked reddish brown or green, depending on the light.

"Tch! So they saw through me. Honestly, nothing to love about those two." Cursing, she leaned back into the sofa, crossed surprisingly thin legs, and dangled a slipper from the tip of her bare foot.

Relaxing slightly at this change in demeanor, Haruyuki cocked his head lightly to one side and asked, "Wait, have you and Raker met before?"

"Nah. The meeting there was the first time we've come face-to-face. I've just heard stuff about her from Pard."

"S-stuff? Like what?"

At the question, a broad, meaningful grin spread across Niko's face. "You know where her nickname ICBM comes from?" she asked in return.

"Huh? It's not just from her boosters sort of looking like missiles…?"

"There's that, but that's not the whole story. It actually comes from this tactic the old Nega Nebulus used once in a while in large-scale Territory Battles. They would deliberately push up to the enemy team front line and scatter their fighting power. Then Raker, either alone or carrying someone as support, would fly into the enemy's rear base with her boosted jump. And 'cause the only armor in the rear's basically paper, super-long-distance types, they did serious damage with this strategy, the sort of damage you'd get from a missile."

"…R-right." Haruyuki nodded, unconsciously breaking out into a cold sweat despite the fact that the person behind this clever attack was his own ally.

"And you know how Pard is a speed demon." Niko's expression softened as she continued, almost as if she were recounting her own memories. "Whenever she got hit with that missile strategy, she'd head straight to the rear and duke it out with Raker. Over and over. Seriously. I mean, we're talking about the main force of a Legion we got a cease-fire with, but she was so happy Raker'd come back to the front…You know what, Crow? Pard's a fairly longtime Linker, but she's still only at level six and…"

Here, Niko fell silent, so Haruyuki finally leaned forward. The doubt in her was one he'd sensed several times in the past.

"'L-level six and'…?"

"Nah, it's a secret. Ask the girl herself later." Grinning, she offered a quick "Thanks" as she lifted the glass from the table.

He could no longer see the curious helplessness in the little—apparently thirsty—girl as she took big, glugging gulps of the juice. Maybe it had just been his imagination, he thought as he replied, "I totally feel like she wouldn't tell me even if I did ask… Well, anyway. So, Niko, did you come all the way over here just to apologize for the thing in the meeting?"

"What? You don't have to sound so put out." She glared at him over the rim of her glass, and he hurried to shake his head.

"N-no! I'm not put out! It's just sort of out of character, I guess. Oh, uh! I didn't mean it like that, it's, um, actually I've been thinking for a long time that I'm the one who should apologize." Unable to stop the spinning of his mouth once it had started moving, he awkwardly turned into sound the idea he had been planning to communicate in a more polished form. "I-it's just, we worked so hard to destroy the Armor in Ikebukuro, and then I go and make a stupid mistake and now it's still around. And on top of that, you had to give the old owner, Cherry Rook, the Judgment Blow, but I'm still here being a Burst Linker—"

Haruyuki's words did not entirely miss their mark, and Niko listened with a serious face. Eventually, however, she shook her head lightly and interrupted him. "Nah." The young king set her glass down, crossed her legs again, and sat back deep in the sofa. "I'm not holding a grudge against you or anything for that. I didn't give Cherry the Judgment Blow because he was the owner of the Armor. I did it because he was swallowed up by the Armor's controlling power and then he attacked—no, *devoured*—a ton of Burst Linkers. If Cherry had maybe been able to make the Armor surrender and control it with his own power, I would have done the opposite. I would've protected him. No matter what the other kings said…yeah…" Niko's voice slowed unnaturally.

Haruyuki blinked and looked at the pale face turned to the floor. The same dark shadow he had seen outside in the hallway again clouded her large eyes, a deep green at that moment. This time, Haruyuki understood what it was: fear. And anger at herself for being afraid. And a tiny bit of resignation. The look that must have come onto Haruyuki's own face in the past at those times when he clutched his knees, unable to do anything under his own power.

"N-Niko." He called her name in a strangled voice.

The girl raised her eyes momentarily and then dropped them again with a weak smile. "I had the power to actually protect Cherry. I've believed that these last six months. But, the thing is…" Abruptly, she clutched the arms poking out of the sleeves of her T-shirt tightly. Almost like she had been overcome by a fierce chill in the middle of the sweltering June heat. "Crow. You didn't feel it at the meeting?"

"F-feel what?" Haruyuki timidly asked in reply.

"That inside those kings there," Niko—the second Red King, the Immobile Fortress, Scarlet Rain—groaned in a cracking voice, "are real monsters. That information pressure…It's impossible… Like, I really planned to just protect you there. I mean, I owe you for saving Cherry for me. So, like, I proposed that compromise at today's meeting. But…if they had seriously pushed for execution, I…" She shut her mouth and pulled her knees up onto the sofa.

For a while, Haruyuki could say nothing to her in reply. It wasn't that he didn't believe it right away; he just couldn't actually understand it. The fact that Niko was calling another Burst Linker a monster, complete with a look of real fear…

To Haruyuki, the Red King was an absolutely elevated presence. He was convinced that they could fight a hundred times under the same conditions, and he would lose each one of those hundred times. The dreadnought long-distance firepower she had when she deployed all of her Enhanced Armament was no doubt one of the greatest attack powers in the Accelerated World. After all, with one shot of her main armament, she had sent half of the Shinjuku government building flying.

But even in just her small avatar body, equipped with a single handgun, Niko's strength was fathomless. At the meeting of the Seven Kings, Haruyuki had in fact felt an enormous pressure from the Red King, one that did not pale in any way in comparison with that of the other kings.

"Th-that's..." Haruyuki finally rebutted her hoarsely, shaking his head in several short jerks. "I mean, for me, every single person in that place was up in the clouds, but I can't believe there was anyone there who could make you say that. I—I mean, you're a level niner just like them, right? 'Same level, same potential,' that's the main principle of the Accelerated World, right?"

The redheaded girl glanced at Haruyuki over her small kneecaps and moved her head slowly from side to side with a bitter smile. "Exceptions to every rule, you know. Listen. For all intents and purposes, level nine's the cap for Brain Burst. 'Cause no matter how many points you earn, you can't get to the next level from there. The road to level ten is hunting five other level-nine Linkers...which basically equals making five people lose all their points. To put it another way..."

She dropped her eyes once more and said softly, "No one else knows how much time you've spent in the Accelerated World, how much experience you've had after getting to level nine. I thought those other kings couldn't beat me on that one. I thought I had the power to at least not have the things I lost in the real world taken from me again in the Accelerated World. But...that was wishful thinking. Those guys, the 'originators,' have transcended stuff like the hurts I'm clinging to. And if you don't call that *monstrous*, what is it..."

"...'O-origin'...?" Baffled, Haruyuki could only repeat to himself the unfamiliar word. But Niko simply set her cheek down on the knees she had her arms around and offered nothing in the way of reply.

The living room fell back into silence, with just the faint hum of the air conditioner reaching his ears. The cloudy sky beyond the windows was concentrated lead, and headlights began to pop on here and there in the lanes of EV vehicles flowing along Kannana.

Niko went to a boarding school, and she would soon be in danger of breaking curfew, but the body curled up before him showed no signs of moving. Even the hair pulled up into thin bundles on either side of her head hung limply, as if it had lost its usual vigor.

*I should say something*, Haruyuki felt, and fumbled earnestly for the words. Now that he was thinking about it, he had a hard time believing that Niko would have brought herself all the way to Suginami just to apologize for what she had said during the meeting. Maybe right now, the look on her face under that red fringe was one she couldn't show to her friends in the Red Legion, not even her closest aide, Pard.

"……"

He was completely unable to think of something appropriate to say, but even still, he had to say something, and so took a deep breath. But before he could get any words out, Niko popped her head up. Her entire face radiated with an unexpected smile. Her lips moved and her high-pitched voice came rushing out, her tone a complete one-eighty from what it had been until that point.

"Sorry for suddenly talking about all this weird stuff, big brother!"

"…Uh, n-no, it's…" He simply darted his eyes about in confusion. Even knowing that Niko's suspicious "Angel mode" was a trick to tease Haruyuki and throw up a smoke screen, for an only child, being called *big brother* with a big smile was a shot straight through the heart.

"Just forget all that! Ah! I gotta get going! Thanks for the juice!" She launched the words in a voice so adorable, he could practically see a stardust effect at the end of each sentence, and then bounced off the sofa and trotted across the living room.

Here, Haruyuki finally pushed through his surprise and stood up. "H-hold on, Niko!" he called after her slim back. "Didn't you…Wasn't there something else you wanted to talk about?"

The small girl stopped dead in her tracks in front of the door. After a moment's hesitation, she whirled around abruptly. He was wholly unprepared for the broad grin and the speech that accompanied it.

"Look, big brother Haruyuki. If one of us—or maybe both of us—loses Brain Burst, we'll probably forget it all, everything about each other, you know?"

"Huh…?"

Total erasure of related memories. The final rule of Brain Burst applied to those who lost the game, a rule Haruyuki had discovered a mere two months earlier. Even Kuroyukihime had only had rumor-level information about this rule before then; how long had Niko known?

Haruyuki held his breath as Niko peered up at him and then suddenly thrust her right hand out, extending just her surprisingly slender little finger.

"So let's promise. That when we find a name we don't know in the address book of our Neurolinkers, before we erase the data, we'll send one mail. And then maybe, one more time…"

"…rita. Arita! Hey! Are you listening to me?"

A thick voice suddenly calling his last name dragged Haruyuki out of his memories of the previous day. He intently swallowed down the pain rising up in his chest and took several breaths, somehow managing to change gears in his brain.

"Y-yes!" he responded hurriedly, reflexively half standing at the same time, and bumped his legs into the reinforced plastic desk, making both desk and chair clatter.

Here, he finally remembered that this was not his own living room, but the classroom of grade eight's class C. Nervously shifting his gaze, he saw his homeroom teacher Sugeno making a sour face at the podium, and the students around him snickering at his overreaction.

He couldn't hear the scornful echoes of seventh grade in that laughter, although there might have still been the tiniest undercurrent. But the Haruyuki of this class, despite still being at the bottom of the hierarchy, had somehow established himself as the harmless round guy. Naturally, he was not dissatisfied with this. He would almost say it was ideal, in fact.

Which was why he had to make every effort to avoid drawing unnecessary attention to himself as he had just done with his silly mistake. He wouldn't be able to handle it if, because of this, some secret punk in the class decided it would be a good idea to relieve some stress by sending a little light bullying Haruyuki's way. Thus, he moved to sit back down with an embarrassed smile befitting someone who had gotten a bit too carried away and done something awkward.

However, for some reason, he sensed in his classmates a certain expectation directed toward him, and he froze. They all looked like they were waiting eagerly for Haruyuki to say something.

*Wh-what's going on? Am I supposed to do something now? Do they want me to make a joke? Did I accidentally activate the super-difficult mission of making them laugh?* Mind racing, Haruyuki broke out into a cold sweat.

"Oh, Arita. So you're standing up. Can I take that to mean you're announcing your candidacy?" Sugeno said unexpectedly.

*Candidacy? For what?*

He had let his homeroom teacher's words flow right past him, so he had no idea how what connected to what. Stiffening at the surprising turn things had taken, Haruyuki focused his eyes to the rear of his teacher. But there was nothing written on the virtual blackboard.

*Don't panic. Think. So the kind of jobs you recruit for in homeroom...Right, someone to read out the announcement texts from the school. Nine times out of ten, that's what it is.* Haruyuki turned his gaze back to his virtual desktop and noticed that at some point a document file had arrived in his new message area.

He definitely wasn't good at reading out loud. But he had to do it sometimes in language arts or English class, and it was way better than having to state his own thoughts on anything. In this situation, the less messy choice was to own his carelessness and take the role of reader instead of sitting down with a *no* and making the whole thing worse.

Having arrived at a decision on how to act, Haruyuki raised his head and met Sugeno's eyes. "Y-yes, I'll do it!" he replied in a clear voice.

An impressed "Ohh!" abruptly rose up from the entire class, followed by applause like heavy thunder.

"...Sorry?"

*Th-this reaction. Why would anyone applaud just because I said I'd be the reader?* Freezing once more, Haruyuki watched Sugeno nod.

"Mm-hmm, mm-hmm. I knew you were the type to step up when push comes to shove, Arita! I'm honestly delighted someone's come forward in class C. Classes A and B will no doubt end up drawing names."

*What?* A very ominous feeling settling over him, Haruyuki clicked on the newly arrived file. The document that opened with a crisp sound effect was:

NOTICE OF ESTABLISHMENT OF ANIMAL CARE CLUB: A TOTAL OF THREE MEMBERS, ONE FROM EACH GRADE EIGHT CLASS, ARE TO BE ELECTED.

—In a rather cold font.

"A-Animal Care Club?!" Haruyuki's shriek was drowned out in the ongoing applause.

*Animal Care Club. So then, looking after animals?*

Belatedly coming to the obvious conclusion, he looked around the class and saw Chiyuri shaking her head in exasperation and Takumu grinning wryly with a *you've done it now* look.

"Look, Haru. Even if you are always daydreaming..." In the short period after school before team practices started, his childhood friend Chiyuri Kurashima appeared before Haruyuki, who was still limp with exhaustion at his own desk. She turned a hard gaze on him as she continued. "If you don't know what's going on, then at least open the handout! Why would you just charge in on a gut feeling like that?!"

"Come on, Chi. It's not like this is the first time Haru's let his thoughts just run wild," Takumu Mayuzumi said, standing next to Chiyuri.

*You don't have to rub my nose in it*, he thought, although he couldn't actually deny the truth of what they were saying. He slowly slid down on his chair and said lifelessly, "It's fine. Whatever. I'll just do it. The animal caretaker thing, anything."

"If someone had, like, forced you, we could maybe have said something. But, I mean, you stood up and proudly declared your candidacy. There was nothing we could do." Chiyuri let out a sigh, and then the expression on her face changed abruptly. A serious light shone in her catlike eyes, and she brought her head in close, large barrette glittering. "But, actually, you do have the time for some kind of club, right? I mean, within the next week, you'll—"

"You have to 'purify' that parasite, whatever it takes," Takumu interjected to finish the thought in a low voice.

Exactly.

That week—Monday, June 17, to Sunday, June 23—was the "stay of execution" Haruyuki/Silver Crow had been given.

Two resolutions had in the end been adopted at the meeting of the Seven Kings the previous day. First, they would continue to gather information on the attack by the mysterious Acceleration Research Society. In his heart, Haruyuki was indignant at this too-lukewarm proposal, but it was true that a counterattack was impossible, given that they had absolutely no real details about the nature of the group; there was really nothing else they could do.

And then, as if to counterbalance that tepidity, a harsh decision was made about Silver Crow's transformation into Chrome Disaster: If he didn't completely remove the parasite that was the Armor of Catastrophe within that seven-day period, the five kings would place a large bounty on his head. And that enticing sum of burst points would be distributed according to the number of times a Linker defeated Silver Crow. Once that happened, the instant he took even one step outside of Suginami Area, he would be assaulted by waves of Burst Linkers, including high-level ones, and Haruyuki's points would run dry in a flash. They did have, after all, the just cause of the destruction of the armor on their side. No one needed to hesitate about pitting a large group against one person.

Naturally, if he copied Kuroyukihime, who had a similar bounty on her head, and shut himself up in Suginami, he could refuse duels even while connected to the global net, but if he did that, he would no longer be able to earn points. He would stop leveling up, which was the very definition of a slow death for a Burst Linker.

All of which meant an erasure ordered by a king, as long as it was lawful, was essentially the same thing as a death sentence. Kuroyukihime had managed to live for two whole years due, of course, to her iron will and her steadfast refusal to connect her Neurolinker globally, but the fact that she was already level nine played a big part. Haruyuki obviously lacked the latter and most likely the former as well.

"...One week..." Haruyuki looked down at his hands on his desk. Unconsciously, he overlaid on them the gleaming, smooth silver of his armor. Silver Crow was his other self; becoming his avatar was entirely natural. The idea that he would no longer be able to be that person, no longer able to be a Burst Linker, felt unreal.

*Wait. Maybe I just feel like that because that's the real world now?* Real *for me is maybe in that world now? So then, if I lose Brain Burst, where the hell will I go...?* The instant this thought came into his mind, Haruyuki was overtaken by something like a chill, and a shiver ran up his spine. Deep in his ears, he heard again her clear, high voice.

*So let's promise. That when we find a name we don't know in the address book of our Neurolinkers, before we erase the data, we'll send one mail…*

Haruyuki didn't know just how serious Niko had been, since she'd said it in Angel mode, which was supposed to be a performance. She had forced Haruyuki to pinkie shake and then left, practically running out the door.

But how could he forget? They could erase his memories of the Accelerated World, but there was no way he'd forget the people he had built bonds with in the real world. He tried to feel this confidence, despite the sharp unease in his heart. What if at some point he had lost sight of the reality of the real world? What if the memories tagged with *reality* had become empty without him noticing it?

Clenching both hands tightly at the fear suddenly rising up in him, Haruyuki's head started to sag even lower, but a small hand entering his field of view was faster than his head, wrapping itself around Haruyuki's left fist.

"It'll be okay, Haru."

Lifting his face again, he found Chiyuri's usual smile there.

"Right. I'm sure we'll be able to work it all out," Takumu said crisply, standing next to her, and stretched out a hand blistered from his wooden kendo sword to rap Haruyuki's right fist. His two childhood friends exchanged brief glances and nodded as if confirming something before looking back at Haruyuki.

"And, okay, Haru? We talked about it, and we made a decision. If the week does go by and that bounty gets put on you, Taku and I will share our points with you, so you can keep leveling up at the same pace. So you don't have anything to worry about." Haruyuki stared hard at Chiyuri's face as she spoke.

He quickly rose up out of his chair and shook his head fiercely. "Y-you can't!" he half said, half shouted, keeping his voice at minimum volume. "If you guys do that, you might end up with bounties, too! They're just waiting for an excuse to turn all of us into targets!"

"Hey, whoa, Haru. I've been in this longer than you, okay? I know a dozen ways to transfer points in secret." Takumu grinned as he touched the bridge of his glasses and quickly ran his gaze over to the lower right, moving his body as if to close off any objections from Haruyuki. "Yikes! I gotta be getting to practice. Haru, let me know if the animal thing takes too much of your time. I'll switch off with you whenever I can. At any rate, this week, your priority should be the purification plan Master came up with."

"Yeah. Thanks, Taku." Haruyuki swallowed a bunch of different words and lowered his head.

The Armor of Catastrophe purification plan. After the handling of Silver Crow had been decided at the meeting of the Seven Kings, Kuroyukihime had come up with a mission to eliminate the element of Chrome Disaster parasitizing him, fuming all the while. Her plan apparently had three stages, but she still hadn't told Haruyuki and his friends the whole of it. "I don't know the details, but...," he said half to himself, lifting his face. "Anyway, I'll just do everything I can."

"Yeah. And we'll do everything we can to help. Okay, see you guys later." Takumu patted Haruyuki's elbow lightly, turned, and trotted off to the kendo area.

Watching him go, Chiyuri said quickly, "I have practice, too, but tell me if you need anything. Don't be shy about it. We... um...We're not friends...or kindred souls...ummm..."

*Family. Right.*

Almost as if she could hear Haruyuki's thoughts, Chiyuri stopped talking and offered him a big smile before raising her right hand briefly and racing out of the room.

Left alone, Haruyuki murmured in his heart as he shouldered his bag, *It's not such a basic problem as real or virtual or whatever. Me and Taku, me and Chiyu, me and Kuroyukihime and Raker. And Niko and Pard, and so many other people. What ties us all together is always here, inside my heart.*

*I want to protect that. I don't want to lose it. As Haruyuki Arita. And as Silver Crow.*

Glancing at the clock, he saw that he only had five minutes until the meeting time noted in the file. Even as he hurried to the exit on the first floor, Haruyuki was steadying his resolve anew.

This week of grace was precious time Kuroyukihime and Niko had won for him by fighting the Yellow and Purple Kings, who both had insisted on immediate execution. He absolutely could not waste it. He had accidentally nominated himself for the unexpected job of caring for some animals, but there had to be a hint for him somewhere, even in that. Right now, he had to simply focus his everything on his problem.

"Right!" he shouted softly, and went outside to find that at some point, the rain had stopped.

# 4

The private Umesato Junior High School was on the east side of Tokyo's Suginami Ward, quite close to the corner of the streets of Oume Kaido and Itsukaichi Kaido. Although the school was small in scale with three classes per grade, the campus was reasonably large. On the north side of the grounds, which featured a three-hundred-meter track, the three-story first classroom wing stretched out east–west, connecting in the center with the north–south sports wing. On the opposite side stood the second wing, also in the east–west direction. In other words, the entire school was in the shape of a sideways *H*.

The classrooms and the student cafeteria were concentrated in the newer first wing. The fairly older second building held the principal's, teachers', and guidance counselor's offices on the first floor, while the second floor was made up of storerooms and the now barely used special classrooms. Thus, students almost never ventured into this building. Which was why Haruyuki had used the boys' washroom on the third floor of this wing as his "shelter" when he was in seventh grade.

However, there was one place students went to even less frequently, a place they weren't even aware of. A long, narrow space enclosed by concrete walls and a high fence even farther north than the second wing. The place Haruyuki had been called as a new member of the Animal Care Club was past this damp gap, a corner in the northwest, the deepest of recesses at Umesato.

"I didn't even know this place existed...," Haruyuki murmured, staring at the building.

It was really too small to be called a building. The floor was at best four meters each way, and the ceiling maybe two and a half meters up. The side and interior walls were presently boards of unfinished wood, and the roof was probably straight shingles. The front was entirely made up of chicken wire with a three-centimeter mesh. A cage, in other words. Naturally, it was not used to lock up students who had done bad things; it was a hutch for keeping animals.

However, no matter how close he brought his face to the chicken wire or how he strained his eyes, he could see no animals inside it. There was just a thick pile of leaves that had come in through a hole in the mesh. He had no doubt that plenty of microscopic creatures lived under it, but they couldn't possibly be the animals he was meant to care for.

"You can have an Animal Care Club and a hutch, but the animals are really the key," he said to himself, cocking his head to one side. If they were going to be brought in later, he couldn't understand why the club was being formed now.

At that moment, he heard the crunch of feet behind him. Turning with a start, he saw two students coming toward him from the direction of the front yard. One girl, one boy. Their ribbon and necktie were the same blue as Haruyuki's, but he didn't know their faces, which meant they were probably in different classes. Which also meant they had to be his colleagues, newly assigned to the Animal Care Club like him.

He took a step forward, thinking to at least say hello, but before he could, the boy shouted loudly, "Uuuugh! The hell! It's filthy! And there's a ton of leaves there!"

"I know, right?!" The girl followed his declaration with an emotional announcement of her own opinion. "What's even the point of cleaning a mess like this? Seeeeeriously."

From the way they were talking, neither had come of their own volition; they'd likely been selected by lottery. But Haruyuki was in a similar position. He had stood up with such force entirely by accident.

However this ended up, having come this far, he had no choice now but to amicably work on this club with these two. He took a deep breath and yet called out in a relatively weak voice, "Um... Anyway, let's decide who does what."

According to the document he had been sent after being assigned to the club, there were two items of work for that day. One was the selection of a president, and the other was cleaning this hutch. They wouldn't be able to go home until they completed both and submitted a signed log file to the in-school server.

It was obvious from looking at the disastrous state of the hutch that the cleaning would be fairly tough, so he wanted to at least quickly knock out the job of assigning jobs. Haruyuki waited a few seconds with the faint expectation that one of them would say, *I'll do it.* Club activities were an extra bit of grading data and also had an impact on high school entrance, so students generally wanted a positive history of being the president of whatever club.

But they hadn't volunteered for this, so obviously, no one there cared about any of that. After a full five seconds had passed, he checked that neither of them were going to open their mouths before smiling weakly and saying, "Okay, then I guess I could take it on. Being the president, I mean."

Annoyed with himself that he couldn't have phrased it more like he was doing them a favor (which he was), he waited for a reaction. The boy, who was rather tanned for being in the go-home club, and the girl, whose hair was permed so that it curled inward, both got unabashedly relieved looks on their faces and nodded together.

"Great."

"Thanks."

All three ran their fingers over their virtual desktops at the same time, opening the newly appearing club activity tab and setting Haruyuki's name in the position column before touching the SIGN button. And with that, Haruyuki was registered in the school local net as the president of the Animal Care Club.

Taking the opportunity to check the names of the other two, he saw the boy was Hamajima and the girl was Izeki. Since there were only three people in the club, a vice president and any lower positions were not required.

*If I knew this was going to happen, I would've volunteered for library aide at the beginning of the term.*

Grumbling to himself, he wiped the window away with a wave of his right hand. At any rate, that was one job done. But the problem was the other job—cleaning the hutch.

He looked over at it again. It was pretty clear that the layer of leaves would indeed be a difficult task, not to mention the filthy plank walls. The leaf layer was at least five centimeters thick, and there was nothing they could do about it without tools of some kind. According to the document, they had been given permission to use the equipment in the cleaning shed in the courtyard.

"Okay, first we need a broom and dustpan. I'll go get them. Just wait here, okay?" he said, and trotted off toward the courtyard on the opposite side of the second school wing. He had the thought that this was still way better than having people behind him shouting, *Run! Run! Run!* and forcing him to go buy bread and things, like they had in seventh grade.

When the three of them actually got to work, the job of cleaning out the hutch was far more difficult than he had expected.

If the matted leaves had been dry, they might have been able to simply sweep them up, but it was the rainy season. And the leaves had apparently been piling up bit by bit for years, so that the ones toward the bottom were basically mulch glued to the floor. With the old-fashioned bamboo brooms—and of course, they were not actually made of bamboo, but hard plastic fibers fashioned to look like bamboo—they were just scraping the surface; they didn't even make a dent in the sticky layers.

"Aaah!" the girl, Izeki, abruptly cried out, after battling the mess of mulch for twenty minutes or so. "Geeez, my hands and my butt seriously huuuuurt!"

"Heh-heh-heh! You're like an old woman!" the boy, Hamajima, jeered, and received a fierce glare, a look that would have turned Haruyuki to stone.

"God, you're seriously annoying. I mean, you've been barely sweeping the same place over and over for forever," Izeki half demanded, half snapped.

"Tsh!" Hamajima clicked his tongue. "Shaddap. All you're doing is putting outside the leaves that *we* sweep up, and you're taking your time at it, too. Taking it easy, huh?"

"What? I don't get your point, though. Are you seriously talking to me like that?"

The exchange between his fellow club members was growing stormier by the second, and Haruyuki started sweating profusely, moving his broom at top speed. He knew he should interrupt and defuse the situation before it turned into a full-blown fight, but he couldn't lift his head, much less open his mouth.

*No. No matter how it happened, I volunteered for this club. I even went further than that: I volunteered to be president. I can call these two out, be harsh. I have a responsibility here, don't I?*

"Uh, um!" Haruyuki called out, this resolution filling his heart. Izeki and Hamajima, both about to explode, turned their gazes on him together.

"...Uh, um." He took a deep breath, put some strength into his abdomen, and readied himself for the harsh law he was about to lay down. "At any rate, we're not going to finish before it's time to go home, so...if you guys just sign the log, you can go now. I'll just hang around so we look good."

In less than a minute, his comrades were retreating at top speed with smiles of pure joy, leaving only their thanks. Alone in the small yard, Haruyuki heaved a deep sigh.

If he were to confess the truth—

He had to say that somewhere in his heart had been at least a milligram of the hope that the other two club members would turn out to be kindhearted, animal-loving girls, and that the club work would be unexpectedly heartwarming. But now that he thought about it, this Animal Care Club would have been formed long ago if there were actually any students like that at Umesato; disgruntled and reluctant comrades were the only logical outcome of a hastily ordered club. In the worst-case scenario, the other two members could have been the type of outlaw students who had so mercilessly bullied him last year. He should be grateful for his good fortune.

With this consoling thought, Haruyuki looked around the hutch once more.

Half of the leaves on the floor were still untouched. The clock in the lower right of his field of view indicated that it was 4:15 PM. The school closed at six, which was when everyone was kicked out, so he did still have some time, but it was pointless to try and attack with his lone broom that black layer, which had practically turned into dirt. If he seriously wanted to make the hutch clean, at least.

"Well, we don't need to get it all done in one day. I mean, there aren't even any animals, so..." Muttering, Haruyuki tossed the broom in his right hand to the ground. He would just kill time with some game app until school closed, put up a show of having tried but still been unable to get it finished, and pick up where he left off the next day. He was about to sit down on the steps at the foot of the exterior wall, when—

*Kuroyukihime.* Her name flashed through his mind, and he stopped dead.

Kuroyukihime had to be still there, too. In the distant student council office, she was no doubt busy with work for the school festival coming up at the end of the month. And Chiyuri and Takumu, too. They were on the field and in the kendo area, moving their bodies with determined focus.

"So after classes end every day, they're here doing stuff like this."

A hoarse sigh of admiration slipped out as he took a hard look at his dirty hands. It wasn't as though anyone was going to high-five him or give him some kind of reward for working hard now. So then why on earth do extracurricular activities anyway?

Kuroyukihime had told him before that she joined the student council so that she could have a hold on the in-school local net as a Burst Linker, but he had a feeling that wasn't the only reason. Right: Kuroyukihime, Takumu, and Chiyuri must have been constantly proving something to themselves. And yet Haruyuki was very close to abandoning the resolution he had made not even an hour earlier to actually work hard on things now.

"Honestly. What is with me…" He let out a long breath, stooped over, and picked the broom up off the ground.

After about five minutes of work, when he had gotten rid of as many of the leaves in the hutch as he could sweep up, he stopped and thought for a while. Ditching the whole project to play games wasn't going to help anything. To take care of the mulch layer before the school closed, he needed to find a better way of doing this. The best thing would likely be to flush it out with a lot of water, but the only thing nearby was the tiny faucet in a corner of the hutch, apparently for drinking water for the animals.

He turned it on to test it, but as expected, the dribbling, unreliable stream of water was basically nothing more than droplets. Filling even one bucket would take far too long. Racking his brain, he finally remembered that club presidents were given the right to higher-level access in the in-school net than regular students were.

He called up a map of the school grounds on his virtual desktop and used the infrastructure information to display an overlay of the water lines. A very thin light blue line stretched up into the hutch, but a thicker pipe and a stopcock were apparently buried in the ground very close by. When he tapped on the position and looked around, his AR displayed an arrow pointing downward in a corner of the campus about three meters away.

"So the water line's there…Um…," he murmured, reset the map, and then selected hoses five meters or more in length from the list of school equipment. When he overlaid the positional information on the map, he found there was one in the tool locker in the first-floor boys' washroom in the second school wing before him. He clicked on a flashing mark and in the window that popped up, requested permission to use the hose. Normally, students were not permitted to touch equipment outside their authorized access, but a second later, his request was approved.

"Ooh," Haruyuki said unconsciously. "The rights of a club president. And now..."

He scrolled through the equipment list again and pulled up a large shovel. There was one in the tool shed in the courtyard, so using it posed no permission problems. Last, he searched for a deck brush, found one for scrubbing tiles in the tool shed in the front yard, and got permission to use it.

"And that's everything. So now gotta fight, maaan!"

If a certain someone had heard him, he would've cried out angrily, *Hey! No imitating my masterful self!* Haruyuki set his sights on the front yard and trotted off.

Tackling the leaves on the floor with the water jetting out of the hose connected to the garden spout was unexpectedly fun, and Haruyuki found himself wondering if this was what Reds felt like with their long-distance attacks.

Naturally, however, the strict school system was not allowing him unlimited access, and the bar showing his water allotment dropped before his eyes. He took careful aim and peeled away one glued-on section after another. But he couldn't very well use up all the water now, given that he would need to scrub the floor with the deck brush later, so he turned the tap off when he still had about 20 percent of his water left.

The floor of the hutch was covered in a muddy soup of old leaves melting in huge puddles, making him think he had only made things worse. He very nearly regretted his choices, but he steadied himself and traded hose for shovel before stepping into the hutch. Fortunately, he was wearing high-cut, water-resistant sneakers to fend off the damp of the rainy season; the dirty water didn't penetrate into his shoes. He would, of course, have to wash them thoroughly once he got home, but he could think later about things that had to happen later.

"Oookay!" he shouted and thrust his shovel into a mass of dirt. The tip sliced straight through to the floor, encountering no resistance. He started scraping away, shoveling up hunks of the black dirt. He staggered under the weight as he tossed his shovel-load outside through the doorway.

It was just barely twenty by forty centimeters, but a piece of actual floor had been revealed. Haruyuki stared, and a somehow strange sensation came over him. A profound reaction, different from when he finished off some troublesome homework or took down a boss character that had killed him countless times. Involuntarily, he very nearly shed a few thin tears, and he hurriedly shook his head. It was way too early still to be feeling any sense of achievement.

He stuck his shovel back in the dirt and tossed out another shovelful. Then another. He took a step forward, tossed out another. His shoulders and back were starting to hurt already, but Haruyuki kept working as though something were spurring him on. He could feel his strength being consumed each time he threw out a heap of dirt, but at the same time, he was learning how to use the shovel and how to put his back into it, so his efficiency gradually improved.

While he was focused on the repetition of this straightforward task, he abruptly felt a prickling stab in the corner of his memory. He had done work like this before sometime, somewhere, hadn't he? But even in childhood, he had barely touched real dirt, and cleaning the house was left to a housekeeping service his mother hired to come in once a week.

Forgetting the pain in his back, he dug intently around in his memories and after about five minutes, he finally hit on it. This wasn't a memory from the real world. It was the Accelerated World—the higher-level Unlimited Neutral Field.

Two months earlier, on their first meeting, Sky Raker had pushed him from the top of the old Tokyo Tower. To climb the sheer face of that three-hundred-meter wall, Haruyuki had undergone serious training. He had held the image of swords in his hands and pierced the wall, hard like steel, thousands, tens of thousands of times. The exact moment when he stood on the threshold of the ultimate power in Brain Burst, the Incarnate System…

"……?" He had the sudden sensation that his thinking had gotten close to something very important for the briefest of moments, and he furrowed his brow. He tried to catch the tail of that thought as he continued to scrape the floor with the shovel.

The Incarnate System. A logic to influence the truth of the Accelerated World and overwrite actual phenomena with a strong imagination, the very definition of tremendous power. The Incarnate of a master surpassed the limitations of the rules of the game and cracked the earth, ripped open the sky. Obviously, a supernatural power, not something that actually existed in the real world.

But…

But the real root of it. Cause leads to effect—this simple structure was perhaps…

*Crack!* The tip of the shovel hit the wall, making the nerves in Haruyuki's hands sing. "Ow!" He started blowing on his palms. Once the pain had passed, he lifted his face.

At some point, the mass of old leaves, which had been piled so high, had been almost completely removed from the hutch. A small mountain had appeared instead on the other side of the chicken wire, a mountain Haruyuki couldn't actually believe he'd made himself with a single shovel.

"When you put your mind to it, you can do anything!"

The aggressively positive thought sprang up from nowhere, and he stretched long and hard as he shouted it. His stiff back creaked and cracked, but not only did he not feel pain, he felt almost refreshed. It would be incredible to just collapse into sleep like that, but he still had one thing left to do. He needed to take care of the remaining dirt and leaves on the floor.

Coming out of the hutch, he changed the weapon in his right hand from shovel to deck brush and readied the hose in his left. The place would shine if he brushed the floor now, applying water bit by bit as he went. The hands of the clock were swinging around to five PM, but summer solstice was near, so it was still plenty bright out. It was totally possible for him to finish this job before six, when the school closed.

Returning to the hutch in high spirits, Haruyuki gasped at a sudden realization. To turn the stream of water from the hose on and off, he had to turn the stopcock on and off. But he would have to head back to the water pipe each time he did so, which made the whole enterprise extremely inefficient. But if he just left the water running, he would quickly use up the water the system had allowed him.

"Hmm." He put his brain to work on the problem, glancing back and forth between the hutch and the spigot. This time, at least, however, no clever solution came to mind. He had the chiding thought that if they were going to go so far as to monitor water usage, they should set it up so that he could open and close the stopcock from a distance, but it was too late for that now. The only thing to do was go back and forth between the hutch and the valve, even if it would take a lot longer that way. He readied himself for this unpleasant end and trudged toward the door.

He had walked a few steps around the mountain of mulch when in the center of his field of view, a yellow radio-wave icon flashed. This was followed by a display below it: AD HOC CONNECTION REQUEST.

An ad hoc connection was used to connect several Neurolinkers wirelessly without passing through a server, but it was almost never used at school. Transmission speed and anonymity were worse than with a wired connection, and more importantly, if you were logged into the in-school local net, it was a fairly pointless function.

*Who on earth could be—?* Haruyuki whirled his head around to both sides before finally turning and looking directly behind him.

For a while, nothing made sense.

A child was looking at Haruyuki. So far, so good. It was a girl. Well within the realm of possibility. But he had definitely never seen her face before. Not only was she clearly not a student at Umesato, she didn't even seem to be in junior high; both the top and bottom of her outfit were genuine snow-white gym clothes. Arriving at this stage of understanding, Haruyuki couldn't help but wonder if his eyes or maybe his brain had malfunctioned. He blinked rapidly and shook his head in sharp, tiny bounces, but the girl before him didn't disappear, so he had no choice but to raise the hand holding the brush and touch the ad hoc connection icon with an outstretched finger.

Instantly, the radio-wave mark and text disappeared, to be replaced by a large-ish window and a blinking cursor—a text-based chat window to converse, instead of speech.

The moment the connection with Haruyuki's Neurolinker was established, the girl—clearly younger than Niko, maybe ten, maybe not—raised both hands. Ten small, too-slender fingers stopped, loosely spread out in midair. The home position for a holokeyboard, Haruyuki realized. The following instant, those fingers flashed, blurred with speed, and a row of characters glowing cherry pink flowed across the chat window in his field of view.

UI> HELLO, NICE TO MEET YOU. YOU'RE A MEMBER OF UMESATO JUNIOR HIGH'S ANIMAL CARE CLUB, RIGHT? MY NAME IS UTAI SHINOMIYA. I'M IN FOURTH GRADE AT MATSUNOGI ACADEMY. THANK YOU SO MUCH FOR ACCEPTING OUR SUDDEN REQUEST. I DO SINCERELY APOLOGIZE FOR ANY BOTHER OR TROUBLE. I'M SOMEWHAT LATE, BUT I'LL ALSO ASSIST IN THE CLEANING.

"……?!" Haruyuki stood rooted to the spot, enormously shocked, but not by the details of her message.

*She's fast!!*

Her typing skills were absurd. It hadn't taken her even a full four seconds to input all those characters. If he hadn't actually seen her type it out, he would no doubt have thought that she had copied and pasted a message prepared in advance.

Haruyuki was secretly proud that his typing speed was number one, or maybe number two, in the school, just barely losing out to Kuroyukihime. At the very least, he had been at the top of his class by a wide margin when he took the mock typing exam in his information processing class. And although he got no par-

ticular respect for this skill, he still held it as a natural virtue. However, the fingers of the small girl before him were obviously twice as fast—or even faster—as Haruyuki's own. He gaped at her, wondering exactly what kind of practice you had to do for technique like that.

No matter how he looked at it, he couldn't believe that the girl who had called herself Shinomiya wasn't a master of Linker skills. She was on the small side for fourth grade. The limbs stretching out from the short sleeves of her gym shirt and the shorts that stopped above the knee were almost worryingly thin. Her face was stereotypically Japanese with a crisp structure, as though a master carver had in one quick session chiseled out the single-lidded eyes, the nose, the mouth. A jet-black fringe hung neatly slightly below her eyebrows, and her hair was pulled up in a high position. On her back, a chic brown leather backpack; in her right hand, a fairly large sports bag.

Haruyuki stared vacantly for a while at this figure with an air of refreshment about her—he could almost forget the humid heat of the rainy season just looking at her—before he finally noticed the questioning look she was giving him. He remembered that he hadn't actually responded to her yet.

He opened his mouth to say *hello* at any rate, but then thought he should maybe answer her in the chat window, too.

He hurriedly called up his holokeyboard and went to type out a reply, but he was still holding the brush and the hose. He quickly placed them on the ground and had lifted his arms back up when characters began flowing across the window once more.

UI> IT'S PERFECTLY FINE FOR YOU TO SPEAK TO ME.

"Oh…r-right." His idiotic first words slipped out of him, arms still slightly raised.

The whole situation was full of things he didn't understand. Why was the girl speaking in chat? What was this "sudden request" she mentioned? And why would a kid from another school—an elementary school to boot—show up there to begin with? About the only thing he could surmise was that the text tagging the beginning of her messages in the chat window was probably a nickname, a shortening of *Utai* to *Ui*.

Scratching his head with his right hand, which had nowhere to go now, Haruyuki set his confused thoughts free as vocal output. "Oh, umm. N-nice to meet you. I'm Haruyuki Arita…I'm in grade eight at Umesato. I guess I'm the president of the Animal Care Club…although I just started today…"

Immediately, the sentence UI> Yes. I know that the Animal Care Club here was established today scrolled out at high speed.

"Huh? Y-you do? How? And…why would you go out of your way to come to some other school and help?"

UI> Because the club here was launched due to a request for cooperation from Matsunogi Academy's elementary division.

"Huh? I-it was?!"

In contrast with the stunned Haruyuki, the elementary school girl was utterly calm as she explained to him why they were there in a way that was easy to understand, keyboard work increasingly brisk.

Umesato Junior High was a private, and at any rate, academic school in Suginami Ward in Tokyo. However, an education-related business, headquartered in Shinjuku, operated the school instead of an incorporated educational institution. This company also owned a girls' school that went from grade one all the way through to grade twelve in Suginami: Matsunogi Academy, the school Utai Shinomiya attended.

Although Umesato had an almost thirty-year history, this paled beside Matsunogi Academy, in its ninety-fifth year since its founding. Put briefly, it was a rich girls' school. Nevertheless, unable to avoid the nationwide wave of declining birth rates, the school had, due to management difficulties, been bought up ten years earlier by the current owner. The drastic countermeasures that had been taken to streamline school operations had been insufficient, so that finally, the company had decided to sell a part of the grounds that summer and build a new combined school building to house the elementary and junior high sections with the profits. Given that it was a school with a long tradition, parents naturally raised their voices in opposition, but the parent management organization was a publicly traded company with a bottom line. The decision was not overturned, and the current elementary school building would be demolished at the end of the first term.

However, the majority of the students welcomed the change because of the cutting-edge educational environment—starting with a high-spec VR local net—that was going to be introduced to the new school building, which the same corporation had cultivated at Umesato Junior High. But this move would reduce the total area of the school, and several facilities would not be transferred to the new building. One of these was the old animal hutch standing quietly in a corner of Matsunogi Academy's elementary school.

UI> Naturally, I protested to the teachers and the management company. The Animal Care Club has as its members not only the students, but also the animals we care for. The students might be able to move to another club or team, but the animals cannot. However, the company simply kept replying that "The animals being cared for will be handled appropriately based on the law." Which is to say, that they would be killed.

"They wouldn't!" Haruyuki called out reflexively, the instant he read that far into the smoothly scrolling text. However much profit-chasing was the mission of a publicly traded corporation, killing the animals because there was no longer a place to keep them was just too much. He couldn't even imagine how great the shock must have been for the children who had been caring for them for such a long time. If they were going to do that, then—then…

Haruyuki's righteous indignation slammed up against a thick wall and raced emptily.

He could also picture the situation on the management side: Building a new animal hutch would be difficult when the school site shrank to reduce costs. He felt like the students could maybe take the animals into their homes, but keeping animals was impossible unless you had a passion and the appropriate environment for it. That said, releasing them into the wild outside the city or something was out of the question, and more important, it was also a crime.

The girl with the old-style name of Utai looked at Haruyuki biting his lip, sunk into thought, and seemed just the slightest bit troubled. Her fingers started moving once again, and the text flowed quickly before his eyes.

UI> You have no need to worry. None of the animals have actually been disposed of yet.

"Huh? Th-they haven't? Good..." Unconsciously, he let out a sigh of relief.

Utai's fingers continued to dance out their explanation. UI> A farm family who keep free-range birds in their garden out toward Sayama were kind enough to take in the seven bantams we were raising. We also found a reliable person within the ward to adopt our two rabbits. But there's one animal we can't seek out a new home for due to certain circumstances.

"You can't...look for a new home? Not you can't find one?"

Utai nodded sharply. Her hair, tied up with a white ribbon, swung above her shoulders. The ends were so neatly aligned that rather than a ponytail, her hair looked like that of a girl from a samurai family in some period drama. A thoughtfulness flitted across her similarly traditionally Japanese face before the elementary school student ran her fingers over her holokeyboard. Quite a bit of time had passed since this strange conversation had begun, but she hadn't made a single typo so far, and her word choice was excessively adult.

UI> His situation is a little complicated, and he now will not eat his food unless it comes from my hand. Once,

I TRIED TO FAMILIARIZE HIM WITH ANOTHER MEMBER OF THE CLUB AND ENTRUSTED THE FEEDING TO THAT STUDENT, BUT HE ESSENTIALLY WOULDN'T EAT AT ALL AND QUICKLY LOST WEIGHT. I'LL GO OVER THIS IN DETAIL AGAIN TOMORROW WHEN I BRING HIM HERE, BUT BECAUSE OF THIS SITUATION, THE ABSOLUTE NEED AROSE TO FIND A NEW PLACE TO KEEP HIM WITHIN A RANGE I AM ABLE TO COMMUTE DAILY.

"I—I get it," Haruyuki said, his physical voice three times more faltering than Utai's typing, as the situation finally sank in. "So then, Umesato, which is part of the same corporation, has this animal hutch they're not using, so they offered it to you and started an Animal Care Club here, too. But our main job isn't to care for any animals, but to clean out the hutch, which is why only three people were recruited...Is that it?"

UI> THAT'S EXACTLY RIGHT. I APOLOGIZE FOR THE INCONVENIENCE FOR YOU.

"Oh, no, it's fine...But I'm kinda surprised our school was so ready to help out. Maybe I shouldn't say this, but our admin's pretty cold. I got the impression they wouldn't do even a minute of extra work for anything."

*We might be in the same corporate group, but if they can be nice enough to keep some other school's animals here, maybe they could've taken a little better care of me when I was getting beat up last year.* The thought he couldn't actually say aloud went round and round in his head.

Almost as if reading his mind, Utai said—or rather, wrote, UI> I'M SORRY. THERE ARE ACTUALLY CIRCUMSTANCES AROUND THIS. I KNOW SOMEONE ON THE STUDENT COUNCIL HERE, SO SHE WAS ABLE TO MAKE THE ARRANGEMENTS FOR ME.

"Oh, is that what happened?"

That made sense. The majority of students in the elementary division of Matsunogi Academy went directly on to the junior high and high school divisions, without having to deal with entrance examinations, but he had heard that kids from families that really care about those exams sometimes came to Umesato Junior High. In which case, it wasn't at all strange that Utai would know someone at this school.

Having heard—or rather read—the explanation this far, Haruyuki finally understood why he had suddenly become a member of the Animal Care Club. The basic reason was that the club at Matsunogi Academy in the same corporate group had been eliminated, and the reason for that was the streamlining of operations. And the reason for that was the declining birth rate, which showed no signs of stopping; in short, it was society's fault. Although, naturally, ending up president of the Animal Care Club and cleaning the hutch by himself was Haruyuki's own fault.

"Right...You're pretty amazing, Shinomiya. I mean, you go up against a big company, find adoptive homes, and even come all the way to another school for the sake of these homeless animals. When I was in fourth grade, the only things I ever thought about were video games, manga, anime, and snacks," Haruyuki murmured, heartfelt.

Utai shook her head quickly, a serious expression on her face. Slipping her backpack off her shoulders, she dexterously tapped away at the keyboard. UI> I play games, too. And now that I've been able to go over with you the circumstances leading up to this situation, I'd like to help clean the hutch, Arita-san.

"Oh! R-right." He finally remembered that he had been in the middle of the club work and hurried to pick up the hose and deck brush at his feet.

He couldn't see the point of it when he had been cleaning by himself, but now all these bits and pieces had been explained to him—and, more important, now that he knew there was actually an animal moving in here—he had to put some real elbow grease into the work. "All right! Let's do this!" he cried out with new resolve in his heart, and turned his eyes to the hutch.

The cleaning would be done once he rinsed away the remaining slush and leaves stuck to the floor, but he had been struggling with how to turn the water valve on and off. He was actually grateful someone had shown up to help him at such a perfect time.

"Okay, then, maybe I could get you to turn that valve on and off for me?" Haruyuki pointed to the base of the hose.

Utai cocked her head, confused. UI> IS THAT THE ONLY TASK YOU NEED ME TO DO? I DID COME IN MY GYM CLOTHES, PREPARED TO GET DIRTY.

Reading this, Haruyuki stared at Utai again—white short-sleeved shirt with the school emblem on the chest, similarly white shorts covering skinny legs—and quickly averted his eyes. The gym clothes at Umesato were navy blue, but basically the same style otherwise, and he should have been accustomed to seeing girls wearing this outfit at school every day. But when he thought about the fact that the girl before him was one of Matsunogi's princesses, he got the feeling he shouldn't be looking at her. If Chiyuri found out thoughts like this had even crossed his mind, she would totally shoot endless super-firepower beams from both eyes.

"Y-yeah. Just gotta scrub the floor with the brush, and it's all done! So, uh, when I give the signal, please open the valve about three-quarters!" he told her, voice slightly raised, before trotting back over to the animal hutch. He decided to rinse it out from the far side and readied the hose and brush before shouting, "G-go ahead!"

UI> I'M TURNING IT ON NOW.

He got an instantaneous reply via text, followed by a fairly modest stream of water coming from the end of the hose. Keeping a careful eye on the water gauge in the edge of his vision, he thoroughly rinsed an area about one square meter and then instructed, "Turn it off!" In lieu of a reply, the valve squealed shut.

Putting his strength into scrubbing, he easily peeled away the last of the leaves and dirt stuck to the floor to reveal the ceramic tile beneath. Fortunately, it appeared to have been given a solid weather- and dirt-resistant coating, and there were relatively few depressions or cracks for how many years it had sat there covered in wet leaves. If they just let it dry out for a day, it would likely return to its original appearance.

Haruyuki deftly shifted between watering an area and brushing it out. If he had had to turn the valve on and off himself, his efficiency would have no doubt dropped significantly. But more than that, just thinking that he had someone working seriously alongside him had the strange effect of strengthening his desire to get the job done, despite the fact that he had been incredibly listless working with Hamajima and Izeki, both of whom made their annoyance plain with their entire bodies.

Twenty minutes later, he was done brushing the entire floor. "All right! Now we just need to put on the finishing touches," he said, stretching hard. He turned around to call out to Utai Shinomiya crouching down by the stopcock. "Okay, I'm going to rinse the whole floor now, so open it all way!"

Instead of nodding, Utai tapped her fingers in space. Pink text rolled into his field of view, somewhat coldly, perhaps not wanting to intrude. UI> If I wouldn't be in the way, would you allow me to help as well? It would be more effective to use the brush at the same time as the water comes out, and I would like to work a little.

"Oh! No, you're working plenty already. But if that's what you want," Haruyuki mumbled and held the deck brush up. Utai got the smallest expression of delight on her face, and then nodded sharply before resting her right hand on the valve and typing adroitly with her left.

UI> All right. I'm coming, then.

"Great!"

The valve squeaked all the way open, and the hose shook forcefully from the base. Utai started running earnestly as if trying to overtake the water racing along inside the hose.

Springing into the hutch a few seconds after the high-pressure water began to gush out, the girl took the brush from Haruyuki and turned her focus on pushing the water flooding the floor out through the mesh. She matched her breathing with this movement, and Haruyuki showered the hutch from front to back with the stream of water, clutching the hose with both hands because it threatened to fly away. The remaining 20 percent in the water meter approached zero before his eyes, but each time the deck brush moved with a forceful scrape, the ceramic tiles beneath took on their original attractive light brown.

Utai's brushwork was actually impressive, the way she put her back into it. She was probably used to this sort of large-scale cleaning. Feeling a curious admiration for the princess school, Haruyuki stayed steadfast with the hose and pushed the garbage floating on the floor to the outside. In mere minutes, the floor was sparkling like an entirely different floor, and at the same time, they had almost used up all of the water allotted to them by the system.

*Perfect rationing, if I do say so myself!* Feeling a certain satisfaction in his heart, Haruyuki looked at Utai with a smile and started, "Okay, now the valve..." before stopping in his tracks.

His partner had been in charge of the valve but was now inside the hutch, and so couldn't reach the spigot. And that valve wasn't automatic, so the water wasn't going to stop when they reached their limit. Which meant they would be over their allotment in a minute or two if the water kept flowing like this. Naturally, he wouldn't be arrested and sent to jail or anything, but a "minor infraction" would be noted on his record in the local net, and that would lead to a teacher having words with him at some later date, words he very much did not want to have.

"Crap." Haruyuki instantly gripped the hose as hard as he could. The dammed water flow shuddered in protest, but the meter essentially stopped. Astutely guessing the situation from Haruyuki's actions, Utai stopped her typing, threw the brush down, whirled around, and ran for the stopcock. And then it happened. Catastrophe.

Haruyuki's thumb applying firm pressure to the hose slipped, and the superpowered water surged out with overwhelming force, a fully charged long-distance attack and—

*Splash!* A direct hit on the gym-clothing-clad Utai from her right shoulder down to her stomach.

His brain overflowed at the magnitude of the disaster he had himself wrought; he froze. In contrast, although the much younger elementary school student did stop dead for a moment, a look of surprise on her face, she quickly started running again. She crouched down by the stopcock in the corner of the school building about three meters away and quickly shut the valve off. The water meter in the right corner of his vision was at 0.2 percent; they had narrowly avoided overusage.

But, unaware of this, Haruyuki remained frozen, the hose in his right hand hanging in the air. He watched Utai trot back over to him, typing as a tiny ocean of water drops trickled down from her torso.

UI> PLEASE DON'T WORRY ABOUT THIS. I CHANGED INTO MY GYM CLOTHES BEFORE I CAME, READY FOR JUST SUCH AN EVENTUALITY. Then, the look on her face not changing, she pulled up a large chunk of the hem of the shirt plastered to her skin and wrung it out with both hands.

The paleness of the bare skin he saw whether he wanted to or not due to this innocent gesture crashed into the transmission of Haruyuki's idling thoughts and got things in gear. The speedometer plunged into the red zone at once. When Haruyuki had finally recovered to the point of his normal reaction to stress and/or embarrassment—increased sweating, redness of the face, heart palpitations—he snapped to attention.

"I-I'm—I'm sorry!!" he shouted in an inside-out voice. "R-r-really sorry! Th-that totally wasn't on purpose. M-m-m-my hand slipped a-a-and the water—the water splashed…"

Utai blinked a few times as she cocked her small head before her fingers flashed along once more. UI> IT'S FINE! I ALSO BROUGHT A CHANGE OF CLOTHES, SO THERE'S REALLY NO PROBLEM.

"B-b-b-but getting hit by water with that kind of power, your N-N…"

*Your Neurolinker will get wet*, he tried to say, looking at Utai's slender neck.

Every model of Neurolinker, an everyday wearable device, was water-resistant to the extent that the wearer could wash or bathe with it on. However, the direct connection terminals and the camera lens were weak points, and there was the risk of water getting in and causing a malfunction if these areas were immersed in water or hit with a high-pressure jet. This was what Haruyuki was worried about. But.

He kept looking at the nape of Utai's neck, covered by the broad-based ponytail, and he kept seeing nothing there. Just the tips of the fine hairs there glistening with tiny water drops; there was absolutely nothing in the way of a device.

"What..." The word slipped out of Haruyuki, struck by a new kind of surprise.

Utai Shinomiya was not wearing a Neurolinker. But that wasn't possible. Less than an hour ago, she had made an ad hoc connection with his own Neurolinker. She'd been talking with him through the chat tool this whole time.

Thinking about it, Haruyuki finally stumbled on the question he should have hit a lot sooner: Why chat? He had just accepted it because they could have a conversation without any lag thanks to her incredible typing speed, but now that he was really thinking about it, Utai hadn't said anything in her physical voice since she showed up. And naturally, there had to be some kind of reason for that.

Utai seemed to intuit the meaning of Haruyuki's gaze. The irises of her eyes seemed to have a bit of red mixed in as she turned them on him directly. She slid the fingertips of her right hand, and instantly, a long vertical rectangle popped up in his field of view.

A name tag. Displayed in the center was UTAI SHINOMIYA and then in a slightly smaller font, SUMIRE CLASS, GRADE FOUR, MATSUNOGI ACADEMY. BORN: SEPTEMBER 15, 2037." However, a resident net-certified name tag was generally horizontal; this one was vertical for an unexpected reason: An unfamiliar certificate was attached below the name display field. The text, in a severe Mincho font, read, CERTIFICATE OF PERMISSION FOR USE OF A DURA-CONTAINED TRANSMISSION DEVICE FOR MEDICAL PURPOSES, and then below that to the right, a stamp of authentication from the Ministry of Health, Labour, and Welfare.

Haruyuki stared at the row of kanji characters, the meaning of which was difficult to grasp at first glance. He went backward and forward, trying to pull out the meaning. *Contained transmission device* was a microchip implanted in the body. And *dura* was probably inside the skull—the membrane surrounding the brain. So a transmission chip implanted in the brain...Then that meant—

A brain implant chip. BIC for short.

"Ngh!" Haruyuki fiercely resisted his body's impulse to jump back in shock.

A mere two months earlier, a seventh-grade student had appeared before him soon after the start of the new school year, a boy with terrifying plans who tried to steal a great number of things from Haruyuki. He, too, had had a BIC. At the end of a long and difficult battle, he—Dusk Taker—had left the Accelerated World forever, but the organization he belonged to was still going strong. In fact, a second assassin, Rust Jigsaw, had jumped into the Hermes' Cord race event the previous week and released a wide-range Incarnate attack forcefully boosted by his BIC, destroying the race itself.

It wasn't difficult to imagine the Acceleration Research Society, the organization both Linkers belonged to, ramping up their attacks on the Accelerated World, so Haruyuki couldn't help but be reflexively on guard against Utai Shinomiya, a BIC user he was meeting for the first time. But before all of this showed up on his face, his eyes finally fell on the last of the words inscribed on the certificate.

*Medical purposes.*

The members of the Acceleration Research Society—Dusk Taker, Rust Jigsaw, and Black Vise—had all had their BICs implanted illegally through black-market surgeries. Naturally, they would not have certificates of approved use from the Ministry of Health, Labour, and Welfare. Even if it was a fake, the complex stamp of authentication glittering on the surface of the tag at least could not be re-created, no matter what kind of hacker you were. Kuroyukihime had once presented a name tag with a revised name, but the tag itself hadn't been created from zero. She had simply rewritten the encrypted name data. Although even that, no doubt, required a seriously high level of skill.

In other words, according to the certificate Utai was showing him, she had a legal BIC for medical treatment. In which case, what on earth was the medical problem?

Seeming to read these thoughts in his eyes with her sharp insight, Utai stroked her holokeyboard with a calm look. UI> I apologize for not explaining sooner. You were chatting so naturally with me, Arita, that I simply missed the opportunity to mention it. Due to expressive aphasia, I'm not able to converse with my physical voice. So I speak with people like this in chat, using my BIC.

"Ex...pressive?" Haruyuki said. He had a rough idea of what *aphasia* was, but was unable to dig out the meaning of the word attached before it.

Naturally, the explanation scrolled out from Utai, who was likely used to typing it. UI> Broadly speaking, aphasia is divided into the two categories of expressive and receptive. Receptive aphasia is a syndrome where the sufferer has difficulty understanding words themselves, and in that situation, a mutual understanding cannot be reached via chat. In contrast, expressive aphasia is a syndrome in which the function to move the vocal organs and speak in words is inhibited. We can understand words, however, so reading and writing is possible.

Haruyuki read the text displayed over and over until he finally digested the difference between the two, and then timidly gave voice to the question that popped into his head. "Umm...So then what about neurospeak with a directly connected Neurolinker instead of a BIC?"

Almost as if she had been expecting the question, Utai promptly typed out a reply. UI> Neurospeak via the Neurolinker is not actually thinking, but a voice that is re-created by reading the movement signals of the speaker attempting to move their mouth, tongue, and cheeks. Some people with a mild form of expressive aphasia are able to do

THIS, BUT THE SIGNALS TO PRODUCE A VOICE ARE COMPLETELY BLOCKED BY NEURONS SOMEWHERE IN MY BRAIN. LIKE THIS.

Here, Utai stopped typing and turned the index finger of her right hand toward her mouth. As Haruyuki stared intently, the small lips the color of cherry blossoms gently opened. He could just barely see the tip of her tongue between her droplet teeth shining like pearls. She took a deep breath and went to expel it as sound. Before she could, there was a hard, sharp *clack*ing sound, and her top and bottom teeth were biting down forcefully. The tendons around her throat popped up thinly, trembling, showing the great effort in her jaw. He heard the creak of her teeth clamped down against her will, and a hint of pain crossed Utai's neat face.

"I-I'm sorry! That's good, that's enough!!" Haruyuki cried out unconsciously, and took a step forward. He stretched a hand out toward a slim, rigid shoulder, but he hesitated to actually touch her and froze in a halfway position.

Fortunately, the tension in her was released a few seconds later. She tottered for a moment and, expelling a deep breath, she lifted her face and began typing only the slightest bit awkwardly. UI> I APOLOGIZE FOR WORRYING YOU. I WASN'T INITIALLY INTENDING TO REALLY TRY AND USE MY VOICE, BUT I GOT THE FEELING THAT PERHAPS I MIGHT BE ABLE TO SPEAK, AND I JUST...THERE'S NO REASON I WOULD BE ABLE TO, AND YET I DID SOMETHING SO STUPID. I DO APOLOGIZE.

"You don't need to apologize." Haruyuki shook his head fiercely. Deeply regretting that a mere minute before he had been alarmed by Utai's BIC, he spoke urgently. "I-I'm the one who's sorry, asking you about all this just to satisfy my own curiosity. I should know better; I know how neurospeak works...If I had just thought about it a little more...I'm the stupid one."

Unable to look at her anymore, he dropped his head, and cherry-colored text scrolled slowly against the backdrop of the hutch's floor tiles shining in the evening light that leaked in.

UI> THANK YOU SO MUCH. I'M NOT BOTHERED BY ANY OF THIS, SO PLEASE, ARITA, I HOPE YOU WON'T BE, EITHER. NOW THEN,

SHALL WE PUT AWAY THE TOOLS? THE HUTCH IS SO NICE NOW. THAT'S MORE THAN ENOUGH CLEANING. I'M SURE MY LITTLE ONE WILL BE VERY HAPPY.

Haruyuki timidly raised his eyes and looked at Utai's small face. Just as she had said—or rather written—there was not the slightest hint of ill humor there, and he finally relaxed his shoulders, nodding. "Right. I'll put everything away. You should hurry and change. There's an emergency exit on that side of the school building, and there's a washroom on the left side a little ways in down the hallway there." He spoke at high speed and had picked up the brush when a fairly forceful objection appeared in his field of view.

UI> I'M FINE. PLEASE LET ME FINISH THIS WITH YOU. I'LL TAKE THE HOS Her words stopped abruptly as she took a sharp breath.

*Choo!* she sneezed, somewhat adorably.

That was the first time Haruyuki heard Utai Shinomiya's real voice.

5:45 PM. Having completed the mission to clean the animal hutch and return the cleaning tools, Haruyuki opened the Animal Care Club activity log file, added his name after the authentications already saved for the other two members, and sent it to the school system.

"Phew." He let out a deep breath and once again looked around the now-clean space.

Although there were still little puddles of water here and there, the ceramic tiles, original light-brown color reinstated, were like a whole different floor from the mulch layer that was there before he started working. The stainless steel chicken wire and the plank walls were dusty, but they would clean up nicely if he took a brush to them the next day.

Of course, the emptiness inside was balanced out by the little mountain of dead leaves and dirt he had made in front of the hutch, but he should be able to stuff that into a garbage bag and throw it away once it dried. Fortunately, the weather forecast was predicting no real rainfall over the next few days, so it wouldn't take too long for it to dry out.

"When you put your mind to it, you really can do it," Haruyuki murmured.

Utai Shinomiya had finished changing and quickly typed out, UI> Yesterday, I actually was allowed to take a preliminary look at the hutch. At the time, I expected that it would take three or four days before it became usable. But the work's gone so much more quickly than I anticipated. It seems I'll be able to bring the animal who'll be living here tomorrow. The administration has been quite insistent about moving things along, so this helps me immensely. Thank you so much, Arita.

"Oh, uh…If I had just been a little more together," Haruyuki mumbled, omitting the words *if I hadn't sent the other two club members home early*, "we could've finished a bit sooner. And…now I'm really curious. What kind of animal are you going to keep here?"

He glanced at Utai standing there next to him, and her large eyes with their red-tinged irises sparkled. She tapped just the index finger of her right hand rhythmically. UI> Not. Telling.

"O-oh. Then I guess I get to find out tomorrow," he fumbled out in reply and once more turned his gaze directly to his side.

The summer uniform at Matsunogi Academy elementary was a straight-line dress with a white sailor collar and two wide darts running down from fairly high up on the waist. The whole silhouette was somehow reminiscent of old-style *hakama* pants.

Haruyuki's eyes stopped unconsciously for a few seconds on this unfamiliar uniform before he brought his eyes hurriedly forward again. "Th-the school closes in ten minutes, so we should get going. Thanks for your help today."

UI> Thank you. I look forward to seeing you again tomorrow. Utai then typed something unexpected. I'm going to give my greetings to the student council office, so please go on ahead of me, Arita.

"Huh?" He whirled his whole body to the right to stare at Utai.

She had indeed said before that she knew someone on the student council, but even still, it took surprising nerve for a fourth grader to march into the student council office of some junior high school.

She met his wide-open stare with a strange look and then dipped her head, typing coolly, UI> WELL THEN, IF YOU'LL PLEASE EXCUSE ME. HAVE A GOOD DAY, ARITA. She spun around and started walking briskly toward the main gate.

"O-oh, I'll come, too!" Haruyuki called out to her back, half reflexively. "I know someone in the student council, too, so..."

He didn't know how many people would still be in the student council office on the first floor of the first wing, but there was a pretty high probability that Kuroyukihime was among them. Kuroyukihime might very well react with the same feelings of alarm as Haruyuki at Utai's BIC. He needed to tell her as soon as possible that there was no way that Utai, who wasn't even wearing a Neurolinker, could be an assassin from the Acceleration Research Society or anything like that.

Utai looked at him trotting up alongside her, a curious expression on her face, but she simply nodded without saying—writing—anything.

They entered the campus through the main gates, and just as he had changed out of his filthy sneakers, a warning announcement from the school system played in his vision and hearing. He frowned at the synthetic voice, rambling on about how anyone who did not leave the school within five minutes would have a third-level infraction of school rules noted on their personal record. Even with the privileges of a club president, this was a rule he could not disobey. The only ones who could request permission to stay after the school closing time were the members of the student council.

His only choice was to get Kuroyukihime to let him stay longer, but he wasn't sure she would approve of mixing business and personal like this. Heart racing, Haruyuki walked down the hallway of the first school wing, while Utai Shinomiya next to him looked as calm as she always did.

*When I was in fourth grade, there's a good chance I would've passed out just taking one step onto the campus of a junior high school I didn't know.* Pathetic thoughts racing through his head, he caught sight of the dead end on the west side. The door in the wall on the right led to the student council office. Now that he was thinking about it, in the year and three months since he'd started school here, he had never once been inside.

When Haruyuki hung back before the closed white sliding door, Utai raised her right hand without a hint of hesitation and knocked at a single point in the air. A holowindow was displayed, and she pressed the entry button.

Two seconds later, he heard the sharp *click* of the door being unlocked. Her expression unchanging, Utai slid the door open and stepped inside after bowing lightly.

*Uh, umm, what should I…*Haruyuki stood still in the hallway, agonizing even now, although he had already made his choice, until a familiar voice reached his ears.

"Sorry, Utai. My work here took longer than I expected. I suppose you're not done cleaning the hutch yet? I'll come and help right away."

*Huh?*

There was no doubt that the voice he had just heard was Kuroyukihime's. And she had called Utai by her first name, as if it were the most natural thing in the world. Which meant the person Utai Shinomiya said she knew on the student council was, in fact, the vice president, Kuroyukihime. Was that it? But what on earth could those two have in common?!

He stopped in his tracks, head reeling in confusion, and a new line of text scrolled across the chat tool still displayed in his field of view.

UI> THE CLEANING'S FINISHED. THIS GENTLEMAN HERE WORKED VERY HARD ALL BY HIMSELF TO FINISH IT FOR ME.

"This gentleman? Where?"

Hearing the suspicion in Kuroyukihime's voice, Haruyuki realized he couldn't lurk in the hallway any longer and so stepped awkwardly out of the shadows to cross the threshold. Head still hanging, he reached a hand behind him to close the door before nervously lifting his gaze.

Seeing the Umesato Junior High student council office for the first time, he found it much larger than he had expected. In the middle of the room was an elliptical meeting table, while a long office desk had been placed farther in by the window, and grid-like wooden racks had been set up on the walls to the left and right. All the furniture was a relaxed, dark-brown natural wood, a thick beige carpet was laid out on the floor, and there was even a large sofa set to the immediate left of the doorway, making it hard to believe that this was a room in a junior high school. The space was conceivably more luxurious than the principal's office (which he had peeked into just once before).

Utai stood by the edge of the conference table in front of him, and Kuroyukihime was on one side of the sofa set. There was no one else in the room. Apparently, Kuroyukihime had been working overtime by herself, but what he hadn't been expecting was her outfit.

"K-Kuroyukihime, why are you wearing that?" Haruyuki asked, instantly forgetting his questions about her relationship with Utai.

Kuroyukihime briskly brought her arms up to hide the form-fitting black T-shirt and the navy shorts—her gym clothes. She pursed her lips, cheeks reddening slightly. "N-no, this is, er," she said somewhat shrilly. "I simply thought I should be dressed to get dirty if I was going to clean that hutch. Anyway, more important, what are you doing here, Haruyuki?"

"Me? Oh…umm…Why am I here again?" Haruyuki mumbled, honestly not knowing for a moment, and Utai's words marched across the chat window, exasperated somehow.

UI> Arita is the president of the Animal Care Club. He cleaned out the hutch for me. When I said that I was

COMING TO THE STUDENT COUNCIL OFFICE TO SAY HELLO, HE CAME WITH ME, BUT I DON'T KNOW WHY.

*Seriously, what was it…*

At almost the same time he sank into belated thought, he heard Kuroyukihime sounding equally surprised and exasperated. "Y-you're the club president?! How did…Oh, I see, the result of a lotto, then? Honestly, at such a difficult time, you do get pulled along with the currents, Haruyuki."

If he said here that he'd volunteered through a misunderstanding, the whole situation would probably get more complicated, so he simply flashed an embarrassed smile. "No, it's not that bad."

Shifting his gaze, he was overwhelmed by the charm of Kuroyukihime in her gym clothes, a different appeal than her usual tidy, uniformed self. Maybe because she had her hair pulled back in a ponytail like Utai, the way she looked made him feel a bursting energy.

He stared vacantly until he stumbled upon the obvious question. "A-anyway, why were you going to clean the hutch out? You can't be on both the student council and in the Animal Care Club…can you?"

"Oh, that. Well…" Kuroyukihime cut herself off as if having realized something and briskly moved her fingers over her virtual desktop. In Haruyuki's field of view, a message scrolled by to the effect that he had been given permission to stay past school closing. Looking at his clock, he saw it was only seven seconds before six. He started to thank her, but she brushed his words away with a wave of her hand and continued.

"I assumed that just three people—all of whom would no doubt be decided by lottery—would be unable to clean that hutch in a short time. I promised Utai to make the hutch usable as soon as possible, you see. And I thought I would help clean until they kicked us out. I never dreamed you would be in the Animal Care Club, or that you'd be able to clean up that mess in a mere two hours. You did well, Haruyuki."

She nodded deeply at him with a gentle smile, and an invisible hand squeezed his heart tightly. He simply stood there and stared into her eyes, not knowing how to respond.

*The truth is, I was gonna skip out. But then I thought about how you were probably working hard at your own stuff, which gave me the strength to work hard, too. And yet you…Once your own work was finished, you were planning to go over and clean out that hutch…*

He didn’t know how far this inner voice of his reached, but Kuroyukihime nodded slowly once more.

Interrupting this magical moment was the cherry-colored font scrolling across the chat window at super-high speed. UI> I apologize for bothering you when you’re staring at each other, but I would appreciate it if you could tell me already. Are you and Arita friends, Sacchi?

Blinking rapidly, Kuroyukihime looked at Utai to the right of Haruyuki. “Oh, right,” she said. “No, I’m sorry. That’s right, you don’t know, do you, Uiui? My mistake.”

*Sacchi? Uiui?* Dumfounded, Haruyuki looked back and forth between the two girls as he listened to Kuroyukihime’s concise explanation.

“He—Haruyuki Arita—is the vanguard of my Legion, my ‘child,’ Uiui.”

“Hng…?! Unh?!!”

*Wh-wh-what are you sayiiiiiing?!* Haruyuki shrieked in his heart.

Utai’s clear response flowed before his eyes. UI> Oh, is that how you know each other? Is Arita that Silver Crow?

“???!!!??!!?!?!”

*I-I’ve been outed in the real before my own eyyyyyyes!*

Reflexively, he started to flee, but the door was locked, and no matter how he pulled and it clattered, it wouldn’t open.

“Look, Haruyuki,” Kuroyukihime called to his back, utterly stunned. “I think you should be able to figure out just how this all came about. It’s obvious she—Utai Shinomiya—is a Burst Linker like us, and that she was a member of the first Nega Nebulus, all right?”

# 5

*I don't trust anyone anymore*, Haruyuki muttered to himself bleakly, like the dark hero in an old manga might say while lowering the gun in his right hand and pressing on a wound with his left.

He crouched in one corner of the sofa in the student council office, a cup of black tea in both hands. Made for him by Kuroyukihime herself, it was Darjeeling, which somehow seemed luxurious, but he still hadn't recovered from the shock enough to be able to enjoy the sweet fragrance.

*Okay, saying I don't trust anyone is maybe too much, but at the very least, I'm suspicious. All the people who show up suddenly and are ridiculously relaxed and treat me like a human being are without exception Burst Linkers. And high-level old-timers. I'm not wrong here.*

He glanced at the sofa across from him; Utai Shinomiya was just pouring milk into her cup, a serious look on her face. She nodded as if she had poured in just the right amount, put the pitcher back, and stirred solemnly with a spoon.

Watching this childish gesture, he realized this was still hard for him to understand. Utai was in fourth grade at Matsunogi Academy, a school in the same corporate group as Umesato; she was born in September 2037; and so, she was currently just nine years and nine months old. Two years younger than the Red King Niko. The first Nega Nebulus vanished two and a half years earlier after the show of insurrection by its leader, Black Lotus, which meant Utai would actually have only been seven at the time. So then at what age exactly had she become a Burst Linker?

Too many questions gnawing at him, Haruyuki sipped his tea, while Kuroyukihime, seated to his left, placed her cup back in its saucer and started the conversation in a rather unexpected way.

"You weren't wearing a Neurolinker yesterday, either. Do you usually leave it off, Utai?"

The smaller girl began typing adroitly with just her left hand while sipping her milk tea with her right. There was no noticeable decrease in her incredible typing speed. UI> Yes. When I have it on, I always end up wanting to go to that world.

"Well, why don't you? Unlike me, there's no bounty on your head. There won't be a parade of annoying players assaulting you if your name shows up in the matching list."

UI> About once or twice a month, I do solo duels in the neutral area of Setagaya. That's enough. I'm not allowed to wish for anything more. A substantial portion of the responsibility for the destruction of the old Nega Nebulus lies with me, after all.

"Huh?!" It was Haruyuki letting out the stunned cry.

He intently examined the chat window floating before his eyes, but no matter how many times he read the words there, he couldn't pull any other meaning from the row of text Utai had typed.

Destruction of Nega Nebulus.

Kuroyukihime had said those same words countless times up to that point.

At a meeting of the Seven Kings two and a half years earlier, the Black Lotus had taken the head of fellow level-niner Red Rider, the Red King, and an advocate of peace, and was now to be forever pursued. As a result, the first Nega Nebulus she had ruled over had fallen into ruin. Haruyuki understood that much at least. But…

He shifted his gaze to one side, seeking an explanation, but Kuroyukihime, sitting there in her gym clothes, left her teacup there on the table. Her eyes were colored with sadness, and she didn't open her mouth. Utai remained quiet as well, left hand on her holokeyboard.

In the heavy silence, the light coming through the window on the north side gradually faded. Although it would be summer solstice soon, the sky was indeed still dim when 6:30 PM rolled around.

Haruyuki bit his lip. He was pretty sure the limit for the student council members was seven. And he *was* worried about the time, but he was far more interested in where this exchange between the two girls had started and where it was going. He wanted so badly to have everything explained in a clear and easy-to-understand manner, but he was essentially an uninvited guest. He hesitated at being too forward.

Fortunately, however, the two veteran Burst Linkers seemed to have reached the seed of an agreement during the period of silence.

Kuroyukihime sighed lightly. "Up to now, I've consciously—or unconsciously—avoided talking about the first Nega Nebulus. I thought if I was clinging to something I'd lost, I wouldn't be able to face you and the others, Haruyuki. And you all are working so hard for me as the new Nega Nebulus. And more than that, I didn't have the courage to face my own crimes. But Raker's come back, and here we are, meeting again, after two and a half years. The time has come to face the past...I suppose."

Haruyuki held his breath and drank in her words, while across from him, Utai's fingers flashed.

UI> If we're going to call them crimes, then they are mine as well. You, me, Fu...we've each turned our eyes away from our respective pasts and hidden ourselves away in different corners of the Accelerated World for a long time. But I'm certain that the reason we're now able to once again face ourselves is because of how hard the

MEMBERS OF THE NEW NEGA NEBULUS HAVE BEEN WORKING. ARITA HAS THE RIGHT TO KNOW WHAT ERRORS WE COMMITTED PREVIOUSLY AND WHY WE HAD TO REMOVE OURSELVES FROM THE FRONT LINE.

"Mmm. You're right. That's exactly right." Kuroyukihime nodded after reading the cherry-colored text and turned her entire body toward Haruyuki.

In the depths of her obsidian eyes was the same shaky light he'd seen the many times she started to talk about her own past before, but this time, it wasn't only that. In the very center of her iris, a small star glittered resolutely.

"Haruyuki." After a tiny pause, she spoke again, her voice edged with a crispness that told of how she'd endured the pain and tried to overcome it. "Just as you know, I pretended to accept the cease-fire agreement the first Red King, Red Rider, insisted upon and took off his head. I then fell into battle with the other five kings. I survived, burst out, and then blocked my connection to the global net for two years. To be more precise, however, just once, the day after the battle with the kings, I dove into the Unlimited Neutral Field. To apologize to the members of the first Nega Nebulus and transfer the majority of the burst points I had accumulated to them."

UI> THERE WAS NO WAY WE COULD ACCEPT THAT, Utai interjected in text, and Kuroyukihime grinned slightly.

"But I had nothing else to offer. You all got so mad at me, despite the fact that I risked my life to exchange my points for items in the shop."

UI> OF COURSE WE DID. EVEN REMEMBERING IT NOW, I GET A LITTLE ANNOYED.

"I was wrong." Kuroyukihime shrugged and smiled once more. "But the story doesn't end there. I confessed what I had done, appointed the next Legion head, and announced my intention to retire from the Accelerated World, but Utai and the other Elements came back with an unexpected proposal."

"E-elements?" Haruyuki parroted.

UI> At some point, the four Burst Linkers positioned as the subleaders of Nega Nebulus at the time were given this rather grand nickname. The reason was that the avatar attributes were divided into earth, water, fire, and wind. As Utai typed, her cheeks reddened slightly.

"*Wind* was naturally Sky Raker. I'll leave you to look forward to finding out what Uiui's attribute is later," Kuroyukihime added, grinning, and Haruyuki glanced back and forth between her and the faintly sour-faced Utai.

Four subleaders taking the separate name of Elements. He could probably take that to mean they had been like the Four Heavenly Kings, the Buddhist gods the daimyo lords had served long ago in the Warring States period. He had expected this to a certain extent; this small girl was powerful, so powerful that she had stood alongside *the* Sky Raker in the past. If she was so strong and living in Suginami as they did, why hadn't Kuroyukihime gotten in touch with her sooner and asked her to come back to the Legion? There were probably some issues he didn't know about, but defending would be a whole lot easier if they could at least get her to help during the Territories.

Haruyuki's thoughts ended up stuck on a rather narrow-minded track. But the look on Kuroyukihime's face changed as she cleared her throat, so he hurried to sit up straighter. Her quiet voice rolled out into the student council office as it sank into darkness.

"The counterproposal from the Elements to my retirement announcement was completely unexpected. They...they said that perhaps there was another way to beat Brain Burst. Something other than reaching level ten."

"What?!" Haruyuki was stunned.

The end point of the online fighting game Brain Burst. Given the severity of the conditions imposed on all players, he had unwaveringly believed there was no other way there than to reach level ten. But was it possible there existed an equally difficult objective? For instance, unifying all the Territories or something?

No, that was just too unrealistic. The majority of Burst Linkers were concentrated in Tokyo, but the areas themselves were spread out all over Japan.

"Wh-what is it?!" Haruyuki asked impatiently, leaning forward, unable to expand his hypothesis beyond this. "The other way to clear the game?!"

"You should have seen it at least once, Haruyuki." Kuroyukihime switched gears, adopting a mysterious tone.

Haruyuki opened his eyes wide. "Seen...seen what?"

"A magical castle existing in the center of the Accelerated World, granting access to absolutely none...a severe and majestic figure."

Instantly...

The sight from only the day before popped up vividly in his mind: the Demon City stage, heavy with thick fog. The group of towers soaring darkly to pierce the clouds on the far side of the city buildings cutting into the sky. The dazzling and dignified silhouette, refusing all comers and yet somehow inviting.

"...The Imperial Palace?" Haruyuki whispered in a shaky voice, and Kuroyukihime and Utai both nodded gently, saying nothing. He blinked frantically several times before hurriedly arguing, "B-but...you said so yourself yesterday, Kuroyukihime! You said no matter what we do, it's the only place in the Accelerated World we can't go!"

"But I believe I also said this: We only know for sure that entry's not possible in the Normal Duel Field."

"Th-that's...So then, umm...somewhere that's not the Normal Duel Field." He gulped loudly before continuing timidly, "That means there's a way in if you're in the higher-level Unlimited Neutral Field?"

For a few seconds, he got no response. Kuroyukihime and Utai exchanged glances, and then both lowered their eyelashes for some reason. However, they soon lifted their faces and nodded like they had earlier.

This time, Utai replied via the chat tool. UI> AT THE VERY

LEAST, SOMETHING THAT COULD BE A PATH HAS BEEN CONFIRMED. AT THE IMPERIAL PALACE IN THE UNLIMITED NEUTRAL FIELD—WE CALL IT THE CASTLE—THERE ARE FOUR GATES THAT THE IMPERIAL PALACE IN THE GENERAL FIELD IN THE CHIYODA AREA DOES NOT HAVE.

"...Are they...the entrance to the Castle?"

"Mmm. Four massive gates rise up, one on the east, west, north, and south of the castle, probably about thirty meters tall. All the other castle walls are indeed set with invisible walls above and below the actual walls."

Haruyuki drew the ground plan for the real-world Imperial Palace in his mind. He was pretty sure there were also gates in the four cardinal directions on the real thing on this side. Some had even been used as metro station names. The one on the south was Sakuradamon; the west was Hanzomon. He couldn't remember the names for the north or east, but since the terrain of the Accelerated World was in principle based on the real world, it was natural to think that these would be the gates on the Castle, too.

"Are these gates...open?" he asked, secretly a little excited.

Kuroyukihime crossed her arms and nodded. "An unopened gate's the same thing as a wall, after all. If it's a gate, it's logical to think that it opens. If we could get there and push on the door, that is."

UI> YES. THE GATES ARE THERE, BUT WE CAN'T REACH THEM. ALL FOUR ARE VERY OBVIOUSLY GUARDED BY FOUR TOP-LEVEL ENEMIES, THE STRONGEST OF THE STRONG EVEN IN THE UNLIMITED NEUTRAL FIELD.

"......!" Haruyuki took a sharp breath, feeling like he could finally see where this discussion was going.

*Enemy* was the name for the monsters that lived in the Unlimited Neutral Field. Similar to general MMORPGs, they were controlled by the system, and the majority of individuals would savagely attack any Burst Linker that entered into its response range. If you took one down, you got burst points instead of experience points, but not only were even the lowest-level Enemies terrifyingly strong, they paid a trivial amount of points. If you were going to put some real effort into hunting Enemies, you would first need to put together a party of a few people and then camp out in the Unlimited Neutral Field for a few days to a week; it was no mean feat. Haruyuki was definitely not averse to some dull grinding, but even he couldn't really muster an interest in taking an active part in a hunt.

He wetted his dry throat with cooling tea. "The strongest. So how strong are they?" he asked.

Kuroyukihime fell into thought. "Mmm…To be honest, there's no way to really explain it…Okay. Haruyuki, perhaps it was just the one time, but you did see a party of about twenty hunting Enemies once, didn't you? I think it was that time we were heading toward Ikebukuro with the Red King."

"Y-yeah. It was a huge one, maybe the size of a building. Was that one of the top-level Enemies Shinomiya's talking about?" Haruyuki asked fearfully, and the two veteran Burst Linkers grinned wryly in perfect sync.

Utai's fingers flashed, and the cherry font flowed with a light sound effect. UI> AN ENEMY THAT CAN BE HUNTED BY TWENTY OR SO PEOPLE IS CALLED A *Beast*. AN INDIVIDUAL APPROXIMATELY TEN TIMES STRONGER THAN THAT IS A *Legend*, BUT PLAYERS ALMOST NEVER ENCOUNTER THESE. IF A PLAYER DID ENCOUNTER ONE UNPREPARED, IT WOULD ESSENTIALLY MEAN DEATH.

"T-ten times…than that…?!" Haruyuki cried out, a chill running up his spine. He had been convinced that going one-on-one with the Enemy they'd seen on Yamate-dori Street on their way to Ikebukuro would mean instant death. His own experiences actually offered no means of imagining just how strong a Legend would be.

However.

Haruyuki couldn't react at all, much less shiver, at what Kuroyukihime followed that with, as smooth as ever.

"And the Enemies guarding the four gates of the Castle are so strong that the Legends look like Chihuahuas. They're called *top-level* because we can't even begin to guess at their status. They're also known as the Four Gods, and just as that name implies, they should be recognized not as monsters but as the true gods ruling the Accelerated World."

The Accelerated World's...gods.

Until that moment, Haruyuki's faith that the strongest beings in the game space produced by Brain Burst were the Seven Kings of Pure Color had never wavered. He had been convinced that no matter how strong the large Enemies might have been, Kuroyukihime, Niko, and the other kings would be able to defeat them even in one-on-one combat.

And if the conditions were right at least, they could probably win against a Beast, or even a Legend depending on the situation. The Blue King's nickname was Legend Slayer, after all. Haruyuki was certain that was proof that he had once defeated a Legend solo. And that this had been such a great exploit, it ended up a title of honor.

But it almost seemed like a faint hint of fear bled into Kuroyukihime's voice as she spoke now.

"Umm." Haruyuki lowered his voice and asked timidly, "So which is stronger: a king or a god?"

"The kings are, in the end, people. In contrast, the gods are far beyond the domain of human beings. If we were to seriously take them on directly, we Seven Kings could muster every bit of power we had and likely not be a match for even just one of the Four Gods."

"Seriously?!" he said, dumbfounded. "So then, um, doesn't that mean there's no way to break through the gates those monsters—I mean, the god-level Enemies—are guarding?"

Utai nodded, shaking the ponytail that hung down to her shoulders. UI> Yes. It's incredibly difficult. It's because of this difficulty that we came up with this idea. The idea that slipping past the guard of the Four Gods, opening

THE GATE, AND GETTING INSIDE THE CASTLE MIGHT BE THE SECOND REQUIREMENT TO CLEAR BRAIN BURST.

"Oh! I—I guess!" Haruyuki cried out unconsciously.

The known requirement—take all the burst points of five other level-nine Burst Linkers and become level ten—was extremely difficult, but he could see it being possible soon, in a certain sense. Five of the Seven Kings simply had to sacrifice themselves and offer their heads to one king. In that instant, a new level-ten Burst Linker would be born, and something would happen in the Accelerated World.

Naturally, however, in reality, that sort of thing was not going to happen. Every Burst Linker fought to make themselves stronger. There was no way any of them would simply throw it all away, not when they had given the game such passionate devotion for such an enormous amount of time to finally reach level nine.

Conversely, breaking past the Four Gods and getting inside the Castle was, at best, a problem of fighting power. It might be possible to break in if, for instance, all the members in a single large Legion were in the king class. This, too, was unrealistic, but there was no need for any self-sacrificing mentality.

So the two requirements of "level ten" and "Castle siege" had different difficulties: The former required strength of heart, the latter strength of fist. Thinking about this contrast, it made sense to think that if someone managed to reach the inside of the Castle, something would indeed happen in the world—that depending on the circumstances, Brain Burst itself would be cleared. Plenty of sense. After all, wasn't the impregnable castle in the middle of the world map the final stage in pretty much all the old games?

"Yeah." Haruyuki leaned forward and bobbed his head up and down, enjoying the way his serious gamer mind was being so enticingly stimulated. "That's possible. That might be it! If it's protected by such incredible monsters, then the Imperial Palace—I mean, the Castle—is the so-called last dungeon! If we can just get inside, some kind of amazing...something amazing might be..."

UI> Depending on how things are set up, there might also be some kind of incredible last boss even more powerful than the Four Gods. At any rate, when Sacchi announced her retirement two and a half years ago, I and the other members of Nega Nebulus insisted on the same idea we explained to you now. If one path to clearing the game was blocked, then we would try the second. Obstinate Sacchi.

"I stopped you," Kuroyukihime noted with a wry grin. "Of course I stopped you. I screamed with all my heart that it was hopeless, that I wouldn't forgive you, that you had to give it up."

Her expression was calm, her tone light and easy. But the slightest hint of pain appeared in her black eyes, and the instant he saw it, Haruyuki had a fuzzy foreboding of how this escapade had ended. His previous excitement receded, replaced with a cold tension filling his chest, and he waited intently for what followed.

"But it wasn't just the Elements; each and every one of that lot in the first Nega Nebulus was obstinate. Not content to merely go against their Master's orders, they even told me to give them all the Judgment Blow if I wanted to stop them. In the end, I lost my temper and sat down in protest, but they left, heading toward the Castle in small groups."

UI> Naturally. Because while we were your subordinates, we were at the same time your protectors, Sacchi.

"Now look, Uiui. You had only just started elementary school at the time! Really, each and every one of you..." The end of her sentence melted tremblingly into space. Haruyuki stayed quiet, watching her pale throat moving as she shut her eyes. She soon lifted her lids again; her eyes were slightly wet, but no tears fell.

"With no other choice, I struck out for the Castle with everyone else." Kuroyukihime continued her quiet recollection. "The field attribute at the time was the rare Aurora stage. Beautiful lights shimmered across the night sky...That path we walked from Suginami to the Castle along Shinjuku-dori Street, it was almost like a midnight picnic."

UI> It was fun, wasn't It? It's still one of my cherished memories, that time spent chatting with the Legion members as we walked. Graph gave me a piggyback ride. And Aqua pushed Raker's wheelchair. It's like it was yesterday.

"We reached the Castle so quickly, I thought perhaps we should do another turn around Tokyo. Or wait. Graph did actually say that in all seriousness, didn't he? But, of course, that proposal was rejected, and there on a hill in Kojimachi before Hanzomon, we held our final strategy meeting."

She lowered her long lashes, and her eyes fluttered as though she were looking into the distance. Quiet memories fell from her slightly parted lips.

"The Four Gods are essentially one body split into four parts, so we needed to fight them all at the same time. We split the Legion up into four squads and placed them north, east, south, and west. Before we separated, everyone received a buff from Utai, and with our hearts as one, brimming with courage in the highest of spirits, we charged the guardians of the Castle."

"S-so then...what happened?" Haruyuki asked hoarsely, unable to bear the mere second of silence.

Kuroyukihime straightened up in her seat and placed both hands on her knees. "About a hundred and twenty seconds after the start of the attack, the last of us fell," she said quietly. "The first Nega Nebulus did not disappear through the usual dissolution. It was annihilated in that moment by the hand of God."

*We'll bring in Takumu and Chiyuri and discuss the rest tomorrow*, Kuroyukihime told a dazed Haruyuki and drank the last of her cold tea.

In truth, he still had many, many things he wanted to ask. What specifically did *annihilated* mean? Where were the former members now and what were they doing? Why did they stay silent? Why didn't they get in touch with Kuroyukihime? And why was one of them, Utai Shinomiya, here before Haruyuki and his friends now, after an absence of two and a half years?

But she was right. This was a story that current members Takumu and Chiyuri should also hear. And more important, the chic analog clock hanging on the wall indicated that it would be seven in a few minutes, the hard deadline for leaving school grounds.

After quickly washing up the teacups and picking up her school-designated bag from a corner of the sofa, Kuroyukihime urged the other two on with a "Well, let's go, then" and started walking toward the door. Haruyuki could almost believe that her face in profile was the same as it always was.

Last fall, when she met Haruyuki, back when she cast aside her dummy avatar and returned to the Accelerated World, she had seemed afraid to even glance at her memories of the past. In fact, when the Yellow King had shoved a replay video before her on the battlefield, it caused her to "zero fill"—she lost the will to fight and became unable to move. All of which was to say, even Kuroyukihime, with her transcendent battle skills, also fought her own weakness on a daily basis.

*I've got no time for uncertainty, either.* He stood and followed Kuroyukihime to the door as he made a new resolution in his heart.

He had to get stronger, ever stronger, as a member of the reborn Nega Nebulus. He would chase away that Armor of Catastrophe parasite sticking to his avatar somewhere in days—forget a week—and fight proudly in the Territories on Saturday. Kuroyukihime still hadn't explained to him what sort of "purification strategy" she was thinking of, but he would endure whatever special training or penance was necessary. He secretly clenched his right hand into a tight fist.

At that moment, the chat window still in his field of view offered up a question that proved Kuroyukihime was indeed not as composed as usual. UI> I'LL ASK JUST IN CASE. SACCHI, DO YOU INTEND TO WALK HOME DRESSED LIKE THAT?

*Huh?* he thought, looking over at Kuroyukihime ahead of him: beyond the black hair hanging down her back, a glossy T-shirt of quick-drying material. On her lower half, formfitting shorts and slender legs stretching out from under them. Haruyuki had completely forgotten that during that long conversation, Kuroyukihime was still in the gym clothes she had changed into to clean the hutch.

"A-ah! I forgot. Hold on a minute," Kuroyukihime said, quite panicked—unusual for her—as she whirled around. She pushed through wide-eyed Haruyuki and somewhat exasperated Utai to run over to the lockers in the southwest corner. Abandoning her bag to the floor, she took the hem of her T-shirt in both hands and, without the least hesitation, yanked it up over her torso.

Her snow-white back and the strap of her lacy black bra were burned into his retinas—

"Hnyagh?!" He didn't know whether letting this mysterious yelp out was a huge mistake or just the right thing to do.

At any rate, the moment she heard it, Kuroyukihime looked back with a start once more, and as soon as she saw Haruyuki standing there stiffly, she quickly covered her chest with both arms.

*I'm glad this is the real world*, Haruyuki said to himself seriously, watching as her face grew red hot. *If this were the Accelerated World, she would use the most massive Incarnate attack she had to chop my head off.*

The T-shirt she had sent whirling through the air slapped him in the face, filling his nose with the most wonderful scent and blacking out his entire visual field.

After Kuroyukihime had chased Haruyuki from the student council office and changed at super-high speed, he followed her and an exasperated Utai out of the school gates with twenty seconds left before 7:00 PM, just barely getting a normal record in the school log.

Before he had the chance to even breathe a sigh of relief, he was pelleted by harsh words in a harsher voice. "Haruyuki. It's already dark. You'll walk Utai home! When you're done with

the Animal Care Club tomorrow, convene in the student council office! Make sure you talk to Takumu and Chiyuri! That's all! Now good-bye!"

In front of the school gates, Kuroyukihime gave orders and farewells at top speed, whirled around, and headed off in the direction of Asagaya. The *clack*ing of her loafers grew distant, and, watching her swinging black hair melt into the evening dark, Haruyuki expelled the air he had been holding in his lungs.

"I didn't do anything wrong, though," he whispered.

Next to him, Utai tapped away with the fingers of both hands.

UI> SACCHI'S ALWAYS BEEN A SECRET KLUTZ.

"Yeah, I kinda knew that." He bobbed his head and then shook it from side to side, rethinking the whole situation. A lot of things had happened since school let out that day, but he still hadn't cleared every mission. There remained the task Kuroyukihime had set for him: seeing Utai to her house.

Glancing up at the sky, he saw all signs of dusk were almost completely gone; the lights of the city dimly illuminated the bottoms of the clouds. Even with the social camera network on each and every road, it was definitely not safe for a fourth grader to be walking home alone by herself at this time of day. But more important—

"Um, Shinomiya? It's already past seven. You're okay for curfew?" he asked, and Utai's fingers started moving, the look on her face unchanging.

UI> THAT'S NOT A PROBLEM. I'M ALSO A BURST LINKER, YOU KNOW?

When he finally understood the meaning of this a few seconds later, Haruyuki unthinkingly clenched his teeth.

Essentially all Burst Linkers carried around one shared hurt. That's what Haruyuki's teacher, Sky Raker, had said. And this was the pain of being watched over by Neurolinkers from infancy instead of by a loving parent. Utai's statement essentially boiled down to a question of whether a child raised in this manner would face any kind of reprimand if they were to arrive home late.

Haruyuki had no adult in his house to yell at him, even if he came home past nine, and he knew the answer only too well. "Right. But, well, I guess there's no harm in getting home earlier. You're probably hungry after all that work you did cleaning." The moment he said this, a fairly loud, low-frequency rumble came from Haruyuki's own digestive tract.

Utai giggled slightly and nodded, her bound hair swinging. UI> THAT IS TRUE. I CAN MAKE IT HOME BY MYSELF, SO PLEASE FEEL FREE TO GO, ARITA. HAVE A GOOD EVENING. She bowed and began walking south, the hem of her white skirt fluttering.

"No, I'll walk you!" Haruyuki hurriedly chased after her. "It's already dark and all, and if I go home now, Kuroyukihime will for sure get super mad at me tomorrow."

Utai cocked her head to one side, still walking. UI> THAT CERTAINLY WOULD BE THE CASE. WELL THEN, MY APOLOGIES, BUT I DO APPRECIATE YOU SEEING ME TO OMIYA. She then adjusted her pace slightly to walk immediately alongside Haruyuki.

This was actually a strange journey for him.

Haruyuki was an only child, so naturally, he had no brothers or sisters, and his mother was estranged from her relatives, so he basically had no memory of ever spending time with a small child. If pressed to give at least one example of a child he knew, that would be his cousin Tomoko Saito, in neighboring Nakano Ward, but he hadn't seen her since they'd met at his mother's parents' house five or six years earlier.

But…he could say he had a younger friend in Niko, who had snuck into his house by pretending to be this very Tomoko. However he looked at it, though, she was the Red King, ruling over the great Legion Prominence. He very much did not get the feeling that he was dealing with a small child with her. Moreover, if he did try to treat her like a child, there was a good chance she would burn him to a crisp with a blow from her main armament. Thus, walking alongside Utai Shinomiya—brown knapsack on her back, gym bag in her right hand—in an older brother–type role was an extremely new experience for him.

"Oh! I-I'll carry your bag!" he said, finally noticing after they had already gone over a hundred meters, and Utai handed it to him with a crisp bow. He grabbed it with his right hand and tossed it over to his left in an overly grand gesture.

*Maybe this is what it feels like to protect someone*, he thought absentmindedly, measuring his steps along the elegant residential area path lit by the streetlamp LEDs.

The idea had never before crossed his mind, but one day in the distant future, the time would come for him to exercise his right to copy and install the Brain Burst program. Which meant that, as a "parent" Burst Linker, he would choose someone to be his "child," and he would watch over and raise a little level-one chick, completely unaware of the ways of the world.

*What if, supposing, maybe, that person was a weak-ish younger girl like Utai Shinomiya here? No, take it one step further: What if Utai was my child? Would I be able to do the right thing as her parent? Would I be harsh at times, and then kind, and protect and guide her?*

*I could do it. I should be able to do that. I mean, I managed to say I'd carry her bag and all. And I'm totally matching her pace. Aah, it'd be so great if we really were parent and child.*

His thoughts rambling and racing in this fashion, Haruyuki had already completely forgotten the weighty truths he had been informed of less than an hour earlier.

Making him aware of this heedlessness was the sudden movement of Utai's fingers as she walked next to him and hesitantly typed out, UI> My house is just ahead. And so, I wanted to take this opportunity to ask you the tiniest of favors, Arita.

The feeling of false parenthood still with him, Haruyuki read this, blinked, and then bobbed his head up and down. "S-sure. Anything!"

UI> I realize that you've been so kind as to walk me home and now I ask further favors of you.

"It's fine. Totally fine. Fire away!"

UI> Thank you so much. Then I will take you at your word and indulge myself.

"Y-yeah. So…what?"

UI> Please show me your actual abilities. I wish to confirm with my own eyes whether or not this "Platinum Corvus" is truly someone worthy of bearing the first spear of Nega Nebulus before I follow Sacchi's plan.

"…Sorry?"

*Snap!*

Haruyuki froze in an awkward position with an unnatural look on his face, while before him, Utai slipped her backpack off, opened the flap, and stuck her hand inside before quickly pulling it out again. Clasped in that small hand was an equally small, off-white Neurolinker, with a matte texture like fired pottery.

Watching as she lifted her ponytail with her left hand and set the quantum device on the nape of her slender neck, Haruyuki finally arrived at the facts that he had so completely forgotten.

Utai Shinomiya was a member of the first Nega Nebulus and one pillar of the Elements, the Legion's main force, essentially one of the Four Heavenly Kings. Also among this elite was Sky Raker, all of which meant that far from being a level-one chick, she was a Burst Linker probably—definitely—far, faaaar stronger than Haruyuki.

He was still frozen in place when Utai tugged at his shirt near his waist and invited him to one of the benches set evenly along the lane. He sat down half on autopilot, and she dug around in her backpack again for a few seconds before pulling something out. An XSB cable for direct connections covered in white plastic.

Offering one end to Haruyuki, Utai typed out deftly with her left hand, UI> Will you fight me one-on-one? Or perhaps you'd prefer to join together as a tag team and fight another team two-on-two?

Haruyuki's response came in half a second.

*Tag team, please.*

The promenade bench on which Haruyuki and Utai sat was at the real-world address of Icchome, Omiya, Suginami Ward, and in an area known as Suginami Area Two in the Accelerated World. Because it was neighbored by the "duel spots" of Shinjuku in the east and Shibuya in the southeast, it was on the sparsely populated side. But the hours from six to eight in the evening were the time of day when the most duels happened, and nearby Kannana Street housed several large dive cafés, so there should have been at least twenty or so Burst Linkers on the matching list.

Connected to Utai by a meter and a half of XSB cable, Haruyuki watched the wired connection warning appear and disappear as he clenched his hands on his knees and straightened his back. The girl five years his junior fiddled with her virtual desktop in a relaxed manner, the expression on her face essentially unchanged. She was likely launching the BB console and setting Haruyuki—Silver Crow—as her tag team partner.

UI> ALL RIGHT, THEN: I'LL SELECT AN APPROPRIATE TAG TEAM TO GO UP AGAINST. I'LL TAKE A SUPPORTING ROLE IN THE OPENING, SO PLEASE, ARITA, FIGHT HOWEVER YOU SEE FIT. IF YOU'RE PREPARED, WE CAN BEGIN.

"O-okay! Go ahead!" he replied, mouth dry, and turned his full gaze on Utai's glossy lips. Naturally, he wasn't doing this as some kind of harassment, but rather to shout the "acceleration" command at the same time as she did.

But then Haruyuki came up against a question he hadn't previously considered. Utai Shinomiya had expressive aphasia. She couldn't speak using her physical voice. How on earth could she say the command for the Brain Burst program?

The answer was exceedingly simple.

Utai abruptly closed her eyes. A narrow valley was carved out between her eyebrows, and her slightly parted lips shook, almost convulsing. Teeth clenched beyond those lips creaked. One and then two beads of sweat popped up on her forehead. It was a feat of strength. She was goading her body to force out a voice that couldn't come.

Haruyuki desperately swallowed the word—*stop*—that tried to leap out of his mouth. If Utai was such a high ranker as to be one of old Nega Nebulus's Four Heavenly Kings, then she would have had to have been through an almost uncountable number of battles to claw her way to that position. And they couldn't all have been from Standby mode. This girl had to have done this thing that looked so absurdly difficult over and over, an infinite number of times.

It probably didn't take more than five seconds, but to Haruyuki, the struggle felt like it went on for minutes, until in the end, Utai's lips opened two centimeters. They were then pursed and farther opened to the sides. Finally, she pointed them slightly once more.

*Bur. Ssst. Lin. K.*

Although completely soundless, Utai's actual mouth did in fact carve out those syllables. At the same time, Haruyuki muttered the words with his usual awkwardness.

# 6

As if it had never been, the damp heat of the rainy season turned to a dry, cold wind and caressed his body. Beneath his duel avatar's mirrored helmet, Haruyuki snapped his eyes open. This moment when he checked the attributes of the stage was exciting, no matter how many duels he fought.

However, just then, he had something in his heart that was double, triple, quadruple the concern. So the instant he saw the fiery sunset and the sea of golden grass swaying in the wind, he realized it was a Grassland stage and immediately spun his body around—and swallowed his breath when he saw this quadruple concern in the center of his vision: the appearance of the duel avatar operated by Utai Shinomiya.

To a certain extent, it was what he expected: a fairly small avatar. But she had a dignified silhouette that made the avatar feel larger, fitted with long shields hanging below her arms and an armor skirt that spread out, covering the area from high up on her waist down to her feet. Combined, the armor looked almost like a white robe and red *hakama*—a traditional Japanese outfit.

Furthering the impression was the fact that the top and bottom halves of her avatar had almost entirely different coloring. The torso and the arms were a graceful, semiglossy off-white, like her Neurolinker. But the *hakama* armor was a concentrated red, with both depth and brightness, different from the pure red of the first Red King, Red Rider, and from the transparent crimson of the second Red King, Scarlet Rain. Like the form of the avatar, this red was somehow Japanese—vermilion, perhaps.

The head looked very much like the real Utai's. A fringe-shaped armor covered the forehead of the white mask, and a long stabilizer stretched out from the rear of the head. Eye lenses the same brilliant red as the *hakama* were clear and severe, yet cute.

Haruyuki had never before seen a two-tone avatar. It went without saying that Silver Crow was entirely silver, and the other members of Nega Nebulus were a single color. It wasn't that there weren't avatars with multiple color schemes, but the majority were simply different shades of the same color. The reason for that was that the color name of the avatar equaled the attributes of the avatar, which equaled the body color. The color name was always one word, and the color expressed was inevitably limited to one—or it was supposed to be.

Utai's avatar standing neatly before Haruyuki, however, had her lower half wrapped in a fairly pure long-distance red and her upper half in a similarly saturated, peculiar white; each color represented fairly different attributes. What kind of color name could express both in one word?

Haruyuki forced his eyes away from the Japanese-style avatar and checked the name attached to the second of the two health gauges in the top left of his vision. Ardor Maiden. That was Utai Shinomiya's avatar's name.

He understood *maiden*. Like a young lady or a virgin. And that was actually pretty fitting for Utai. But he couldn't immediately translate into Japanese with his own brain the key to it all, the color name, the English word *ardor*. If he had been in the real world, all he would have had to do was focus his gaze on the word to make a translation window pop up, but unfortunately, that sort of useful function did not exist in Brain Burst. He felt like it was a word he'd seen somewhere before, but he was pretty sure at least that it hadn't been a word in any of his English textbooks before eighth grade.

He gave up on asking what her name meant, since it was just too stupid, and finally checked his tag team partner's level. Seven. So fairly high indeed.

Having spent approximately three seconds collecting all this information, Haruyuki lowered his head. "O-okay, then, I appreciate your help. I'll try not to disappoint you."

When he lifted his head again, he had the sudden thought. Just like it didn't have a translation function, Brain Burst wasn't equipped with a text chat feature, either. How on earth were they supposed to understand each other? Sign language? Or maybe eye contact?

But as soon as this thought struck him, Utai responded in a way that made Haruyuki doubt his eyes—or rather ears. "Looking forward to it. And you don't have to be so polite all of a sudden, C."

*C? Does she mean me? Like C for* Crow?

*Wait, that's not the real issue here. Right now, I'm sure, there's no doubt—she spoke. The mouth area of Utai's avatar Ardor Maiden moved, and I heard a voice.*

"Ah! U-um?! Sh-Shino—no, wait, uhh, what should I call you here..."

"Anything except *Den Den* is fine. In the past, I was mostly called *Mei*."

"O-okay...Mei, uh, just now, you...talked." In his immense surprise, Haruyuki ended up being fairly impolite, but Utai showed no sign of being bothered by this as she nodded crisply.

"I can speak like this only when I'm accelerated. In fact, you could say that that's one of the reasons I visit this world now."

Inside the innocent childishness and clarity of her voice was a strength that cut to the core. Compared with Haruyuki's rattling speech, which wasn't much different from him in the real world, her voice was crisp, as though she had taken voice training, with an overwhelming smoothness and rich inflection.

"B-but being able to talk in this world...I thought it was the same mechanism as talking in neurospeak with your Neurolinker..."

"I don't know the detailed theory behind it, either. Black Lotus once said it was because of the depth of connection with my consciousness, which is different at a quantum level."

"O-oh...I don't actually get what this is, either." Cocking his head, Haruyuki took in the full picture of Utai's duel avatar once more.

Even though just the combination of the vivid white and vermilion was beautiful on its own, paired with the Japanese *hakama*, he almost felt a seed of holiness there, like his soul was being pulled in. Or maybe there was a reason for that—this color and form together called to mind something that existed in the real world. Something he'd seen somewhere a long time ago. He was pretty sure it was before his parents got divorced, and the three of them went out at New Year's...

"Um, C. Although I don't especially mind how long you look at me..."

"...It's...a big shrine...first visit of the New Year..."

"I don't particularly mind if you do your first shrine visit of the year in June, either."

"After we prayed, we got our fortunes...Huh, I was the only one to get terrible luck..."

"The guide cursor has been moving quite energetically for a while now."

"Pretty sure I lost big in that one...Huh?!" Utai's voice finally reached his brain, and Haruyuki hurriedly activated the light blue triangle displayed faintly in the center of his field of vision. It was indeed rapidly changing direction from right to left. And what lay beyond this arrow was, of course, the enemy.

After all, this beautiful grassy field was not a virtual space for chatting, but rather a duel stage produced by Brain Burst.

"Crap! They've gotten pretty close!" Hurriedly readying himself, Haruyuki checked the enemy tag team in the lower right of his vision.

One was a level four, Olive Grab. He was pretty sure this avatar was a member of the Green Legion, but he didn't know them.

Haruyuki gulped the instant he saw the other name: Bush Utan. Level three and also a member of the Green Legion, he was a Burst Linker Haruyuki had fought a few times before. But whenever Utan had appeared in Suginami, it had always been paired up with the motorcycle-using Ash Roller, whom he adored like a big brother.

Haruyuki cocked his head slightly to one side, but he soon pushed aside the weirdness of it. Bush Utan probably couldn't make the timing work out with his big brother every time. At any rate, from the way the guide cursor was swinging, the enemy was already closing in hard, within twenty meters. Just a bit more before contact—or it should've been.

"Wh-where are they?!"

Standing on his tiptoes, Haruyuki stared intently in the direction indicated by the cursor. However, there was nothing but tall grass swaying in the wind as far as the eye could see—no sign of any enemy avatars. They were probably making themselves as small as possible and moving along against the ground under the grass like they were swimming.

As he whirled his head around, Utai next to him whispered, "C, it seems the enemy team's split up into advance and rear guards. I'll keep the rear in check; you handle the advance. Let me see what you've got." And then she quietly pulled away to the right.

Utai prepping him for battle like this and appearing before Haruyuki and his friends now after her long retirement probably meant she was involved in Kuroyukihime's Armor of Catastrophe purification plan. Apparently, Utai was going to watch this battle very closely to determine whether or not she would help.

In which case, he had to at least show her a solid victory, even if he couldn't manage an easy win, but that wasn't going to happen if he couldn't even find the enemy. His opponent seemed to be approaching in spiral to the left and would already be in the ten-meter range before he knew it. When that happened, the guide cursor itself would disappear. Straining his eyes even more desperately, Haruyuki still saw absolutely no difference between grass swaying in the random wind and grass swaying because of the enemy.

*Right, the sound!*

He abruptly closed his eyes and focused every bit of his attention in his ears. There should have been the slightest difference between the noise of the enemy parting the grass and the rustling caused by the wind. He would listen for that.

Two seconds later…

"They sound totally the same!" Haruyuki groaned and opened his eyes again. The *ksh-ksh-ksh* sound effect was essentially uniform in all directions. There might have been the tiniest difference in it somewhere, but he would need some kind of miracle training to be able to pick up on it.

Eyes no good, ears no good. If he used his wings to ascend, he probably would have been able to find his opponent, but his special-attack gauge was still empty, and there were no objects he could smash anywhere around him.

He was gritting his teeth at his mounting frustration when the guide cursor abruptly disappeared from view. Or more precisely, one of them did; another very faint cursor remained, but that was for the enemy rear guard some distance away and no use to him now.

The advance guard—it wasn't clear whether it was Bush Utan or Olive Grab, but whoever it was was currently moving somewhere within a ten-meter radius of him and planning the timing to hammer Silver Crow with a serious advance attack. Haruyuki could also try creeping along the ground himself here, but if he did, he would lose his mobility, Silver Crow's greatest weapon, and there was a serious possibility that he would get pulled into a ground skirmish.

If this had been a normal duel, this would have been the point where he abandoned everything he'd been thinking up to that point and braced himself to be slammed down in the beginning of the fight, all so that he could fill his gauge and bet the rest of the duel on the strength of his wings. It was practically his standard fighting style, in fact. Because Silver Crow couldn't take much of a hit and hit his breaking point quickly, he was not suited to fighting on the ground. He was at a disadvantage when he couldn't fly, and obviously…

From somewhere in his heart, the thought continued. Utai Shinomiya had said she wanted to see Haruyuki's actual power. And his actual power meant his true abilities. And really, he had had no excuses or reason to hold back. Above all else, success or failure of the purification plan hinged on this duel.

*Is that really my only option? I have to have something else I can use to deal with this, don't I?* The moment the thought came to him, a single idea flashed in his heart like a bolt of lightning.

What would *she* do? What would the Black King do? She was basically the same sort of close-range, high-mobility type as Silver Crow. She definitely wouldn't be looking around so feverishly. She would no doubt stand calmly in one place, wait for the instant the enemy attacked, and wager everything on that moment's offense and defense. Right, that was it. If his enemies were a close-range type, too, then they'd at least have to come up out of the grass in the moment of attack.

His first move would inevitably be slower. Even if his enemy became visible, he wouldn't be able to act first. But she had taught him a technique to change defense into offense in that direct duel they'd had a week before. He totally wouldn't be able to pull it off in the same way as she did, but trying and failing was a hundred times better than giving up and just standing there.

Haruyuki relaxed his entire body and half closed his eyes. In the back of his mind, he called up an image of Black Lotus from their fight the week before.

In an almost leisurely gesture, the Black King had caught his right straight, which had all of Silver Crow's speed and power behind it. Her movement had been not so much fast as streamlined; there had been no wasted effort. Instead of repelling the power of her enemy's attack, she pulled it in, changed the angle, and released it. Black Lotus called this technique "the way of the flexible"—a kind of reversal via blocking.

Despite the fact he hadn't moved at all, he became conscious of a high-pitched whine, and the noise around him receded. It was the feeling of acceleration he got when he concentrated with a certain intense focus, but this was the first time he had relaxed his muscles so much and felt this stillness.

A time passed—whether it was long or short, he couldn't tell—and Haruyuki sensed the first blow coming from the enemy finally, from not sound or sight but rather the vibration of his enemy's footstep.

*Behind, to the right!*

He raised his right hand as he turned around.

A small avatar with grass green armor that blended into the background rose up from the grass and launched a punch: Bush Utan. Mask reminiscent of a certain primate, his arms were abnormally thick and long compared to his forward-leaning body and compact legs. He had probably used those sturdy arms to "swim" through the grass instead of run. So, naturally, his feet would have made no sound. He would also have used his shorter height to his advantage.

To Haruyuki, this punch was essentially the ground below the deep grass leaping up into his face. By the time he saw his opponent, that enormous right fist was already closing in on his face, less than a meter away. And given that his footing wasn't very solid at that moment, there was absolutely no way he was going to be able to dodge.

"Hoooh!!" Utan let out a loud battle cry, perhaps certain that his first blow would hit home.

In contrast, Haruyuki remained silent and loosely caught his opponent's fist in his open right hand. He felt the force of his enemy's right hook in his palm, a burning sensation. If he had tried to force a block here, his arm would have been thrown back, and he would've taken a serious blow to the face. But rather than block, he fused his own movement with the fist's, and without resisting his opponent, he changed only the direction of the attack.

The key was probably the circular motion. In the virtual squash game he used to play every day, the already incredible speed of the ball increased exponentially if he simply smashed it as hard as he could with every stroke, so he would sometimes squash his own power and cradle the ball in the face of his racquet.

Remembering that movement now, Haruyuki moved his palm counterclockwise, following his enemy's punch. Unable to completely quench the force, the armor of his right hand creaked and squealed. But at the same time, he felt the trajectory of the attack shifting bit by tiny bit.

At this point, Kuroyukihime had turned the attack vector one hundred and eighty degrees and sent it flying directly behind Haruyuki. He, of course, did not have the skill for that. But if he could turn it a mere ten degrees down and to the left, he could at least avoid a clean hit. He held his breath, clenched his teeth, and carefully, cautiously, pulled in the rotation of Utan's fist.

*Skrk!*

He heard a quiet scraping, and the sharp sensation of heat raced along his left cheek. Several dots were carved off his HP gauge, but the massive fist merely grazed Haruyuki's helmet before flowing off behind him, and Utan staggered slightly. His center of gravity was likely too high when he attacked standing up because of his overdeveloped arms and shoulders.

When he sensed his opponent faltering, Haruyuki unconsciously swung his right leg out to sweep Utan's short ones out from under him.

"Uwaah?!" The grass-colored avatar tumbled forward with a shout, and then hit the ground with his back. *Wham!* The sound of impact. The tall grasses beneath him acted as a cushion, so there wasn't much damage, but Utan's HP gauge did drop a few percent.

*I did it! Something kinda like that block reversal thing!* He shouted to himself gleefully, but his delight was short-lived.

Utan was swimming deep in the ocean of grass once more, and only the slithering sense of high-speed motion reached him; there was no doubt he was planning another surprise attack. Haruyuki slowly crouched down and sharpened his senses.

The second attack came quickly. Mere seconds later, the vibration of the step came, this time from directly behind him. Without taking the precious milliseconds needed to look back over his shoulder, he thrust his right hand back. The instant he felt something, he yanked upward in a circular movement.

When his eyes finally caught up they found Utan, left straight knocked, center of gravity off balance once again. He extended his left leg, perhaps trying to force his fist back onto its original trajectory, and his body rose up even farther. Reflexively, Haruyuki followed Utan's punch with his left hand and brought them both up to his shoulder.

"Haa!" With a short battle cry, he heaved the other avatar into the air with everything he had.

Utan flew even higher than the last time, spun through the air, and slammed into the grass headfirst. The natural cushion couldn't completely absorb the impact this time, and nearly 10 percent of his gauge was shaved away, accompanied by a damage effect.

For a brief moment, Bush Utan's legs stuck comically up out of the grass, but eventually, he pushed himself to his feet using the strength of his arms and whirled around to stand. Looking like he planned to dive back into the grass for Stealth mode, he retreated several steps and thrust a finger out at Haruyuki.

"Oh-ho-ho! Just as one would expect from the eternal rival of my bro Ash, you feel me?"

Haruyuki blinked hard. This was unexpected. "Huh...I—I am?" he blurted, somewhat unkindly, but fortunately, Utan didn't notice his curt tone.

"You sure use a pretty weird defense technique, huh!" he yelled. "This is the first time I didn't get the First Attack bonus in a Grassland stage! But don't go thinking you've won with that, punk! We dump the standing throws and get down to wrestling, and I am totally unbeatable in this stage! Got it?"

"Unh!" Haruyuki had no doubt that this was exactly the case. He felt like he had at last awakened to the "way of the flexible" Kuroyukihime had initiated him into, but he wasn't going to be able to handle throws or locks. If those solid arms suddenly grabbed ahold of his legs from below in the grass, he'd be forced into the ground fight he was so bad at whether he liked it or not.

As Haruyuki panicked, Utan calmly waggled his index finger. "But my fans in the Gallery wouldn't like it one bit if I used a locking technique here, you feel me? 'Cause, you know, they wouldn't be able to see it at all!"

Haruyuki spun around and found the figures of spectators, albeit only three or four—in addition to Utai Shinomiya as Ardor Maiden—watching over him from a little ways off, and his other duel opponent, Olive Grab, still invisible, apparently moving around a great distance away. Because there was absolutely no higher ground anywhere nearby, they were all standing in the same grassy field. And indeed, if Haruyuki and Utan were to wrangle and wrestle in the bottom of the grass, they wouldn't be able to see anything.

"So what now? Oh! And don't even talk about arm wrestling! Not interested, all right?!" Haruyuki said preemptively, and Utan slapped his fist into the open palm of his hand.

"Ohh, nice idea, man. Sucks for you, but those skinny little arms of yours are no match for these powerful guns of mine. That's why I'm gonna use a new trick I just learned!!"

"N-new technique?!" He couldn't help but be on guard. As far as Haruyuki knew, Bush Utan had only two weapons: the sheer brute power of those overdeveloped arms and the ability to stretch them out over three times their length when he used his special-attack gauge. He hadn't gone up a level since they'd fought last week—he was still at level three—so he couldn't have gotten a new special attack or ability. In which case, he had either bought Enhanced Armament with points or come up with some new fighting method on his own. Either was cause for alarm.

Haruyuki crouched, nerves tensed, while Utan approached nonchalantly. "Mwah-hah-hah! If you charged in here now thinking you were in for an easy win like in that Territory Battle, you got another think coming, homie," he sneered, challenging. "I'm not the me of last week no more. You're gonna freak when you see it—this is the power that changed my life!!"

He stopped and made broad circles with his arms to cross them tightly before his chest. He held this position for a moment and then flung both hands out to his sides. "IS mode activate!! Hell yeah!"

*E-eye ess mode?* Although Haruyuki was bewildered by the completely unfamiliar technique name, he still tightened his taut muscles further, ready to dodge a sudden weapon whizzing his way. But what followed overturned any expectations he could possibly have had.

In the center of Bush Utan's grass-colored chest, a bizarre something rose up with a *pop*: a black semisphere, five or so centimeters in diameter. Although it shone with a deep brilliance, it wasn't metal. It made Haruyuki think of plastic, or something more alive. Glittering like light was leaking out. And then, proof that this impression was correct: The surface of the semisphere split at the center into top and bottom, like an eyelid opening. The "eye" that appeared held a deep red light reminiscent of blood and stared hard at Haruyuki.

*Bwaaa!* Waves of pressure shot out from Bush Utan's body, and the surrounding grass was flattened in concentric ripples. From the center of the eye in his chest came a black aura, gushing out to envelop Utan. Although he was nearly ten meters away, Haruyuki felt the prickly stabs of this pressure on his own body.

Clad in the thick shadow of this aura, Utan looked at Haruyuki with eyes that sparkled strangely and charged head-on without the slightest show of hesitation. He brandished his right fist with a war cry, shouting the name of a technique Haruyuki had definitely never heard before.

"Hooooooo...Dark Blow!!"

*Vzzzm.* A heavy vibration echoed through the stage, and the coating of night around Utan's fist grew even thicker. He closed in on Haruyuki, clenched fist raised and radiating a wrecking ball's worth of pressure.

"Hngh!" If Haruyuki had been thinking clearly, he would have had enough time to try for a block reversal like he had before. But he was assaulted by unspeakably sudden shaking and abruptly switched to Dodge mode, flinging himself to the left and just barely avoiding the ominous fist.

And then Haruyuki opened his eyes so wide they nearly fell out of his head, and all thought of a counterattack fell by the wayside. Utan's empty punch plunged into the ground at his own feet, sending that earth and its dense grass flying like his fist was a meteorite impact.

Unlike the buildings and rocks, the ground in a duel stage couldn't be so easily damaged normally. And yet Utan had gouged out a crater that deep with a single blow. Whatever this IS mode was, it was no ordinary power. Haruyuki would have been in serious trouble if he had actually tried to catch and return that blow with one hand.

*What was that?! Special attack—no, Enhanced Armament?!*

Oozing silent astonishment, Haruyuki reflexively checked the thin blue line displayed below Utan's HP gauge—his special-attack gauge.

Doubly shocked, he gasped. Utan's special-attack gauge hadn't dropped. Or rather, it hadn't been charged to begin with. But the black aura tinged with a red phosphorescence still radiated from Utan's body like it was overflowing from within.

A continuous emission of light that didn't use up his special-attack gauge. There was only one word in the Accelerated World to explain such a phenomenon: *overlay.* When a powerful imagination passed through the Image Control System—an avatar control path hidden under the normal Movement Command System—the signal that spilled out was processed as light that could be seen with the naked eye.

Having gotten this far, Haruyuki finally understood exactly what "IS mode" was: It had to be short for "Incarnate System mode." Or to someone used to using it: "Incarnate mode." The aura enveloping Utan at that moment was proof that the forbidden power of the Incarnate System was being invoked.

But why? The number one thing that should have been drummed into Utan's head when he learned the Incarnate System was that using this power first in a general duel was the greatest taboo. And what was that black eye stuck to his chest? Incarnate was a power born from within the heart of the user alone. He shouldn't need to equip an object like that.

Battered by waves of confusion, Haruyuki couldn't react right away to Utan charging him head-on once more, shrouded in that jet-black aura.

"Unh...hooooooo!!" With a low, nasal shout, Utan showily brandished his right fist.

Haruyuki finally opened his eyes wide with a gasp, but he no longer had time to dodge to either side. Painfully aware of the danger he faced, he thrust his open left hand out; he had no choice but to use the "way of the flexible."

"Hoooo! Dark Blow!!" Shouting the same technique name as before, Utan unleashed a punch that roared as it ripped through the air.

Haruyuki caught this fist—the overlay of it even more intense now—in the palm of his hand. It was cold like ice. Almost before he had the time to process this, he heard the screeching of destruction, and Silver Crow's left hand turned into a myriad of metal fragments and danced away on the wind.

"Ngah!" Haruyuki groaned, a fierce pain racing through his body as if his very nerves were being ripped out, despite the fact that this was a Normal Duel Field, where the sensation of pain was suppressed.

But Utan's fist still did not stop; it charged forward toward his face.

He desperately tried to cock his head to one side and dodge the blow, but the thick thumb gouged deep into the left side of his helmet. And again, the burning heat came. The enormous pressure repelled him, and he was slapped onto the grass back first. Haruyuki rolled around, pale sparks shooting out of his right arm where it disappeared at the elbow, a deep wound carved out of his helmet.

Looking down on him, Utan heavily pulled his right hand back while slowly raising his left fist high above his head. In the eyes shining in the slightly humorous mask, there was no sign of that vibrant gleam—his passion for the duel—Haruyuki had seen in their fight the week before or even mere minutes earlier. They only shone now with the excitement of beating Haruyuki down, of destroying him, of making him yield.

The left fist came at him for a third time, shrouded in the viscous aura of darkness. Haruyuki frantically brought his back up, deployed both wings while still on the ground, and vibrated the ten fins with every ounce of strength he had.

Utan's fist pierced deep into the grass where Haruyuki's torso had been only a tenth of a second before and the hard earth beneath it. Feeling his blood freeze as he watched this, Haruyuki ascended, working to put distance between them. Once he had gotten about twenty meters up, he finally went into Hovering mode.

He hadn't fully digested the situation yet. Or rather, he couldn't accept the truth. He managed somehow to move his mouth, frozen solid beneath his mask, and pushed the words out. "U-Utan…Why…That technique…How on earth…"

Haruyuki's answer was an enormous right hand thrust up toward him in the sky. A low, broken howl slipped out from the mouth area of Utan's mask. "Flying's no good either…" He spread his five fingers wide, and the black aura collected and condensed there. Then in a slightly distorted voice, "Dark Shot!!"

A heavy vibration shuddered through the stage while an inky black beam leapt out of Utan's palm.

Beyond surprised, Haruyuki could only watch, dumbfounded, as the lance of darkness closed in on him. Unconsciously, he flipped one of his wings and slid in the sky to avoid the beam's trajectory, but not quite fast enough.

He heard a *crunch* as the center of his left wing was pierced. The metal fins scattered in an instant, the wing of a bird shot with a gun. His propulsion suddenly unbalanced, and with no time to pull himself together, he plummeted to the ground.

If there hadn't been a thick covering of grass below him, his health gauge probably would have dropped into the red at that point. But even with the cushion, it dropped down to nearly 50 percent. He glanced over at it, shuddering at the terrifying force of Utan's Incarnate attack, and somehow pulled his torso upright.

"Whaddaya think 'bout the power of my new technique, huh?" Bush Utan approached him, grass crunching, and stopped to stand directly in front of Haruyuki, a grin cutting his face in half. "Pretty great, yeah? I'm pretty much unstoppable now, y'know?"

The light of the bloodred eye in the center of his chest pulsed. *Throb, throb.* Feeling the hunger in that gaze, Haruyuki asked hoarsely, nearly done in, "H-how…H-how on earth did you get this power…?"

Thinking it through, the only conclusion Haruyuki could come to was that someone had taught Utan how to use the Incarnate System, the way he himself had been initiated into the key points of the system by Sky Raker, as had Takumu by the Red King Scarlet Rain.

But one thing wasn't sitting right with him. Of the four types of Incarnate power—expansions to range, movement, attack power, and defense—an avatar could only master those in line with their original attributes. Niko had said this was a key principle.

And yet, although Bush Utan was a defensive green—the exact opposite of long-distance red on the color wheel—he had used a long-range beam attack to take Haruyuki down from high up in the air, which was clearly a range-expansion Incarnate attack. But right before that, he had used an attack-power-expanding Punch technique, and there was just no way these two Incarnates could exist in the same avatar. Even a master like Niko had acknowledged that she couldn't use the straight attack or defense Incarnates, since they clashed with her own attributes.

These facts that outpaced his own ability to understand in hand, Haruyuki, still flat on his back, could do nothing but open his eyes wider.

Facing Haruyuki, Utan glanced down at the eyeball stuck to his chest, long, sturdy arms hanging loosely at his sides. "Yo, I told you, didn't I?" His mouth moved, and a whisper came out, rich with a ridiculous passion, a child telling secrets. "I got it. Someone I know gave it to me. This IS mode study kit—ISS kit for short."

"S-someone gave it to you? An ISS kit…That?!" Haruyuki muttered, his confusion doubling at the unexpected explanation.

The phrase "study kit" itself was something he was quite familiar with. Any number of education-related companies in the real world sold products for children for every kind of area of interest: piano study kits, gymnastics study kits, even bicycle study kits. If you installed these in your Neurolinker, you could get quite adept instruction from a virtual instructor in a full dive's artificial reality environment. Haruyuki himself had a past with these he preferred not to talk about, having been assisted by how-to-talk study kits and similar aids.

But there was absolutely no way a real-world company could have been selling Incarnate System study kits in the Accelerated World. To begin with, the power of the Incarnate wasn't something that could be learned with an instant method like that. And Utan hadn't bought the kit; he'd gotten it from someone. Some other Burst Linker had probably transferred that black eyeball to Bush Utan and told him he could use it to study the Incarnate System.

So then who had he gotten it from? It couldn't have been…It couldn't.

"So…the one who gave you that, that ISS kit…was it Ash Roller?" Haruyuki asked nervously.

Utan got a curious look on his face momentarily before finally shaking his head from side to side. "Nah, it wasn't. My brother, Ash…It's still a secret from him. This sort of thing, he maybe might not like it, y'know."

The tension in Haruyuki's chest eased a little. Ash Roller was learning the basics of Incarnate from his parent, Sky Raker, although he was still very much the novice. He had no reason to reach out to suspicious assists like this ISS kit.

But his relief was fleeting. "But if I get super strong with this kit," Bush Utan whispered, even more heatedly, bringing his face in toward Haruyuki's, "then I just know my brother's gonna be happy. You think so, too, right, Crow? I got torn apart by you last week, but once he hears how I destroyed you in IS mode, he's gonna be super happy, okay? He's gonna say, 'Giga coooool!' to me, right?"

"……!" Seeing the hard gleam of excitement in Utan's round eyes up close, Haruyuki took a sharp breath. He reflexively shook his head vigorously. "Y-you're wrong. That's wrong. IS mode—I mean, the power of the Incarnate System isn't something you should be learning with a kit like that. First, you have to face your own mental scars…You have to start with learning the source and the meaning of that power. Otherwise, the dark side of Incarnate will swallow you up instead—"

"You lecturing me now?" Utan spit out, and Haruyuki was at a loss for words.

Mask and mask came closer together, covering each other, and the Burst Linker who had only minutes before been a sunny, happy-go-lucky player uttered in a low, hoarse voice, "Crow. Talking like that, it seems like you know a little about this power, too. But you were in the race last week, so I guess you felt it with that body of yours. How Number Ten barged in and rusted us all into oblivion in an instant with the power of IS mode, all our shuttles and even the hundreds of people in the Gallery. IS mode has that kind of incredible power. The ultimate power, skipping over all the rules of Brain Burst, even. And there're some jerks who knew about it and kept it quiet all this time. So what is even the point of worrying about the meaning of that power now? Actually...maybe you've been using this power for a long time, like maybe a little at a time in duels, and winning by cheating?"

Utan's right hand stretched out, an enormous snake, to clamp around Haruyuki's throat and yank him up with overwhelming physical strength. Now incredibly, uncomfortably close, Haruyuki saw in the depths of Utan's normally green eyes a reddish-black light flickering periodically. He realized that this pulsing was in perfect sync with the light in the ISS kit eyeball buried in Utan's chest.

"You gotta be strong or it's all meaningless. If you're not strong, you can't get a win ratio worth anything, and you stay at the bottom of your Legion, your points dry up, you disappear from the secret Accelerated World. But it's not like you could get how us loser Burst Linkers feel, not when you've had a rare ability like flight right from the start."

*I get it. I know that pain better than anyone. I've never ever thought I was a winner, not in the real world, not in the Accelerated World*, Haruyuki wanted to tell him.

But before Haruyuki could open his mouth, Bush Utan rasped, "But this ISS kit makes even losers strong. Like the more of a loser you are, the stronger you can get. You saw, right? It's only been three days since I got this thing, and I'm already pretty great at using IS mode. As long as I have this power, I can't lose against close-range Linkers *or* long-distance types. I can beat all those Legion jerks who made fun of me...and my brother—I mean, Ash Roller, even. I'm strong...right. 'Cause I'm strong!!"

At some point not just the tone of his voice, but his whole manner of speaking changed. Yanking up the hand clutching Silver Crow's throat, Bush Utan shouted, howled, "Strong! I'm strong! I don't need a tag team partner anymore! Olive Grab, once this duel's done, you and I are facing off! I'll show you whose IS mode is stronger! Where are you, Olive? You better watch me finish this guy off!!"

Unable to follow the deeply incomprehensible situation or the extreme change in Bush Utan, Haruyuki's numbed mind wandered absently.

Olive Grab was the name of Utan's tag team partner. They were probably friends from the Green Legion, and from the way Utan was talking, Olive had this ISS kit, too. So then, Olive would also be able to use this astounding all-attribute Incarnate Haruyuki was being pummeled with. In that case, what was happening with his own partner, Utai Shinomiya? She couldn't also have been taken down so helplessly like he had…

Before he could check the health gauge in the top of his field of view, he heard footsteps coming from his right and abruptly turned his head.

An unfamiliar duel avatar was slowly coming toward them, parting grass that swayed in the cool wind.

His armor was green mixed with tan, just like the avatar's name—olive green. His entire body was slim like a tree branch, but his hands alone were incongruously large. And in the middle of his chest, a jet-black semisphere, just like Utan's.

But the eyelid was almost entirely closed; only a sliver of the "eye" inside was exposed. The red light blinked irregularly, looking like it might go out entirely at any second.

When Haruyuki looked closely, Olive Grab's movements were extremely awkward. He staggered frequently, just barely catching himself each time, and managed to advance somehow. It was almost as if…It was like he was running from something.

"Olive?"

The slender avatar raised its graceless head at Utan's doubtful voice, two eyes open wide behind the vertical slits cut into the long mask. "Utan…H-help—" The hoarse voice was neatly cut off. He looked back abruptly and thrust out his right hand fearfully. A thin, shadowy aura enclosed angular fingers like tree roots. "D-dark Sh—"

The name of the technique was interrupted by a light *fwp*. The sound of a long, thin stick covered in flames—a flaming arrow—piercing the left side of Olive Grab's chest.

Immediately, the avatar's body shattered and disappeared. His health gauge had dropped to zero.

Haruyuki reflexively looked up at the four—no, three bars remaining in the top of his vision. Bush Utan's gauge had a little over 80 percent left. Silver Crow's was about half emptied. And the gauge of Haruyuki's partner, Utai Shinomiya—Ardor Maiden—had not dropped a single dot since the start of the duel.

He had also seen that "eye"—the ISS kit, according to Utan—on Olive Grab's chest, so Ardor Maiden had to have been hit with a preemptive Incarnate attack. In fact, Olive had, in his dying moments, tried to release the same long-distance technique Dark Shot that Utan used. That couldn't have been the first or the last attack. So how could Maiden have not even gotten a scratch?

Forgetting even to breathe, Haruyuki slowly lifted his gaze from where Olive had disappeared.

Twenty or more meters away was the small figure of a duel avatar clad in the two colors of a white robe and vermillion hakama. The armor of her entire body gleamed, not a single dull spot to be seen. But her slight left hand was gently gripping something that had not been there at the start of the duel: a long, slender stick as tall as she was. The top and bottom curved gently, a thin string connecting the two ends. It was a bow.

Ardor Maiden glanced with cool eye lenses at Silver Crow and his missing hand and wing, and then at Bush Utan, holding him in the air by his throat. Her left hand gently lifted the large bow. She placed an empty right hand on the string and pulled lightly.

Instantly, in the space by her hand where there had previously been nothing, a thin line burning red materialized—an arrow. Straightening her back, Utai raised her right arm high and drew back the string in a lovely, almost charming motion. A moment of stillness passed, as though time itself had stopped. Then her right hand flashed as she flicked her wrist back.

The flaming arrow came flying, howling, and plunged deep into Bush Utan's right forearm.

"Unh!" Crying out, Utan threw Haruyuki aside and yanked out the flaming arrow, which instantly burned into nothingness in the air. But not before Utan's gauge had dropped more than 10 percent.

Rooted to the spot, Haruyuki—and likely Bush Utan as well—was awed by the imposing figure of Ardor Maiden launching the arrow from her bow, not to mention the power of that missile and the accuracy of her aim. The Japanese-style avatar approached, gliding through the ocean of rustling, swaying grass. Size-wise, she was smaller than anyone else there, and yet the overwhelming sense of presence she radiated didn't allow him to feel this smallness; it scorched the air. To borrow Niko's words, it was an unbelievable "information pressure."

Coming quite close to Haruyuki and Utan, Ardor Maiden held her longbow low and horizontal. "This is an unexpected development," she said in a nonchalant, ringing voice. "I had intended simply to contain the situation until the contest here was concluded, but I was forced to dispatch Olive." She shook her head gently, as though victory with no damage was distasteful. She continued, a thoughtful monologue: "This ISS kit…If something like this is being freely disseminated, then the situation is indeed serious. We have to locate the source immediately."

She lifted her face and looked at Utan with harsh eyes. "Bush Utan, who gave you that?" She cut directly to the heart of it.

The grass-colored avatar took one step, then another backward, overawed. Perhaps connected to his mental state, the light of the "eyeball" in his chest flickered irregularly, and the black aura over his body began to shudder violently. "I—I can't tell…ya," Utan replied hoarsely, shaking his head back and forth over and over. "I promised I wouldn't say."

"You did? If you promised, I suppose there's nothing to be done, then." Utai nodded briskly, and then shot an even harder look at Utan. "I will tell you this: That power steals more than it gives you. Bush Utan, if you so desire, the fire attribute of my avatar can purify the foreign body parasitizing you. There's still time if you do it now. Unfortunately, Olive refused me, but…what do you say?"

Haruyuki didn't immediately realize the significance of the fact wrapped up in those words, but after a second, his eyes finally flew open.

She could purify a foreign parasitic body. That was definitely what Utai had said. But that ability wasn't readily available. Hadn't Kuroyukihime and Fuko been talking about that before? That only people with the rare ability of purification could remove an object with parasitic characteristics?

So then Utai Shinomiya, Ardor Maiden herself, was someone with the purification ability. The keystone in Kuroyukihime's plan to purify the Armor of Catastrophe. The person who would get rid of the element of Chrome Disaster clinging to Haruyuki.

He forgot the pain of missing limbs and simply stood there, while before him, Utai nodded her head slightly, as if to encourage Utan.

Several meters away, the black aura around Bush Utan weakened even further. "I…I just…wanted to be stronger…like my brother…strong," he muttered feebly, taking a step forward. His arms hung by his sides, and his head shook in tiny increments; he was definitely about to return her nod.

But…

The eye in his chest opened up to a nearly perfect circle. The sharp red pulsed fiercely. Then in Utan's own eyes, a crimson light began pulsing in perfect sync. Haruyuki felt almost like the eyeball—a supposedly simple object—was actually interfering with Utan's nervous system.

"No…This power is mine…It's my power…my strength…" His voice gradually grew lower and slightly distorted. The concentration of the aura covering him increased once more. His loosely open hands were abruptly clenched into tight fists. "I'm not giving it to anyone…You're trying to steal it…You want to take it from me...No...You can't...," Utan muttered incoherently and abruptly threw his upper body back. The dark red light in his eyes and the third spot on his chest turned into thin, gushing lances. "It's *my* power, *my* IS mode! If you wanna steal it...this is what I'll do to you!!"

He flung his right fist up into the air, dark aura condensing around it. "Aaaaaaah...Dark Blow!!" he yelled, as he moved to bring his fist down and smash the smaller Ardor Maiden.

"Ah!" Haruyuki reflexively stepped forward to fly out under that fist. But before he could, Utai raised a gentle hand and stopped him cold. At the same time, she threw an empty hand up above her head. Compared with Utan's enormous rocklike punch, those five digits were thin like fresh buds only just sprouted. There was no way she could stop that fist, Haruyuki thought. But...

In an instant, Ardor Maiden's right hand glittered an indistinct orange. Fire. Cleanly transparent flames covered her small hand.

When the invincible fist was on the verge of shattering her slender palm, Haruyuki heard a terrifying crash. The pressure of the impact surged outward, shaking Haruyuki and the grass around them ferociously. But, unaware of this, Haruyuki simply stared, dumbfounded, at the scene before him.

Utan's hand and Maiden's were not touching directly. In the five-or-so-centimeter space between them, the black aura and the transparent flames were engaged in a fierce contest. White sparks dazzled the eye as they flew off from the edges of this battle. Two imaginations were fighting to overwrite each other; Maiden was defending against Utan's Incarnate attack with her own.

But the appearances of the two avatars were a world apart. In contrast with Utan, face twisted with undisguised rage and bloodlust, Utai was simply, calmly extending her right hand. Her expression was even pitying somehow.

Suddenly, he heard her speak in a way that betrayed this impression.

"Bush Utan. You are thinking incorrectly. The power of Incarnate—what you call IS mode—is not something you can be given by someone, not something that can be taken by anyone. It is a projection of yourself born from within your own heart."

"...Shut up. Shut up, shut up!" Utan groaned and brandished his left fist. But before he could bring it down to hit anything, the flames of Utai's right hand grew the slightest bit more intense.

Instantly, the balance was shattered. Utan's fist was violently repelled, and his entire body fell with it into the grass behind him.

They were simply at vastly different levels in terms of strength. Utai's Incarnate was probably a defense expansion. Normally, red-type avatars couldn't use this power, or they weren't very good at it if they could. But given how she repelled that fist of steel with nothing more than her overlay, she was definitely no ordinary avatar.

Bush Utan seemed to sense this unfathomability of Ardor Maiden. Instead of trying to punch her again, he stayed down and began swimming through the sea of grass. *Ksh, ksh, ksh.* The sound drew a circle and finally melted into the infinite rustling caused by the wind. Rather than running away, he was likely intending to get some distance before attacking with that beam of darkness he took Haruyuki down with.

"Ut—I mean, Mei, he's gonna attack with a missile!" Haruyuki whispered hurriedly, and Utai nodded lightly.

She took a few steps over to him and looked around the area. Once again, her clear voice flowed out over the grassland. "Bush Utan, there's one more thing you don't know. If you're going to carry out an Incarnate attack, you must be prepared for something very serious. And that is the fact that your opponent may counterattack with Incarnate." She stopped and glanced at Haruyuki before murmuring in a completely unconcerned voice, "C. You only have to do it once, but please defend against Utan's attack. It takes a bit of time for my Incarnate technique to activate."

"G-got it...Wait, what?!" Haruyuki immediately accepted, only to then panic. Defending against a long-distance attack originating from a place he couldn't see was no easy feat. It was actually more like impossible.

However, Utai had already shifted her gaze away from him and begun to focus her mind. She stood, arms loosely apart, eyes closed, the gentle flames of her overlay enveloping her body.

And then her avatar changed rather unexpectedly.

From below the hair-type parts hanging down on both sides of her face, additional armor slid out with a *clang* and covered her entire mask. Only a thin eye line, tracing an upward arc, existed in the smooth, perfectly white, curved armor. Almost—no, *exactly* like an actual mask. The eyes carved into this new face were both gentle and severe, depending on the angle. At the very least, there was no hint of the innocence of her original mask.

The next change was the generation of the Japanese bow gripped in her left hand. It was no sooner engulfed in a raging fire than it instantly shrank down to a fraction of its length. Utai moved this thing, now a short, flaming stick, to her right hand, and held it out directly in front of her. Haruyuki guessed that it was a gun or something when—

*Bang!* The sharp noise reverberated in his ears, and the stick spread out in a thin layer into the shape of a metal folding fan, its base the center of the bow. It was not a weapon, much less a projectile; it was, just as it appeared to be, a hand fan. He wanted to shout out, *Why'd you give up a good bow for a fan?!* but he couldn't disturb her concentration at this point.

Left with no other choice, Haruyuki prepared himself to defend against Utan's beam attack and sent his eyes racing around his surroundings. If Utan's overlay had been a vivid primary color, he might have been able to see it through the thick grass, but the black aura melted into the darkness of the depths; he could see no sign of it. As before, he could hear nothing in the way of footsteps, so identifying where the attack would come from was many times more problematic than guessing the trajectory of an oncoming punch.

No. Even if he could kill the sound of his movement, Utan would have to make extraneous sound just once before his attack. And that sound would be the call of the technique name. Unlike normal special attacks, this wasn't required for Incarnate attacks, but immediately releasing the attack without the imagination trigger of the voice was a fairly high-level skill. Having only gotten the ISS kit a few days earlier, Utan wouldn't have that level of technique.

Haruyuki snapped out the fingertips of his right hand and focused all his powers of perception on listening. The wind howling, the grass rustling—he eliminated every kind of noise from his awareness. He simply waited intently for Utan's voice, the memory of which still lingered from a few minutes earlier.

Several long, long seconds passed, and then finally it touched Haruyuki's senses:

"Da—"

Haruyuki's eyes flew open. "Laser Sword!!"

"—rk Shot!!"

The two Incarnate names rang out at nearly the same time.

A beam of darkness shot at Ardor Maiden from behind them, and Haruyuki cut sharply upward. From his fingertips, a silver aura stretched out into a sword. The tip touched the jet-black aura—

*Skriiiing!* The sound of the collision was earsplitting. The beam's trajectory shifted upward, and it just barely grazed Utai's shoulder before narrowly disappearing into the night sky. Surprise raced across Utan's mask as he stood up in the distance. But he quickly sank back into the grass and concealed himself with his high-speed movement.

Haruyuki had defended against that Incarnate one time, just as Utai had instructed, but he was certain that a second beam would be closing in on them in seconds. Not knowing what to do, he looked at Ardor Maiden next to him. Utan's fighting spirit didn't seem to be waning at all, despite the fact that Incarnate attacks used an invisible mental strength gauge rather than consuming an avatar's special-attack gauge.

The small avatar was gently moving the fan in her right hand, face still equipped with the actual mask. Her movement was almost like a dance.

The moment this thought crossed his mind, something prickled in his distant memory.

He felt like he had seen this somewhere before. Right, when he was little, he had seen some kind of play at the large shrine where he had gone for his first shrine visit of the year with his parents. While mystical music played, a woman in a white robe and red hakama had danced with a fan in one hand. She had looked almost exactly like Utai did now, with a few important differences: The woman in the play all that time ago hadn't been wearing a mask, and Utai's movements were more dynamic. Her tempo was more varied; she stopped completely at key moments. Her dance was nothing short of incredible.

Taking in the way Ardor Maiden moved, he forgot almost entirely about the beam attack threatening to destroy them any instant.

A sonorous voice flowed from the mouth area of her mask. Not a yell, it still seemed like it echoed from one end of the stage to the other, a clear, strong "song."

"The slight cool of the three heats."

Suddenly, the clearing shimmered gently as far as he could see. Heat haze—no, fire. A gleam the same flame color as the haze enveloping Utai's body blanketed the stage far off into the distance. This was meant to be the light of her Incarnate—her overlay—but the range was just too large. It was on par with or maybe even greater than Rust Order, the space-corroding Incarnate attack Rust Jigsaw unleashed to destroy the Hermes' Cord race the week before.

As he held his breath, her high-pitched voice continued to flood his ears. "Is this the only escape from suffering?"

The world…burned.

Crimson flames roared up in all directions, nearly touching the sky, and the grassland around them instantly went up in smoke. The entire stage shone red, countless sparks flowing across the night sky like stars.

Only a radius of about two meters centered on Utai was apparently safe; the flames didn't cross into this area. But Haruyuki had the illusion of fierce heat, enough to burn him up, and he groaned uncontrollably.

Ardor Maiden moved her fan gently. Before it, the blaze swirled even more ferociously, burning up not just the grass, but even the virtual ground beneath. And then the curtain of flames parted, and he could see a small shadow.

Bush Utan. His entire body was enveloped in the blaze, and both hands had already burned away entirely; they were gone.

But strangely, he himself seemed not to feel the heat. He was looking down at his own avatar curiously, essentially nothing more than a pillar of flame. Haruyuki reflexively checked the health gauge in the top right of his gaze and saw that it was dropping with incredible speed. Soon, it was less than 30 percent, and even when the gauge dropped into a red more concentrated than the flames, it continued to plummet without stopping. Twenty percent, ten. And then zero.

The human-shaped fire flashed for a dazzling moment and then disappeared.

Dumbfounded, Haruyuki brought his gaze back to Utai.

The small avatar was dancing even more fluidly. As he stared wordlessly, Haruyuki felt her dance was bringing him answers to his many questions.

*Maiden* didn't just mean "an innocent girl." It also meant "a woman or girl who serves a shrine." Of course, the white and red armor was reminiscent of a shrine. This was the figure of a shrine maiden, after all.

So then the meaning of Ardor was fire. Hotter than fire, fiercer than flames, a world-destroying conflagration.

Ardor Maiden.

The shrine maiden of the inferno.

# 7

Tuesday, June 18.

Haruyuki scarfed down his usual breakfast of cereal with milk, called out a good-bye to his mother's bedroom, and hurried out of the apartment.

Although the sun had its face out for the first time in a long time, the air was sticky and wet. The discomfort index had gone through the roof, and it was a foregone conclusion that even the slightest bit of exercise would immediately produce in him rivers of sweat, but even still, he headed toward the main road in front of his building at a trot.

But he wasn't late. The destination he was hurrying to was not school, but on the way to school. Coming out onto the ring road of Kannana Street, Haruyuki passed the place where he usually turned right and kept going south, down the wide sidewalk.

He slipped under the elevated Chuo Line tracks and climbed the gentle hill. In a few minutes, he came out at the large intersection where Kannana and Oume Kaido met. He went up the escalator to the pedestrian walkway, stopped in the center of Kannana Street, and glanced at the clock in the lower right of his view. 7:45 AM.

He shifted his gaze to the lanes of EVs passing below him and murmured, "Burst Link."

*Skreeeeee!!* The world froze blue, accompanied by the sound of a collision. The Brain Burst program multiplied the quantum clock generated by his heart and accelerated his consciousness a thousand times, all to produce the initial accelerated space.

The herd of EVs, dyed a single transparent blue, appeared to have stopped completely, but if he looked very, very carefully, they were actually slowly moving, about a centimeter every second. With this strange sight as the background, Haruyuki moved the hands of his pink pig avatar to open the Brain Burst matching list and breathed a sign of relief when he found the name he was looking for in the surprisingly long list of players. He touched it without hesitation and selected DUEL from the menu that popped up.

The world transformed once more: The sky grew black around him. The walls of the buildings and convenience stores on both sides of the road were immediately riddled with cracks, and all the cars disappeared. In their place, countless bits of rubble, sinkholes, and rusted drums appeared on the surface of the road.

An unconscious smile floated up onto Haruyuki's face as he surveyed the uniformly brutal scene of the Century End stage. It wasn't as if he particularly liked this stage, but it was absolutely perfect right then. The backdrop for the first duel he had fought with the opponent he selected a few seconds earlier had been a Century End stage, too, a duel that had also been Haruyuki's—Silver Crow's—very first.

He opened his ears. From the north of the wide main road, he could hear the distinctive rumbling of an internal combustion engine. The light blue guide cursor was basically not moving; his opponent appeared to be racing straight toward him with the throttle fully open. He was tempted to hide himself on the pedestrian bridge and leap down just as his opponent was about to pass under, throwing all his force into ramming the motorcyclist with a drop kick.

But he stuck with his original plan. He casually threw himself into the air and leapt over the railing while his enemy was still invisible. With the wings on his back, he glided down smoothly to land softly on the road surface.

"Huh?"

"Crow just got down. What's he doing?"

The confused questions came from the members of the Gallery dotting the rooftops of distant buildings in twos and threes. They were no doubt suspicious of Haruyuki throwing away a hard-won advantage, but even as he apologized to them in his head, he knew he hadn't accelerated to fight this time.

He put his hands on his hips and waited. A few seconds later, a headlight popped up, dazzling on the other side of the gloom. The roar of the V-twin engine abruptly grew louder. His opponent had also noticed him and seemed to be shifting down for a charge. But instead of readying himself for the first attack and getting into position, Haruyuki thrust both hands high into the air to indicate his complete lack of intention to fight.

Fortunately, his opponent seemed to get the message. The iron steed from beyond the darkness decelerated, sending sparks shooting out from the front and rear brake rotors, while the rear wheel slid. The bike stopped directly in front of Haruyuki, the orange light of nearby bonfires reflected in its chrome-plated body. The rider took his right hand off the handlebars and waggled an admonishing finger.

"So bad, man. You started this, and now you're giving up before the fight even starts?"

Faced with the grim skull mask of Ash Roller, likely the lone motorcycle user in the entire Accelerated World, Haruyuki bowed his head neatly.

"I'm sorry. I need to talk to you today, Ash."

Ash Roller belonged to the Green Legion Great Wall, which counted Shibuya and the areas south of it as their territory. Naturally, his main duel field should have been Shibuya, but for some reason, he appeared on the matching list in Suginami for a short time on weekday mornings and evenings. Haruyuki supposed he commuted to school by bus along Kannana Street and that this time was probably his "trip abroad" from his own territory, but if that was the case, he was actually pretty daring. If the bus he was riding on was ever identified from where his duel avatar tended to appear, it could lead to his being outed in the real.

But now that he was thinking about it, no other Burst Linker could be so perfectly described by the words *daring* and *rough*, so Haruyuki interrupted his thoughts before they could take that detour and took a few steps toward the motorcycle. He lowered his voice. "And if possible, it would be great if we could talk in Closed mode."

"Closed Mode" was, as the name indicated, closed—in other words, a duel that didn't allow the participation of the Gallery. It could be set with the agreement of both duelers, but in general, other players thought this was stingy. One of the fairly significant motivators of a Burst Linker duel was to show the Gallery a cool trick or two, so almost no one used this mode.

Naturally, Ash Roller looked unhappy and sniffed haughtily. But he seemed to be amenable to Haruyuki's will, and he responded with a brief "Gotcha."

The motorcycle rider then took a look around them and called in a loud voice that carried well, "Hey, heeeey! Girls and boys of the Gallery! I know you came all this way to see the great and powerful me win, so sorrrry to disappoint, but we're doing this duel in secret town!"

Several objections promptly rose up from the buildings around them.

"What? Come on, that's booooring!"

"Just fight for us! We haven't seen an Ash-Crow matchup in aaaaages!"

But these voices of discontent changed at once into loud cheers when Ash tossed them a juicy bone: "Got no choice, maaan! This crow kid here's gonna confess his love to mighty me!"

Amidst the applause and whistles showering down on him, Haruyuki grew flustered. "Tha—No, it's—" he shouted, but it was a fact that they had to give the Gallery a bit of a show or they'd never be satisfied. In the end, unsure whether this was real foresight on the part of Ash Roller or if he was just going for laughs, Haruyuki was forced to simply bob his head over and over in a slight bow.

He then touched on his own name in the top left of his visual field and opened the settings screen. He selected CLOSED from the duel mode change menu and tapped the OKAY button. Once Ash Roller tapped the YES/NO window displayed in his own vision, the Gallery—clamoring even more loudly now—vanished, enveloped in light from one end.

A silence filled the stage, like the mute button had been pressed. The only thing he could hear was the irregular pulsation of the V-twin engine idling quietly.

Ash Roller pulled the ignition key out, and then even that engine noise stopped. "So? What's this whatever you wanna talk about? You lose your wings again…Nah, doesn't look like it's that."

"Umm…well…It's just…" Struggling with exactly where to begin, Haruyuki opened his mouth to tell Ash Roller the facts in order. "Yesterday, I was in a duel with Bush Utan from the Green Legion—" he managed to get out.

"Wh-what did you say?!" Ash Roller's reaction was completely unexpected. He slipped down from his bike onto the ground, practically falling out of his seat, and the fierce-faced rider very nearly slammed his skull-design face mask into Haruyuki's, shouting, "Where?! What time was this?!"

They sat down facing each other on some concrete blocks handily placed on the side of the road, and Haruyuki explained the events of the previous evening's duel as best he could.

The fact that, after school, sometime past seven o'clock in Suginami Area Two, his team had challenged the tag team of Bush Utan and Olive Grab. The fact that, although in the opening stages of the duel Bush Utan had stuck to his *you feel me?* punk act, once he equipped the mysterious ISS kit in the middle, his attitude had changed to one of violence, as if he were an entirely different person. The fact that someone had apparently given Utan this kit three days earlier.

The only thing he didn't mention was the name of Ardor Maiden, with whom he'd been teamed up at the time, and her abilities. There had been a few people in the Gallery then, so Ash would probably hear rumors about her at some point, but he still couldn't indiscriminately leak information about his own Legion friends to other Legions. Ash, for his part, didn't ask any questions related to this.

After the fairly lengthy explanation, Ash Roller rested his arms on his kneepads, leaned forward, and expelled a deep, long breath. "IS mode study kit," he murmured like a groan before looking up at Haruyuki. "This IS mode is *that*? You know, the Incarnate System?"

"Y-yeah. I think it's the same thing. Ash, you already know about…?"

At Haruyuki's half-truncated question, the skull helmet swung slowly from side to side. "Just the name, from my master. When I was stuck on figuring out the V-twin Punch before, she taught me that this thing exists, but I didn't do any training in it. Dunno… I was freaked. Someone tells you you might get swallowed up by the 'darkness of your heart,' you know…And plus, now that Master's back in Negabu, it's kinda ridiculous for me to go and tell her to teach me."

The "master" Ash Roller was talking about was his "parent" and Haruyuki's own instructor in the Incarnate, Sky Raker. In April of that year, she had formally returned to her old home, the Black Legion Nega Nebulus, so she and Ash Roller, a member of Great Wall, were essentially enemies now. Certainly, the two didn't seem to be too concerned about it and fought hard against each other in the Territories, but Ash's position of having trouble leaning on his own parent was certainly a difficult one.

His thoughts drifted off into a bit of a tangent, but this spurred him to ask about something that had been bothering him for a while. Haruyuki opened his mouth. "Um, Ash, why GW?"

"Come on, why the sudden interrogation? Honestly? 'Cause in the beginning I thought it was a freaking huge Legion. And my house is over that way, too, and the kid who invited me was pretty decent. Once I joined, turns out GW's totally way more free than Blue or Purple, so I got no regrets. Our LM doesn't go around giving orders or making rules, either."

The LM—Legion Master—of Great Wall was, of course, the Green King. Haruyuki nodded in understanding, remembering the thorough reticence of Green Grandé he had caught a glimpse of at the meeting of the Seven Kings the other day. Putting aside this question, he finally got to the heart of the matter.

"So about Bush Utan…Is he maybe your 'child,' Ash?"

Apparently, this was not a question Ash Roller had expected. He yanked his skull face back before shaking his head quickly from side to side. "As if. I'm not child-having caliber yet. That kid U's parent is…gone. Beginning of the year, lost all his points."

A shiver ran up Haruyuki's spine. In his ears, Utan's monologue from the night before roared back to life:

*You gotta be strong or it's all meaningless. If you're not strong, you can't get a win ratio worth anything, and you stay at the bottom of your Legion, your points dry up, you disappear from the secret Accelerated World.*

As Haruyuki sank into silence, Ash Roller let out one deep sigh before moving abruptly and unexpectedly. Placing his right hand on the mouth area of his helmet's skull shield, he flung his entire face to the rear with a *clack*.

Ash Roller watched, bare-faced and invisible eyebrow arched, as Haruyuki threw himself back in surprise. His pale green eye lenses were fairly thin, and combined with the pointed chin of his faceplate, the structure of his helmetless head was somehow that of a science-loving boy. At the very least, the impression was one hundred eighty degrees from the usual cackling Century End rider act. From that mouth came his real voice, with an unexpectedly subtle tone.

"...Whut?"

"N-no, nothing!"

"Then get back on topic. When he lost his parent, Utan was still level one. And after that...y'know, stuff happened, and I ended up looking after him. Wasn't like I was the perfect guy for the job, but I couldn't just leave him, right?"

"Right. You're a great big bro."

"Dunno. Maybe I never really saw the first thing about what was going on in that kid's head. I mean, the last little while, I knew he was sorta stuck, but...I been busy with stuff, too, and I just kept putting it off. And then maybe since the day before yesterday or so, I basically hear nothing from him. He's never on the Shibuya matching list when I connect, and he totally doesn't answer any of my mails. Then I start hearing weird rumors."

"Rumors?" Haruyuki leaned forward, and Ash Roller dropped his shoulders once again.

"I heard Utan'd teamed up with Olive Grab and was using this weird tech to win in empty areas like Setagaya and Ota," he responded lifelessly. "So I went over that way yesterday. I never thought he'd be in Setagaya...And the truth about this 'weird tech,' I didn't think it'd be something serious like that—an item you can equip that lets you use the Incarnate System. And one someone else could *give* you."

Haruyuki waited for this break to ask ever so timidly, "Ash, do you have any idea who the Burst Linker that gave Utan and the others the ISS kit might be?"

But the helmet with the shield still up simply shook from side to side. "Can't pin it on anyone. I could tell you the names of all the kids I know Utan hangs out with, but...Look, Crow, maybe there's no point in figuring out who gave the thing to Utan, you know?"

"What? That's not true," Haruyuki hurriedly objected. "We have to at least stop the distribution of something so dangerous!"

Figuring out the identity of the Burst Linker who gave Utan the ISS kit was exactly the purpose of talking with Ash Roller like this in Closed mode. Even if he couldn't immediately narrow it down to one person, if he made a list of the Burst Linkers Utan had contact with and went through it in order, there was a possibility he could take down the source of the kits.

But Ash Roller's next words smashed Haruyuki's hopeful hypothesis. "That bit about how the ISS kit you saw looking like a living creature, that is totally tripping me up. I mean, in the Accelerated World, living-type equipment and items have pretty specific characteristics. Like automatically healing when it gets broken…or splitting with the passage of time. What if…what if this kit being handed out is…a copy, or a copy of a copy?"

"Ah!" Haruyuki unconsciously cried out. He hadn't even considered the possibility.

The ISS kit someone had given Bush Utan. Although he had no grounds for making this assumption, he hadn't wavered in his belief that it was a single person handing the kits out. If, like Ash Roller said, that black eyeball had the ability to duplicate itself and randomly distribute copies to other people…and then assuming there was some kind of compensation for this action…

It might already be too late.

While he was sitting here like this, the ISS kit was continuing its boundless expansion, the number of Burst Linkers able to use the terrifying power of a dark Incarnate attack steadily increasing. And all the while, none of them were being taught the first thing about what the Incarnate System even was. Naturally, they wouldn't have a clue about the most basic first rule—"You must never use Incarnate unless you are attacked by Incarnate"—so they'd have a field day using it in duels. This was already essentially the collapse of the Brain Burst: strategies in line with the characteristics of the stage, techniques to take advantage of your own abilities—all these would lose their meaning, and the fights would devolve into simply trading Dark Shots at long distances and Dark Blows closer up.

Haruyuki shivered bodily at the future's savage portrait.

He tried to find some basis for refuting it, but before he could, Ash Roller whispered, "The truth is…I've heard about two or three other cases besides Utan and Olive where someone's suddenly started using 'weird tech.' And one of them apparently came out of the Edogawa Area. And now hearing this from you, it all makes me wonder if maybe there isn't more than one place these ISS kits are coming from."

"What? Edogawa Ward?" he repeated, stunned. That was on the opposite side of the Imperial Palace from Utan's base of Shibuya and Setagaya. It was too far. Unfortunately, this only strengthened the doubt that maybe instead of being distributed, they were being disseminated.

*But who's doing it, and for what?*

Frustrated, Haruyuki chewed on the question in his mouth that had been plaguing him since the night before. Of course, absolutely no answer came to mind. He hung his head low, and he looked down on his own shadow swaying in the light of the fire in the drum, his mind starting to wander.

Finally, Ash Roller muttered, "Even sitting here talking like this, thirty minutes is too short, eh?"

Reflexively checking the timer in the top of his field of view, he saw that the 1,800 seconds they had started with was already down to 300. Of course, it was possible to do the duel over again from the matching list, but any more discussion than this and they'd just be putting speculation on top of speculation.

Haruyuki bowed his head, ready to thank Ash Roller for agreeing to his sudden dialogue request and wrap things up.

But before he could do anything else, Ash Roller lowered the skull shield of his mask with a *clack*. "Crow," he said quickly in an effect-laden voice. "Before we go, I got something to talk to you about, too."

"Huh? What is it?"

"Aah, 'kay…I shouldn't be the one bringing this up, but…we got no time, so I'll be straight. You don't think something's been weird in your duels this week? Other than the thing with Utan, I mean."

"Huh? Weird?" He immediately scanned his memory, but there was nothing particular that caught his attention. If he counted the fights to defend his Territory three days earlier, he had fought about twenty normal duels, but the battle with Utan the day before had made such a strong impression that he couldn't even remember how many of those he had won. Bewildered, he started talking. "No…All my duels were just regular, I think. What do you mean by 'weird'?"

Ash Roller hesitated oddly before replying awkwardly, "That 'regular' bit."

"R-regular is weird? Ummm. I'm sorry, I've been worried about a bunch of things since the race last week, and to be honest, I haven't actually dueled that much."

The things he was worried about were, of course, the meeting of the Seven Kings that had taken place two days earlier, and the handling of Silver Crow as an item on the agenda there. If he didn't purify himself within a week of the element of the Armor of Catastrophe that was believed to be parasitizing his avatar from somewhere, Haruyuki would, in light of the situation, be banished from the Accelerated World. Haruyuki might not get the chance to see with his own eyes the massive confusion the ISS kit would bring about…

The instant his thinking got to that point, Haruyuki finally grasped what Ash Roller was trying to say to him.

Regular was weird. Right, that was exactly it. Basically, Haruyuki shouldn't have been in any position to be able to duel like he regularly did. Because the week before, in the Hermes' Cord race, Silver Crow had transformed into Chrome Disaster before the eyes of more than a hundred members of the Gallery. Talk that Haruyuki was the sixth owner of the cursed armor should have raced through the Accelerated World. The real mystery was that no one was refusing to duel him or fiercely cursing him out or anything at all.

Every Burst Linker he had dueled that week, even Bush Utan the previous day, had acted like they had no idea about Haruyuki's transformation into Disaster. Which was basically not possible, when he thought about it rationally.

"Right. That is weird. Every duel I've been in, no one's said anything to me," Haruyuki said hoarsely.

Ash Roller started chattering at top speed. "But, like, the reason for that is that all those hundreds of people in the Gallery who saw that fight between you and that rusted bastard made a pact before they logged out."

"What? A pact? What kind of pact?" Haruyuki asked in reply, unable to comprehend this statement.

Ash Roller's answer was surprising. "'We will never offer a single word of reproach to Silver Crow for equipping the Armor of Catastrophe in Hermes' Cord.'"

"...What..."

"Because...you saved the race. That event the rusted bastard would have totally wrecked, at the very last of last moments, you brought it back into our hands. So for just this one transformation, we'll all keep our mouths shut, and we won't think about how you managed to get ahold of the Armor. Everyone in the Gallery then just said it sort of spontaneously and agreed unanimously, I guess. And that's why in all your duels this week, no one has even said the letter *D* of *Disaster* to you."

"......" Deeply surprised and slammed with another, even more massive emotion than that, Haruyuki opened his eyes wide, speechless.

Among all those people, more than a hundred, who watched the fight between Silver Crow and Rust Jigsaw, there had to have been tons who belonged to the kings' Legions. Haruyuki should have been an enemy to them. It was only natural they would reproach and fiercely curse Haruyuki as the summoner of the detested Armor of Catastrophe. And yet, despite that...

"Before we're members of the different Legions, we're Burst Linkers. That's what it is," Ash Roller said distinctly, staring at Haruyuki before continuing in an unprecedentedly serious voice. "Crow, that's why right now, there's no real hostility toward you. I heard a bit about the judgment at the meeting of the Seven Kings from some guys up top in GW, but sounds like there're some peeps saying it's too harsh. So now that that's all out there, I wanna ask you..."

The briefest of instants.

Suddenly sensing something ominous, Haruyuki's voice was strangled as he urged Ash Roller on. "What is it...?"

"There's more to the rumors I heard. This 'weird tech' Utan and Olive are using...I heard it's a copy of Chrome Disaster's power."

Having finished his irregular closed duel with Ash Roller, who was likely on one of the buses running along Kannana Street, Haruyuki crossed the pedestrian walkway to the south and headed for school. During the time he walked westward on Oume Kaido, and even after he slipped through the school gates, changed his shoes, and arrived at his desk, the shock and questions squatting in his brain showed no signs of going anywhere.

The Incarnate attack from the weird tech Bush Utan used—the ISS kit—was a copy of Chrome Disaster's attack power.

It wasn't possible. He'd never heard of anyone reproducing someone else's abilities and loading them into a parasitic item. But now that he was thinking about it, he also hadn't even heard the words *parasite* or *purify* until very recently. It wasn't at all strange that there would be logic he still didn't know about in the Accelerated World.

And the black overlay of that Dark Blow and Dark Shot did look a lot like the aura of darkness that covered the Armor of Catastrophe...

He shuddered on his hard plastic chair. Putting aside whether it was true or not, if this rumor spread far and wide as ISS kits were disseminated, the anger of Burst Linkers who loved the Accelerated World would probably become something explosive directed squarely at Haruyuki, the sixth owner of Chrome Disaster. He had no doubt that the pact the members of the Gallery in the Hermes' Cord race had gone to the trouble of making would be undone in an instant. They might even come to believe Haruyuki had betrayed them and harbor an enormous hatred for him.

"Why is this happening...?" Haruyuki muttered silently, listening to the bells signaling the start of the day ringing off in the distance.

Where and when exactly had this crisis begun? He almost believed there was an invisible force somewhere, separate from the judgment of the Seven Kings, that was closing in on him. Was it simply a series of strange coincidences? Or was someone making it happen...? If it was the latter, this way of preparing scrupulously, of carefully controlling information to back him into a corner, brought a certain character sharply to mind. He had appeared before Haruyuki as a new student at Umesato that spring and tried to destroy him with devilish means: the Twilight Marauder.

Glancing up at the ceiling—and the seventh-grade classroom beyond it—he shook his head slightly. There was absolutely no way that guy was maneuvering here again. Once someone lost all their burst points and had Brain Burst forcefully uninstalled, they lost all memories related to the Accelerated World. The day after their final battle, Haruyuki had seen this hidden rule with his own eyes when he tried to talk to the Marauder.

But. Supposing he had learned this method of attack from someone else?

Supposing this "teacher" had started to move finally?

"Haru."

Haruyuki jumped at the pat on his right shoulder. Whirling around with incredible force, he found the familiar face of his good friend, eyes blinking rapidly behind blue glasses.

"Taku."

"What's wrong? Time to head to the next class."

At these words from his childhood friend and fellow Legion member, Takumu Mayuzumi, he hurriedly looked around. Apparently, morning homeroom had finished; his classmates were leaving the classroom one after another. First period on Tuesdays was Music, so they had to move to the soundproofed music room.

"Oh…r-right."

Takumu watched Haruyuki jump to his feet, eyebrows knitted. "Haru," he whispered in Haruyuki's ear, shrugging his lanky shoulders. "If you're worrying about the bounty thing, it's like I said yesterday: You don't need to make yourself sick about that. Chi and I, and Fuko, and of course Master, we'll protect you."

"Y-yeah. Sorry. Now I'm getting you worried and all." He managed to bring a smile to his face, and as he stood up and began to walk, Haruyuki got to thinking.

Takumu probably hadn't yet heard the rumor that the IS kit was a Chrome Disaster copy. But he'd find out if he did his usual dueling after school. Haruyuki should explain the whole thing before then. And not just to Takumu, but to Kuroyukihime and the other Legion members.

Stepping out into the hallway, he nudged Takumu's arm with his elbow and replied in a low murmur, "So, uh, once you're done with practice today, come to my place. I got something I need to talk to you about, but we probably won't have enough time for it at school."

"Got it." Takumu nodded immediately without any awkward questions, for which Haruyuki was thankful.

"Can you tell Chiyu for me?" he continued. "I'll mail Kuroyukihime and Fuko."

"What time?"

"Right. Uh, six thirty."

"Roger."

With this brief exchange, the chill clinging to Haruyuki's spine finally seemed to fade a little. He clenched his hands and told himself silently, *I'm not gonna lose. As if I* could *lose. I've got such solid friends. No matter what plan gets cooked up, no matter what happens, nothing can break my spirits. No way.*

However, at the terror Takumu unleashed immediately after this, Haruyuki heard the distinct sound of something snapping in his heart.

"That reminds me, Haru. We're supposed to be presenting our vocal solo assignments in music class next. Did you practice?"

# 8

After school.

In addition to first period's vocal solo presentations, Haruyuki was forced to play softball, his absolute worst sport, during fifth-period gym class. The day had done serious physical and mental damage to him by the time Haruyuki staggered, exhausted, out to the animal hutch in the yard.

Because the cleaning of the hutch was finished, the only duty in that day's journal file was something the club president, Haruyuki, would do alone. A tiny part of him expected words of passionate appreciation and gratitude from his colleagues, Hamajima and Izeki, who he had sent home early the day before, but what he got when he stepped through the entrance earlier were just the briefest of messages: "You worked hard, Prez" and "Yup."

"It's fine, whatever. A man doesn't go out looking for gratitude." Muttering and grumbling in a tone far from the hard-boiled sentiment it was attached to, Haruyuki passed behind the gloomy old school building and walked over to the hutch.

Thanks to a day of sun, the tiles on the floor were completely dry. And the mountain of old leaves piled up in front of the chicken wire was also well on its way toward total dryness; he'd probably be able to stuff them in a bag and throw them out the next day. Checking out the results of his own work felt pretty good, so he stood there for a moment, staring vacantly at the hutch.

So when a window requesting an ad hoc connection abruptly appeared in the center of his gaze, he was just as surprised as he had been the day before. His head flew back momentarily before he looked around and saw a small figure standing a little ways off: sharply trimmed front fringe and a ponytail tied back tightly. Brown backpack shouldered on a snow-white dress-type uniform. Fourth-grade student at Matsunogi Academy elementary section, Utai Shinomiya.

"Oh! H-hello!" He quickly tapped the OK button in the request window while he greeted her.

Instantly, characters started flowing across the chat window that opened automatically. UI> Hello, Arita. I apologize for being late. I asked the administrator here to receive some equipment and record some data, which took a while.

As before, she was a demon with the keyboard. He had to read the characters twice, they were input so fast; his eyes couldn't keep up with it. But unable to completely understand their meaning regardless, Haruyuki raised his face and asked, "R-receive equipment? What do you…?" It was then that he noticed a fairly large carrier at Utai's feet. Given that the whole thing was made of a hard-looking plastic, he couldn't actually see inside of it, but Utai must have had a pretty hard time getting it over here by herself.

"Oh, that? If you're going to take out whatever's in there, I'll help you," Haruyuki said, and started to walk over to the case.

But for some reason, Utai thrust her right hand out in front of her, and typed at the same time with her left hand. UI> This is not that. I am terribly sorry, but I'd like you to please not come near this carrier for a while. I'll explain the reason later. And the equipment…It looks like it's coming now.

Just as she said—or rather, typed—the sound of footsteps

crunching along the ground reached Haruyuki’s ears. When he turned his gaze, walking toward them was a young man in a delivery company uniform. He was carrying long and slender treelike things on both shoulders.

“Is this where these go?” the delivery guy asked.

Utai moved both hands quickly. She apparently had an ad hoc connection with him, too. UI> YES. I’M SORRY, BUT PLEASE CARRY THEM INTO THAT HUTCH. PLEASE PUT ONE INSIDE TO THE LEFT AND THE OTHER TO THE RIGHT.

“Sure thing!” With the energetic reply, the deliveryman walked briskly in front of Haruyuki. The things on his shoulders looked like trees—no, they *were* trees, complete with several thin branches stretching out, from the end of a trunk about a meter and eighty centimeters long. The branches had no leaves, and a heavy-looking brace was attached at the base of each. They were artificial.

The delivery man brought the two long trees deftly in through the open entrance, placed them inside in the shade, and turned around.

Utai typed out detailed placement instructions. UI> MOVE THAT ONE TWENTY CENTIMETERS OR SO TO THE RIGHT. YES, THERE’S PERFECT.

When the deliveryman came out of the hutch, he presented a receipt holotag, and Utai signed it electronically. “Thanks!” he said, and raced off, leaving just Haruyuki, Utai, the strange trees, and the mysterious carrier.

From the other side of the chicken wire, Haruyuki stared upward, dumbfounded, at the tall trees. The trunk of each was probably around seven or eight centimeters in diameter. The surfaces were smooth and polished, but they definitely were not new. Most likely, the animal that was going to live in this hutch used them. Now that he was thinking about it, Haruyuki still hadn’t been told what type of animal it was.

Usually, it was a rabbit or a chicken or something of that nature in a school Animal Care Club. But if this animal needed these big trees…Some kind of monkey? A chameleon? It couldn't be a sloth, could it?

Haruyuki gulped, and Utai next to him typed briefly.

UI> Now then, I'm going to put this one into the hutch. I'm sure he'll fly around for a bit, so once I'm inside, please close the door firmly behind me.

Reflexively, he looked at the large carrier. Her words meant that what was inside was the problem animal. And it flying around meant—some kind of bird. Those things that had been brought into the hutch were perches. Thinking about it, he realized an elementary school Animal Care Club wouldn't have a monkey or a chameleon. It was probably a parrot or a mynah or some other big bird.

In his heart, with the doubtful thought *Seriously?* Haruyuki watched as Utai cautiously carried the case in. Once she was through the door, he asked abruptly, "Um, Shinomiya, can I come in, too?"

Utai took a moment to think before nodding decisively. UI> It should be okay. But you can't scare him, so I want you to just stand quietly. He's a bit shy.

"O-okay, got it." He followed Utai into the hutch, closed the chicken wire door, and slid the bar over to lock it.

After checking this herself, Utai put the carrier on the floor, followed by her backpack. From inside, she took out something unfamiliar—a long, sturdy leather glove. She slipped it over her left arm with practiced ease and then opened and closed her hand a few times. Next, turning toward the carrier and crouching down, she gently opened up the sliding doors on both sides. Slowly, cautiously, she put her left hand into the darkness inside, enveloped in the leather glove a soldier-class character in an RPG might equip.

Excitedly wondering if it was a parakeet or maybe a bigger parrot—since you wouldn't need a solid glove like that for a little bird—Haruyuki watched Utai move. She peered into the carrier and seemed to be saying something. Naturally, her voice made no sound and her lips weren't moving, either, but even still, Haruyuki felt like he could hear a gentle whisper calling the creature.

A few seconds later, she started carefully pulling her arm back out. Her wrist appeared, the back of her hand, then loosely stretched-out fingertips, and on those, two feet holding on tightly. Just as Haruyuki had expected, it was a bird. Its feathers were gray, almost white. It was big, but not to the point of huge. Maybe a little over twenty centimeters in length. So then it was a parrot—

Or not.

Utai stood up slowly, and the instant his eyes locked with those of the bird resting on the fingers of her left hand, Haruyuki desperately struggled to keep himself from shrieking in shock.

Round, full face. Large, downward-curving beak, and feathers sticking up on both sides of its head like ears. And more than anything, the perfectly round eyes with reddish-yellow irises.

It was an owl—no, a horned owl...a bird of prey. A carnivore, a hunter, a tough number, a bird that could easily take a crow in a fight.

Of course, this was not the first time he had seen this kind of bird. When he had been taken to the Ueno Zoo a long, long time ago, there had been much larger owls and even larger eagles. But it was a completely different story when he was facing one with nothing separating him from it, and certainly not so close up, only a meter and a half apart. It could come flying at him at any second and peck at his cheeks in lieu of a snack.

Caught up in these imaginings, even his fingertips frozen, he was unable to pull his gaze away from the large eyes of the horned owl.

In the chat window in the lower part of his vision, cherry blossom–colored characters spelled out words. UI> YOU NEEDN'T BE SO AFRAID. IN FACT, THIS LITTLE ONE IS MORE AFRAID OF YOU RIGHT NOW.

"What...R-really?" he said, extremely quietly, and relaxed his shoulders the slightest bit. When he did, the horned owl also slackened its gaze ever so slightly and cocked its round head. This gesture was unexpectedly cute, and Haruyuki involuntarily softened his lips. “That’s…a horned owl, right? What species?”

The answer was immediately displayed before him. UI> It’s called a northern white-faced owl. It’s not a species native to Japan, but one that’s imported as a pet or bred in captivity.

“Wow. So then Matsunogi’s Animal Care Club imported it?”

*Of course that’s the kind of animal they’d have at a rich-girl school*, he thought as he asked the question, but Utai shook her head softly.

UI> That’s not the case. The situation is somewhat complicated. It’s a long story, so I’ll explain it to you another time.

He nodded and looked back at the horned owl. The way it whirled its head around to look at the interior of the hutch, it did somehow look uneasy. But when he thought about it, it had just been brought from the living quarters it was familiar with to this unknown place, so it was probably no wonder it was scared.

Haruyuki had never had anything resembling a pet. In fact, he basically had no memory of even touching an animal that was someone else’s pet. So this was his first attempt to imagine what an animal before him might be feeling.

“There’s nothing to be scared of.” At some point, a quiet voice had slipped past his lips. “This is your home. Shinomiya and I worked really hard to clean it up. No one’s gonna pick on you or anything here.”

Its safe place had been taken from it. Haruyuki knew only too well how hard and scary that was. During the worst period of the previous year, the only place at the school for him in the real world had been a stall in the boys’ washroom on the third floor of the old school building, and the squash corner on the local net’s virtual world.

But someone had suddenly come to Haruyuki one day, flapping black butterfly wings, and pulled him up from the bottom of that deep hole. In that moment, everything in his life changed.

He learned about an incredibly wide new world, met so many people, and gained a precious place of his own.

The horned owl—no, white-faced owl—before him had had its home taken away by the logic of a heartless corporation and had very narrowly avoided being killed. However, thanks to Utai's earnest efforts, it had found a new place here. *I want to do whatever I can, no matter how small, to make sure it lives a long and happy life in this hutch, this time for sure.* Although he had no idea whether or not the owl understood his feelings.

Abruptly spreading both wings, the owl flew forcefully from Utai's hand and drew circle after circle in the four-by-four-meter space of the hutch. The evening sun bathed the white-and-gray plumage of its flapping wings, and Haruyuki almost gasped at how beautiful it was. It was just for a few seconds, but he felt his own body become light as if he were flying around with it himself. Eventually, the snow-faced owl grabbed on to a branch of the perch on the left side with sturdy talons, flapped its wings two or three times, and then quietly settled down.

The large reddish-gold eyes narrowed suddenly, the ear-like feathers flattened, and it pulled its right leg up to stand on one leg. It stayed in this position and stopped moving, as though it had gone to sleep.

UI> IT SEEMS AS THOUGH HE LIKES THIS PLACE.

"H-he does? That's great," Haruyuki murmured in reply.

UI> PERHAPS IT'S BECAUSE YOU SPOKE SO KINDLY TO HIM, ARITA. THANK YOU. Utai dipped her head neatly, causing her ponytail to swing.

"Th-that's totally not it." Haruyuki hurriedly shook his head and waved his hands in tiny increments. "Shinomiya, you've done so much for him. A-and, right, what's the snow-faced owl's name anyway?" he asked.

Utai lifted her face and blinked several times before grinning.

UI> THAT'S RIGHT. I HAVEN'T TOLD YOU THE MOST IMPORTANT PART. HIS NAME IS HOO. IT WAS DECIDED BY A SCHOOL-WIDE VOTE. HE'S MALE, PROBABLY ABOUT THREE YEARS OLD.

So "Hoo" because it was an owl; that was a fairly obvious name. But did this snow-faced owl actually say *hoo hoo*? And what exactly was the difference between a snow-faced owl and a regular one?

Because he was scrolling through questions like this in his mind, Haruyuki didn't immediately realize that there was something he should have been more curious about in Utai's explanatory text. By the time he stopped short with a "Huh?," Utai was already clutching the carrier and heading toward the door. Having no other choice, Haruyuki followed her.

After cautiously opening the door so that the snow-faced owl, Hoo, didn't fly out and stepping outside before closing it again, Utai pulled a small plastic container from the bottom of the carrier, put some water in it, and went back inside. She gently placed the dish on a branch of the perch and came back out.

UI> WE CAN LOCK UP FOR TODAY NOW. I'LL SET UP THE POOL FOR HIM TO PLAY IN AND THE SENSOR TO MANAGE HIS WEIGHT TOMORROW.

"Wh-what about food? You don't need to feed him?"

UI> I FED HIM BEFORE WE LEFT THE OLD HUTCH. HE GETS FED ONCE A DAY, SO I'LL COME AND FEED HIM EVERY DAY AFTER SCHOOL.

Her words reminded him of Utai's explanation the day before that, due to certain circumstances, the bird would no longer allow anyone else to feed him. He wondered what these circumstances might be, while the nagging doubt he had felt earlier came back to life. He scrolled up in the chat window and double-checked Utai's messages. It was definitely there at the end of the sentence with Hoo's name and sex: "probably about three years old."

Cocking his head inwardly at the idea that they wouldn't know the age of an animal kept at the school, Haruyuki went to execute his duty for that day as the president of the Animal Care Club. He opened his bag and pulled out the brand-new, stainless steel, electronic U-lock he had gotten at the administration office on the first floor of the second school building. After turning it on and connecting it to his Neurolinker, he entered the code to unlock it that was given only to members of the Animal Care Club.

It snapped open. He slipped the U part through the metal fixture on the door of the animal hutch and set the bar in it, automatically locking it again. Haruyuki yanked on it to check it was securely locked, and then turned back to Utai.

"Okay, then, I should give you the lock code, too, Shinomiya."

UI> PLEASE DO.

He copied the code from the lock menu window and sent it to her. That way, even if he wasn't there, Utai would be able to come and feed Hoo. And that completed that day's club activities. He signed the log file and submitted it to the in-school net.

Finally, he turned his gaze one last time on the snow-faced owl sitting in the gloom inside the hutch, and its large eyes looked at Haruyuki for an instant before closing once again.

*From now on, I'll be taking care of Hoo, too. I have a responsibility to work hard to make sure he has a happy, comfortable life here.* With this thought, a nervousness strangled him, but it was accompanied by a strange warmth blossoming in his chest. As he stood there, stock-still, hands clenched, Utai's cherry-colored font flowed soundlessly before his eyes.

UI> NOW THEN, LET'S TURN TOWARD OUR NEXT TASK, ARITA.

"Huh? Our next task? But today's club work's already—"

UI> IT'S NOT A CLUB TASK. IT'S ABOUT WHAT TO DO ABOUT THE ISS KITS AND THE ARMOR OF CATASTROPHE.

"......Oh." His mind spinning momentarily at the abrupt and enormous change of topic, Haruyuki looked at Utai Shinomiya's small, uniformed figure.

Now that he was thinking about it, she wasn't just a younger girl who loved animals—she was the level-seven Burst Linker Ardor Maiden, owner of a wide range of attack powers of terrifying force, and one of the Four Elements who had been executives of the first Nega Nebulus.

Even after the tag team match the day before had ended and

he had returned to Suginami Ward in the real world, Haruyuki had remained preoccupied for a while. He watched absently as Utai tucked the direct cable away in her backpack after calmly pulling it out of her Neurolinker before he finally came back to his senses, and immediately asked about the thing that had been nagging at him during the duel. "Your avatar has the power of purification, Shinomiya? You can get rid of parasitic objects?!"

However, the answer that came back to him in text was not definite.

UI> Even if I can, it takes a very long time. A minimum of thirty minutes for a little object like the one we saw before. For a stronger parasite, there's definitely not enough time in a normal duel. Let's talk in more detail about this tomorrow. And then she had stood up, typed, My house is just over there, so I'll be fine from here, and bowed her head deeply before disappearing into the residential area.

"Uh, umm." Struggling to reconcile the figure of the shrine maiden dancing gently in the center of a grassy field enveloped in roaring flames with the slender girl before his eyes now, Haruyuki somehow managed to make his mouth move. "R-right, we have to talk over a bunch of stuff in regards to that today. We probably won't finish up before seven at school, so at my house—I mean, I already told Kuroyukihime and the others that, but…is that okay with you, Shinomiya?"

For some reason, her brow twitched and stiffened, and she typed out fairly slowly, UI> If that is the case, then I believe I would also like to intrude upon you.

"Oh. Maybe it's tough for you after all, if it gets too late?"

UI> No, that's not a problem. Will all the current members be coming together at this meeting? Specifically, Fu?

Fu—i.e., Fuko Kurasaki, aka Sky Raker. Kuroyukihime had asked him to get in touch with her, too, and she had readily assented to join them. Haruyuki nodded—"Of course"—

and Utai looked downward with an even more complicated expression.

*Maybe they don't get along? I didn't really get that impression when they were talking about old times in the student council office yesterday, though…*

While Haruyuki hemmed and hawed with these thoughts, Utai raised both hands with a curiously determined look and tapped at her holokeyboard. UI> UNDERSTOOD. TO RESPOND TO SACCHI'S CALL, THIS IS A ROAD THAT I, TOO, CANNOT AVOID PASSING DOWN. ALL RIGHT, SHALL WE GO? She waved a hand at Hoo in the hutch and started walking while clutching the carrier, and Haruyuki hurried after her.

He took the large carrier with a quick "Let me get that" and then said quietly, "Um, if there's some kind of problem, you can explain it to me."

But Utai simply shook her head and made no move to answer him.

Why would Utai Shinomiya be so afraid of Fuko Kurasaki?

The answer came in an unexpectedly easy-to-understand form twenty-five minutes later, in the Arita living room on the twenty-third floor of a mixed-use condominium building in Kita-Koenji.

"U-Uiiiiiiiiiiiiiiiiiiiiii!!"

A shout that was more like a scream was the first thing uttered by Fuko, the last to arrive of the six people gathered there that day. She threw her bag onto the living room floor and charged at top speed, skirt flying back, at Utai, who was on the sofa. Utai's face froze as Fuko lunged with a force like a tackle and covered her and squeezed her to her chest. "Uiui! I missed you, you know, Uiuiiiii!!"

The thin right hand thrust up from under Fuko's body tapped

at the air, almost convulsively. UI> PLEASE QAIT, NP, FU, I CAN'T BRWSGE.

"You've gotten so big without me even knowing...! But it's okay, I'll still spoil you senseless like I used to in the old days!!"

UI> SOMEONI, PKWASE HEKP

"Aaah, Uiui...Uiuiiiiiii!!"

*...I've never seen Shinomiya mistype before*, Haruyuki thought absently, standing dumbfounded by the kitchen. To his left, both Takumu and Chiyuri were also stunned, eyes wide, while to his right, Kuroyukihime was shaking her head in indulgent exasperation.

It didn't look like the scene of carnage on the sofa was going to end any time soon, so Haruyuki bobbed his own head before saying to Kuroyukihime in a quiet voice, "Um, Kuroyukihime? Before, you said that you only met Fuko and one other person in the real from the first Nega Nebulus, right? So then the other person was Shinomiya?"

"Mmm. You have a good memory. That's exactly right."

"But you also said that Fuko was the only person you were tied to by friendship even in the real world. It seemed kinda like a contradiction, so it bugged me, but...So then, um, this situation..."

Kuroyukihime grinned wryly and nodded at Haruyuki's words. "Hmm, well, that's it, I suppose. Of course, I think of myself as Utai's comrade in arms, but more than that, Utai is Fuko's...How can I put it—" She interrupted herself momentarily, turned again toward Haruyuki and the others, and continued in an explanatory tone. "Perhaps you all already know the reason why Fuko was once called ICBM?"

"Oh, yeah, Niko told me. Because in the Territories, her strategy was a kamikaze attack to the very rear of the enemy line with a single support on her back," Haruyuki replied, and Kuroyukihime nodded once more.

"Exactly. It was actually very effective when the line of battle was stretched out, but the support clinging to Raker had a truly terrible time of it. Dropped from up in the air to a point suit-

able for support, chased around by huge numbers of the enemy, sometimes thrown down right in the middle of enemy territory instead of a warhead...You may already have an inkling of who got that job. It was Utai. She was the Raker Special Option."

"O-option," Haruyuki repeated, cheeks stiffening. Looking over at the sofa once more, he watched Utai's arm, flailing for help, flop down onto the sofa.

Approximately three minutes later.

They all lowered themselves into their seats, Kuroyukihime at the head of the dining table, Chiyuri and Takumu facing her on the right, Fuko and Utai on her left, and Haruyuki directly opposite her. On the table were cups of the tea Haruyuki had made and a big plate of Chiyuri's mom's homemade sandwiches that Chiyuri had brought from home: a mountain of ham sandwiches stuffed with lettuce and pastrami, vegetable and cheese sandwiches combining cheddar cheese with arugula and asparagus, sandwiches putting smoked salmon and avocado between slices of black rye bread, and more—a truly magnificent sight. Having survived Fuko's passionate hello, Utai took in the dish before her, eyes round.

"Sorry for always putting you in this spot, Chiyuri. Please convey my warmest thanks to your mother."

"It's fine! Mom's happy that Haru's got more friends!"

Once the formal motions of Kuroyukihime bowing her head, Chiyuri grinning in response, and Haruyuki making a complicated face were complete, they all sang out a hearty "Let's eat!" At once, six sets of hands reached out for the pile of triangle sandwiches.

Utai finished one of each type and then made her fingers dance with unusual speed. UI> THESE ARE VERY GOOD. FROM WHAT SACCHI SAID BEFORE, I ASSUME KURASHIMA'S MOTHER IS ALWAYS KIND ENOUGH TO PREPARE FOOD BEFORE EACH LEGION MEETING?

"You can use my first name!" After that statement, Chiyuri nodded as if embarrassed. She had been told in the initial self-introductions that Utai couldn't speak because of expressive aphasia, so she continued talking without any confusion. "I only joined Nega Nebulus two months ago, so I still haven't been to many meetings. But my mom's always made food for the three of us whenever Taku and I came over to Haru's place. When I asked her to make enough for six, she was super surprised. That's double the old days, she said."

UI> THAT REMINDS ME. YOU, MAYUZUMI, AND ARITA HAVE BEEN FRIENDS SINCE CHILDHOOD, CHIYURI? Her fingers hovered there momentarily, as Utai looked at each of them sitting across from her in turn with large, clear eyes before adding, UI> IT'S A MARVEL THAT THREE CHILDHOOD FRIENDS WOULD ALL BECOME BURST LINKERS AND ON TOP OF THAT, FIGHT ALONGSIDE ONE ANOTHER IN THE SAME LEGION. OUR BONDS IN REALITY DO WIELD GREAT POWER OVER US. I, SACCHI, AND FU ONCE CREATED A BOND IN THE REAL WORLD, BUT A LONG, LONG TIME WAS NEEDED FOR US TO GET TO THAT PLACE. MOST LIKELY, TOO LONG.

The instant they read this, Kuroyukihime and Fuko spoke.

"Utai..."

"Uiui."

Utai glanced over at them, and a gentle but somehow poignant smile crossed her lips.

UI> WE COULDN'T SYMPATHIZE WITH THE DEPTH, THE ENORMITY OF THE FEAT SACCHI CHASED AND THE DESIRE FU CONTINUED TO SECRETLY HARBOR. THUS, SACCHI ENDED UP HUNTED BY THE SIX KINGS, AND FU'S AVATAR LOST BOTH LEGS. IN THE END, THE LEGION ITSELF FELL TO RUIN. IF ONLY MANY MORE MEMBERS, NOT JUST THE THREE OF US, HAD BEEN ABLE TO BUILD BONDS BONDS IN THE REAL WORLD, THEN PERHAPS THERE WOULD HAVE BEEN ANOTHER PATH. IT'S SOMETHING I REGRET EVEN NOW.

Utai's hands froze, and Fuko, next to her, gently clasped them. This gesture was the exact opposite of her earlier enthusiasm, this one full of a gentle sympathy. "But we were able to meet again like this, Uiui," she murmured, smiling. Utai opened her eyes wide, almost gasping. "Two and a half years have passed. That little corvus there taught Sacchi and me that there's nothing we can't recover from. Sacchi stands once more as a king in the Accelerated World, and I've got my legs back. So that's why..."

"We are confident." Kuroyukihime picked up the thought. Wiping her mouth with a paper napkin and snapping to attention in her chair, the Black King said determinedly, "Utai, your real body is still sealed in the Unlimited Neutral Field, but we are going to get it back...even if our opponent is an invincible God."

# 9

When the mountain of sandwiches had been neatly decimated, the large plate cleared away, and more tea made, Haruyuki raised his voice with a question he could no longer keep himself from asking. "Um. What did you mean by what you said before, Kuroyukihime? That Shinomiya's real body is locked up in the Unlimited Neutral Field? I had a tag team duel with Shinomiya in the Normal Duel Field yesterday, and…Is there some separate problem in the Unlimited Neutral Field?"

To his right, Chiyuri similarly cocked her head. But Takumu seemed to have hit on something, and he opened his mouth, albeit hesitantly. "Master. Is it perhaps 'unlimited EK'?"

"Oh, just like you, Professor! Quite knowledgeable." Kuroyukihime nodded, but Haruyuki had absolutely no clue what that meant.

"U-unlimited EK? Taku, what is…?" he asked, leaning his whole body forward.

"Haru." Takumu replied with a question, pushing on the bridge of his glasses with a finger as he did. "Did you know that there are several ways in the Accelerated World to make a Burst Linker disappear—i.e., to push them into total point loss and the forced uninstallation of Brain Burst?"

"Huh? There's just dueling and winning over and over," he

responded reflexively, before remembering the fact that he himself had fallen to the brink of annihilation two months earlier and adding, "Wait. There's also a big fight in the Unlimited Neutral Field. Both sides charge all their points onto a Sudden Death Duel card, and the winner gets them all. Oh, and speaking of sudden death, there's also that special rule for level niners."

"Right. So that's three. Anything else?"

"There's also that…PK…I think?" Chiyuri said with an expression like the tea in her mouth had turned to salt water. "Physical kill? The one where you attack in the real, lock 'em up in a car or something, and steal every last one of their points in a direct duel. Which is totally not okay."

Takumu nodded with a severe look and added, "I guess in a broader sense, you could call that guy who came after us in April a PK. Anyway, that's the fourth. And the fifth is the 'unlimited EK' I mentioned, formally known as 'unlimited Enemy kill.'"

"Enemy kill…Not killing Enemies, right? So then killed *by* Enemies?"

"Right. That's exactly it," Kuroyukihime interjected, so the three closed their mouths and looked her way. After bringing her cup of tea to her lips, their black-clad Legion Master began to speak quietly. "I already explained to Haruyuki yesterday that there are Enemies in the Unlimited Neutral Field with incredible attack power, called Beasts and Legends. However, the ones at the very top, the ones that are truly a force of nature, stay within predetermined Territories, rather than wandering the field freely, so they pose no danger as long as you don't approach their areas. But conversely, if by some chance you are thrust into their territory and killed, escape is extremely difficult."

"Uh, umm?" Haruyuki let his gaze wander and tried to remember the rules of the Unlimited Neutral Field, a place he had visited countless times.

In that world, a player's HP gauge dropping to zero—the player dying, in other words—didn't mean the Burst Linker was returned to the real world. You remained in the place of your death in a "ghost" state, your field of view colored gray, and were revived after an hour. And you couldn't use the "burst out" command in the Unlimited Neutral Field. The only way to "drop" into the normal full-dive VR game and automatically return to the real world was to slip through one of the "leave point" portals set up at landmarks like stations or famous tourist spots.

Taking these two rules into consideration, he thought about the situation Kuroyukihime mentioned. Assume you carelessly charged into the territory of a fixed-position enormous Enemy, were targeted and hit with an attack of overwhelming force, and then died instantly. Then You are dead would be displayed in your vision, and you'd wait for the regeneration gauge to fill, as a ghost tied to that spot with no physical body. An hour later, you would finally come back to life and be able to move—but that spot was still within range of the enormous Enemy. You would, of course, quickly be attacked again, and die once more. An hour later, you'd come back to life…and die again, and…

"Th-there's no end to it, is there?" Haruyuki shouted, and Kuroyukihime nodded with a gloomy look.

"None. Which is why it's 'unlimited.' The unlimited Enemy kill deliberately creates this situation. In other words, another method of causing a Burst Linker to lose all their points is to leave them deep in the territory of a massive Enemy and have them killed over and over and over, every hour. Naturally, the chances of escape are not necessarily zero. After all, once you come back to life, if you can move even the slightest bit before your immediate death, you'll regenerate in that location next. You can gain distance bit by bit, and perhaps at some point, make it out of the Enemy territory, but with a single death, you lose ten points, as is the case with any Enemy. Die ten times, it's a hundred. A hundred times, and you lose a thousand points. You can't hold out against that for long."

A chill ran up his spine as he imagined himself plunged into such a situation, and Haruyuki assented her point in a hoarse voice. "Th-that's true. Especially after you've used up a lot of points like right after leveling up or buying an expensive item or something." However, he quickly realized something and furrowed his brow. "B-but this 'unlimited EK'...Wouldn't it be pretty risky to set up? I mean, *you* could die before you managed to leave your opponent in that territory."

"Exactly. Which is why people usually use methods such as throwing their opponent in from outside the territory or sending them flying in with an explosive attack." The answer came from Fuko. Still with a gentle smile playing on the edges of her lips, she added, somewhat terrifyingly, "Once, I used Gale Thruster to drop this PK jerk—whose name I was lucky enough to find out—right on top of the head of a Legend. At any rate, in a normal unlimited EK, it's not that easy to carry the other player that deep into the territory, so you can usually escape if you really fight and work hard. And since the stronger the Enemy, the riskier it is for the Burst Linker planning the kill, the distance needed to escape is usually shorter, too."

Haruyuki nodded in understanding, alongside the two other junior members of the Legion.

At that moment, Utai, who had stayed silent until then, moved her fingers surreptitiously. UI> But there's an exception to every theory. Clear eyes still turned on some far-off place, the fourth grader with the mysterious air slowly continued typing. UI> One of the three people who charged into the very depths of the territory of the largest and most powerful Enemy in the Accelerated World died, never to return again. A Burst Linker who can never dive into the true essence of the Accelerated World, the Unlimited Neutral Field, even if able to enter the Normal Duel Field. I am her.

Haruyuki had already told Takumu and Chiyuri the gist of the story he had heard the day before in the student council office about the decline and fall of the first Nega Nebulus. About the absolutely impenetrable Castle in the middle of the Unlimited Neutral Field, and the most powerful Enemies that guarded its gates, the Four Gods. The members of the first Nega Nebulus had set their sights on reaching the Castle under the assumption that this was the second requirement for clearing Brain Burst and attempted to break past the Four Gods. And then they were annihilated.

That was as much as Haruyuki had been told. He still didn't know the crux of it, the reason why a single defeat had led all the way to the collapse of the Legion. However, from this talk now of unlimited EK, Haruyuki was arriving at a guess, albeit a hazy one. He took a deep breath, looked at Kuroyukihime, Fuko, and Utai in turn, and then opened his mouth. "Then that means… Shinomiya, two and a half years ago, you went deep into the territory of the Four Gods and died, and now you can't come back alive. Is that it?"

Nodding sharply, Utai tapped at the air. UI> YES. HAVING A HIGH RESISTANCE TO FIRE, I LED A SQUAD TO CHALLENGE THE GIANT FIRE BIRD SUZAKU, GUARDIAN OF THE CASTLE'S SOUTH GATE. IT WAS A DIFFICULT OPPONENT, WITH PHYSICAL ATTACKS FROM ITS LONG-RANGE FLAME BREATH AND TALONS, AS WELL AS A BROAD-RANGE FIRE ATTACK IN ALL DIRECTIONS. HOWEVER, WE HAD ALL THIS INFORMATION, SO WE DEVISED A STRATEGY TO RESPOND, AND WE SUCCEEDED IN PENETRATING TO A POINT WHERE WE COULD ACTUALLY SEE THE GATE. BUT THERE, SUZAKU'S ATTACK PATTERN CHANGED. IT ENVELOPED ITSELF IN FLAMES AND CHARGED AT HIGH SPEED. WE WERE UNABLE TO MEET THE ATTACK, AND OUR BATTLE LINE CRUMBLED. MY OWN RESISTANCE TO FIRE WAS ALSO LITTLE COMFORT. TO AT LEAST CREATE A ROUTE OF RETREAT FOR MY COMPANIONS, I LURED SUZAKU INTO THE DEEPEST PART OF THAT TERRITORY AND DIED THERE.

"Apparently, the attack patterns of Seiryu at the east gate and Genbu at the north gate also changed for the worse halfway through," Kuroyukihime murmured, and bit her lip before continuing. “It was the same with Byakko at the West gate, who I went up against with Raker. By all rights, we also shouldn’t have been able to make it back from so deep in Byakko’s territory. But using the last of her power, Raker carried me and flew us out.”

“Because at the time, I had already lost my legs and wasn’t any use in battle.” Fuko moved her mouth with the same look on her face, as though she were enduring a certain kind of pain. “I mustered every ounce of my will and flew desperately to ensure that Sacchi at least made it out alive. Even now, I sometimes have dreams where I hear Byakko’s teeth *clack-clack*ing right behind me…Although that punishment is too light for me, the only one of the Four Elements to survive.”

UI> I know I’m grateful for how hard you worked for us, then, Fu, as I’m sure are Graph and Aqua.

“That’s right, Raker. If you and I had been locked away at the gates of the Four Gods, we wouldn’t have been able to even think of having a ‘child.’ Without a doubt, Silver Crow and his honorable rival Ash Roller would not have been born. And without the formation of the second Nega Nebulus, we would never have met again like this. Your decisive flight led us to the future.”

At Kuroyukihime’s gentle yet firm words, Fuko raised her lowered eyelashes and nodded softly.

Feeling something welling up in his heart, Haruyuki silently watched over them, but at the same time, unable to suppress a question that had popped into his head, he saw his opportunity and timidly opened his mouth. “Um, Kuroyukihime? I understand that Shinomiya’s duel avatar is actually sealed away at the south gate of the Castle in the Unlimited Neutral Field. But yesterday, I teamed up with Shinomiya—with Ardor Maiden—and fought a duel. Which means that Shinomiya is still a Burst Linker. She didn’t lose all her points two and a half years ago, right? How is she protecting her burst points from the unlimited EK state?”

“A good question,” Kuroyukihime said, and turned her gaze on Takumu once more. “So then perhaps I’ll ask the pride of our

Legion, the brains, to give us another lecture. Takumu, you must have already guessed how it works?"

To Utai, whom he was meeting for the first time, the look on Takumu's face was rather complicated, but still, his professorial character steadily taking root, he replied obediently, "Yes, Master," and turned back to Haruyuki. "Okay, Haru. This time it's about how to withdraw from the Unlimited Neutral Field. Do you know how many ways there are?"

"Hey, even I know that much, okay?" Pursing his lips, Haruyuki raised his eyes to glare at his childhood friend, who was again pushing his glasses up. "I mean, it's common knowledge, right? The answer is 'one.' You can only leave the Unlimited Neutral Field through a leave point portal. This general principle means that unlimited EK can happen, doesn't it?"

"Eennnnh! Wrong!!" It was, of course, Chiyuri shouting. His other childhood friend, sitting across from Takumu, had a playful grin floating to her lips that was reminiscent of a cat. She shoved three fingers into Haruyuki's face. "The answer's threeee."

"Ngh—N-no way. Th-three?! Like with an item or something?! Or a special attack?"

Chiyuri made the *ennh* sound of the wrong buzzer once more at the flustered Haruyuki before folding down fingers to enumerate her response. "The second way is to cut your Neurolinker's global connection. The third's to take your Neurolinker off your neeeeck."

"Wha..." He was temporarily speechless at this unexpected declaration. Finally, his thinking rebooted, and he groaned desperately, "Th-that's cheating! I mean, okay, it's not cheating, but...That's in the real world, though!"

"Goodness, Taku didn't say anything about a method you could do in the Accelerated World, did he?"

"I—I guess not, but I mean, taking off your Neurolinker while you're accelerated...No one can do that themselves!"

"Oh, my, he didn't say anything about a method you could do by yourself, did he?"

If he got into one of those endless back-and-forths he'd had with Chiyuri since they were kids…

Abruptly, gentle laughter came up from his left. Turning his eyes that way, he saw that it wasn't just Kuroyukihime and Fuko giggling delightedly; even Utai was spilling with soundless amusement.

They laughed for a dozen seconds or so before Kuroyukihime opened her mouth. "Ha-ha-ha! You really are a wonderful trio, you three. Chiyuri is right. Leaving the Unlimited Neutral Field through an internal route voluntarily is indeed one way, but there is also passively being made to leave from the real world." *Koff.* Clearing her throat, she recomposed her expression. "Two and a half years ago, the general members of the first Nega Nebulus took on the Castle attack, knowing it was reckless. However, it was most certainly not a group suicide. Thus, we set up a safety. We decided that rather than the normal wireless connection, we would go through a wired connection, with either a home server or a leftover PC as a stepping-stone."

"Stepping-stone," Haruyuki murmured, and Utai supplemented with the chat.

UI> When a mail with a specific subject line arrives at that intermediate machine, the machine is set to automatically disconnect from the global net. Theoretically, when a squad is destroyed, the first person to return to the real world through a leave point sends that mail to all Legion members. In that instant, everyone automatically bursts out, disconnected. In other words, should one fall into a state of unlimited EK, at the very least, they would escape without losing all their points.

"Huh…M-makes sense." A sigh of admiration slipped out of his mouth. The thought that you could get out of the Unlimited Neutral Field with such methods had never even crossed his mind.

But looking back on it now, that time two months earlier when he had visited that cake shop in Sakuradai in Nerima Ward with

Takumu so that Takumu could get Incarnate training from the Red King Niko, they had indeed made their global connection directly rather than wirelessly. He had no doubt that the same safety was installed on the router device in that room as well.

*There's still so many things I don't know, huh?* Haruyuki wondered absently as Takumu next to him raised his hand lightly.

"Excuse me, Master. I don't know the details of a disconnect departure from the Unlimited Neutral Field, either. What happens to your duel avatar in that case?"

"Mmm. Well, the situation becomes slightly complicated. When you depart the Unlimited Neutral Field using an irregular method such as disconnecting from the net or removing your Neurolinker, your duel avatar does indeed disappear from the field. After that, you can fight a normal duel without any issues, but if you dive once more into the Unlimited Neutral Field, you will appear not at your location in the real world, but in the coordinates where you disappeared."

"Uhhh?" Haruyuki said, unable to digest this.

"Corvus." Fuko popped a single finger up. "You do remember the house on the top of the old Tokyo Tower in the Unlimited Neutral Field where I lived for quite a long time, don't you?"

"O-of course. How could I forget? You pushed me down from there."

"I haven't forgotten. At any rate, since my real-world house is on the southern edge of Suginami, it's a bit far to the old Tokyo Tower in Minato Ward. But when I went to the house on the tower, I didn't actually go to all the trouble of heading over there from Suginami. I fixed my avatar's positional data on the top of the tower by automatically disconnecting from the global net with a timer so that I would appear in that place the next time I dived."

"O-ohh. So that's it!" Nodding deeply, his thoughts moved forward.

Utai Shinomiya—Ardor Maiden—had made it deep into the territory of Suzaku, one of the super-powerful Enemies of the Four Gods, two and a half years earlier. Normally, immediately following her regeneration an hour later, she would have been killed again, a cycle that would repeat infinitely until finally she lost all of her burst points. However, thanks to the safety of an automatic disconnection with the arrival of a mail, she had been disconnected before her points were used up and had returned to the real world. Which was why she had been able to team up with Haruyuki in a normal duel the previous day.

But this return was limited. The moment she called out the "unlimited burst" command to dive into the Unlimited Neutral Field, the ultimate battleground for a Burst Linker, Utai would appear not in the position of her physical body in the real world, but directly in front of the god Suzaku guarding the south Castle gate. Naturally, she would instantly be hit with a fierce attack and immediately die. She would descend once again into that terrifying state of unlimited EK.

"So that's why you're 'sealed,' then. For you to be released from that place, someone would have to go right up to Suzaku and rescue your avatar immediately after you dive," Haruyuki murmured hoarsely, finally understanding.

Nodding sharply, Utai sent her ten fingers smoothly racing. UI> It's not just me. Aqua Current, another of the Four Elements, is sealed in front of Seiryu at the east gate, and Graphite Edge is similarly sealed at the foot of Genbu at the north gate. To ensure the escape of the other members, we three—no, Sacchi and Fu taking on Byakko at the west gate as well—we all continued to make ourselves the target for the Four Gods as long as we could. Fortunately, no one else ended up in a state of unlimited EK; they were all able to escape the territory, but they died over and over and over in the process, losing a significant number of points. It was completely impossible for them to maintain the Legion territory. We had no choice but to abandon all our territory and disband the Legion itself. And this is how the former Nega Nebulus disappeared. It was no one's fault.

No one was to blame. Utai's fingers seemed to Haruyuki to creak loudly here.

Lifting his eyes with a gasp, he saw that the nine-year-old girl, who had until that point maintained essentially the same expression, had twisted up her face and was biting her lip hard. Her fingers moved once more and typed fiercely, as though to rip holes in the air. UI> No. If I was forced to say, it was that person. The one who deceived Sacchi, pressed her, and then betrayed h

"Utai."

"Uiui!"

The two voices stopped the string of characters. Utai clenched her hands above her holokeyboard and hung her head low, while Fuko next to her gently hugged her.

Kuroyukihime watched from her slightly removed seat with an expression that suggested she was enduring something. "Utai," she said finally, quietly. "I'm the one to blame. All the responsibility for the destruction of the Legion is on me. The fact that I created the initial opportunity with my impulsiveness. And the fact that once it was all over, my spirit was broken and I locked myself away in the local net for two years. But I met him—Haruyuki—and gained the strength to stand up once again. I will no longer vainly fear the past or turn my eyes from it. At some point, she and I will settle things. And to that end as well, Utai, I want to break your 'seal.' I want you to come home. To the new Nega Nebulus."

It wasn't as though he were able to understand all of the words exchanged. Who was "that person" Utai was talking about? What had happened with Kuroyukihime back then? But this didn't feel like the time to be asking about it, so Haruyuki leaned forward and started speaking in utmost earnestness to Utai.

"Shinomiya, I second that request. I'm sure you already know, but right now, my avatar is parasitized by an Enhanced Armament called Chrome Disaster, and if I don't 'purify' it this week, the kings are going to put a bounty on my head, and I won't be able to duel in any real way anymore. I—I have to get way stronger. I can't be standing still for even a second if I want to keep fighting alongside Kuroyukihime and everyone else in the Legion. Please…please help me."

The Haruyuki from just a little while ago would never have given voice to such words; his twisted pride would have gotten in the way. But during his many difficult battles, he had learned, albeit only slightly, what it meant to fight together with your comrades. There were times when you had to stand your ground and insist on your own way. But acting tough, like you could do everything by yourself, was foolish hubris. After all, everyone, without even knowing it, was always being helped by someone.

As if unable to take in Haruyuki's heartfelt words, Utai cast her gaze downward. For a brief period, silence. Then fingers were raised slightly to tap at the air hesitantly.

UI> The reason I so firmly refused all communication with Sacchi and Fu and the other Legion members for more than two years was exactly this proposal. I was afraid of the words "break the seal." Given that all the limiters have been released for the Four Gods, they hold attack power that defies imagination. The risk of falling into the same unlimited EK state is simply too great for anyone who would go to recover my avatar. In fact, we were fortunate that it ended with only three of us sealed at the four gates. No more of my companions can be sacrificed. I—and I'm sure Graph and Aqua do as well—believe this and so I've refused contact. Really, I

Here, her fingers froze. The lips that Utai shouldn't have been able to move were trembling slightly. Haruyuki sensed rather than heard the words that flowed out into the still air.

*I missed you.*

Two drops slid down her white cheeks. Fuko squeezed her small body tightly, the corners of her own eyes wet. This time, Utai put up not a hint of resistance, instead burying her face in Fuko's chest, shoulders shaking violently. He heard a faint but

definite sobbing. Haruyuki, Takumu, and Chiyuri, who had no direct knowledge of what had happened back then, had to blink several times themselves.

Releasing the embrace after a mere thirty seconds or so, Fuko wiped Utai's cheeks with a handkerchief she pulled from a pocket, and the girl continued to face downward, as though embarrassed, as she started to type again.

UI> I'm sorry. I'll continue. I had no intention of contacting the new Nega Nebulus myself. As long as I could watch over Sacchi's fight in a corner of the Accelerated World, that was enough for me.

But then the Animal Care Club at my school was eliminated, and I couldn't find anyone to take in the animals we had cared for that would be without a home. After wrestling with it, I sent a request mail to Umesato Junior High, the school Sacchi went on to. On the one hand, I never thought Sacchi would notice my name, while somewhere in my heart I wanted her to.

"I noticed. Your name stands out, Uiui," Kuroyukihime said, smiling.

Although her eyes were still red, Utai pursed her lips sharply. UI> I didn't choose my name. When the reply to my mail came not from the school administration but in the name of the vice president of the student council, I truly didn't know what to do. But I told myself it was for the sake of the animals and contacted Sacchi with a dive call. And then her first words were

"Conditions of an exchange. I would convince the administration and have the animal hutch readied. In payment, I would have you come back." Everyone gaped at these words, reproduced by Kuroyukihime herself. Surprise quickly changed into knowing, wry grins.

Utai also connected a smile with text. UI> Sacchi, your impatient, insistent side has not changed at all. I apparently wasted my time thinking up what I would say to you, given that you simply attacked me head-on. So I replied that I would at least hear what she had to say. After that, I gradually got pulled in by the pace of things, and before I knew it, here I was. It is exactly the same as when I was forced to meet in the real in the old days.

Reading the words, Haruyuki remembered fondly the time Kuroyukihime had “invited” him to the upperclassmen’s lounge. She had just shown up all of a sudden in the virtual squash corner. Her first words were “Don’t you want to go further, boy…to accelerate?” *And I wanted to know what she meant, so I went to the lounge, and we’re all of a sudden directing, and she’s already sending me Brain Burst. I didn’t even get a chance to breathe.*

*But if she hadn’t invited me like that, I totally wouldn’t have gone. She really is impatient and insistent, but more than that, she’s totally serious about everything. I mean, with this Armor of Catastrophe plan, too, she’s been hard at work without my even knowing it.*

Haruyuki abruptly felt a question and he turned to Kuroyukihime, who was sitting directly across from him, and raised a hand timidly. “Uh, um, Kuroyukihime…”

“Mmm? What is it?”

“Umm, after the race ended last week, when we were here talking about what to do about the Armor of Catastrophe parasite, you said you had an idea about someone with the power of purification, so we should leave it to you. Did you mean Shinomiya?”

“Yes, I did.” She nodded crisply, and he pushed with another question.

“But did you have a way to get in touch with her? Shinomiya said before that she totally refused all contact for over two years.”

UI> It is exactly as you say, Arita. I discarded the address I used before. There should have been no way for a message to come to me from Sacchi. If I hadn’t mailed Umesato Junior High about the animal hutch, what had you been planning to do? Utai cocked her head curiously as she typed.

A gentle grin slid across Kuroyukihime's face. "Isn't it obvious? Even if you deleted your mail account, I at least know the school you go to and what grade you're in, Utai. All I had to do was go directly to the grounds of the elementary division of Matsunogi and find you from the edge of the fourth-grade classroom. Right?"

The instant she heard this, the color drained from Utai's cheeks, and she responded with awkward fingers. UI> When I was trying to decide whether or not to ask Umesato about the animal hutch, I heard a voice telling me to do it. It had to have been the voice of Heaven.

And then Haruyuki and his childhood friends, together with Fuko, laughed out loud. Utai's head was still pulled back fearfully, and Fuko patted her on the back.

"Right, Uiui? The time came for you to return to the place that needed you. It was like that for me, too. When a troubled and injured little bird appeared in my small garden at the top of the old Tokyo Tower, I felt it, too. That a wind would blow once more in a stagnant world."

"Exactly, Utai. It's true that I'm impatient, but I no longer live as recklessly as I did in the past. I'm saying this precisely because I believe that now a strategy to free your avatar from the seal of the God is possible. Come back." Kuroyukihime stared directly at Utai with her jet-black eyes.

Utai met that gaze with eyes singed by the color of flames. UI> I, too, would like to release my avatar from its sealed state not just for my own sake, but also to purify Arita's avatar. If it is The Disaster parasitizing him, then thirty minutes most certainly will not be enough to purify it, so it would have to happen in the Unlimited Neutral Field rather than the Normal Duel Field. Yesterday, I dueled in a tag match with Arita and saw very clearly his latent power. We definitely cannot allow the Kings' plans to move forward.

Haruyuki read this and unthinkingly raised his voice. "What?

B-but I didn't do anything good yesterday. I just got hammered down, basically."

Utai turned back to Haruyuki, ponytail swinging, and smiled with a look that made him feel a mysterious love in her innocence. UI> Arita. Did you learn that "way of the flexible" from Sacchi?

"What?" Kuroyukihime furrowed her brow.

He glanced over at her and pulled his shoulders in, answering frantically, "Oh! No, uh, she didn't, uh, teach me. It was more like she showed me once, and then I just...I figured I'd try practicing it, too."

UI> Just as I thought. Even though the trick was the same as Sacchi's technique, the form was different. In your dueling, I felt the intent to aim for the far-off distance and continue. That fight contained the feeling that even if you lost yesterday and lose today, you would try and fight again tomorrow, without losing heart. There are not so many Burst Linkers like this, who have reached level five and still have not forgotten the importance of moving forward step by step.

"Huh? No, that's...I'm...It's..." Completely unaccustomed to being complimented, Haruyuki was unable to endure it and dropped his head. He then heard Chiyuri's voice and the grin it held.

"Plodding ahead is Haru's signature move! Ever since we were kids, even if he was worse at something than Taku and me, before we knew it, he'd have gotten good at it. Although that's limited to games!"

Inwardly grateful for the life raft his childhood friend had launched for him, Haruyuki immediately retorted, "I-it's not just games! I mean, in the who-can-clean-off-a-corn-cob-the-best contest, I was number one in the e—"

"Haru, there's not much difference there in terms of practical use, you know." Takumu's crisp jab got them all laughing brightly.

Once the laughter died down, Utai sat up straight and looked at each of them in turn before bowing her head deeply. UI> Right now, I'm full of doubt and fear and hesitation. But if I don't take a step here and now, I'll likely never be able to move forward from the place I'm currently in, not in the Accelerated World and not in the real world. With the world beyond and the current world—front and back—becoming one, and my duel avatar becoming frozen, my real-world self hasn't been able to get anywhere, either.

"That's exactly it, isn't it?" Fuko, sitting next to Utai, nodded softly. "During the time I lived in hiding on the old Tokyo Tower, before I even knew it, I got the feeling that the me in the real world was also living hunched over, holding her breath. So much so that these last two months since Corvus appeared have felt much longer than those two years."

This time it was Kuroyukihime nodding her head deeply in assent. Her obsidian irises glittered as though they contained an infinity of swirling stardust. "It's only natural to feel that, Fuko. Because even when we haven't launched Brain Burst, when we're heading toward a single goal with friends, we're always accelerating. The excitement that makes our hearts pound strongly also fiercely drives our consciousness."

And then finally, Utai set her ten fingers dancing lightly once more. UI> I want to feel my heart pound again like it used to. I want to pursue with all of you the continuation of that dream that was interrupted. Sacchi, Fu, Chiyuri, Mayuzumi, and Arita. After a moment's hesitation, her slender, smooth fingers tapped out determinedly:

UI> I'm asking you now. Please release me—my other self, Ardor Maiden, from the seal of Suzaku.

# 10

The plan to purify the Armor of Catastrophe that Kuroyukihime had put together was apparently made up of three phases. The first was to contact Utai Shinomiya in the real world and somehow drag her into talks. The second was to persuade Utai to help them and rescue her avatar from the unlimited EK state in the Unlimited Neutral Field. And the third was to eliminate the element of Chrome Disaster parasitizing Silver Crow with Utai's purification ability.

At 7:20 PM on Tuesday, June 18, in the living room of Haruyuki's apartment, when asked by Fuko when the second phase was to begin, Kuroyukihime replied immediately, without the slightest shred of doubt, *This very instant, of course.*

Once the six Burst Linkers had moved to the sofa set and sat down again in relaxed positions, they attached five XSB cables to their Neurolinkers to form a daisy chain. In general, it wasn't necessary to go so far as to connect directly when diving into the Unlimited Neutral Field, but this time, they had to set up the aforementioned disconnection safety. Thus, they all turned off their wireless connections to the global net, their host, Haruyuki, deciding instead that they would go in via a direct connection to the Arita home server. This way, if some unforeseen accident did occur and someone ended up in an unlimited EK state, the first person to return through the portal could yank out the cable connecting to the home server, and at that moment, they could all burst out.

Of course, this would be the worst outcome—not rescuing not only Utai but her would-be rescuers imprisoned alongside her—but they had already passed through the stage of fearing this. At the moment, after making every possible preparation, they could only march forward, convinced of their inevitable success. Or rather, this was what Kuroyukihime said at the end of the real-world meeting.

UI> ALL RIGHT, THEN, EVERYONE. I'M GRATEFUL FOR YOUR HELP.

Kuroyukihime, Fuko, Haruyuki, Takumu, and Chiyuri nodded firmly together. The plan was for the five of them to dive first and then have Utai dive once all the preparations inside were complete. Sitting on the sofa, they closed their eyes and took a deep breath. Kuroyukihime started the countdown from ten. When she hit zero, they all shouted the command to fly to the true Accelerated World, permitted only to Burst Linkers at levels four and up.

"Unlimited Burst!!"

His first view in a while of the Unlimited Neutral Field was of a world frozen a snowy white, all the way to the horizon in the distance—an Ice stage. The sky was blanketed with leaden clouds, tiny snowflakes glittering as they danced on the cold breeze.

"Good. A fortunate omen to start," Kuroyukihime—the Black King, Black Lotus, said, the tips of her sword legs loudly piercing the thick ice covering the ground. "A Drizzle or a Storm would have been ideal, because of the hindered long-distance visibility. But given that we're aiming for a single moment, this might actually be quite good."

"You're right. And this much sleet's not going to block our view." Standing next to her, Fuko—Sky Raker—nodded, her sky-blue hair swinging.

Unable to immediately understand what they were talking about, Haruyuki cocked Silver Crow's round, helmeted head and asked timidly, "Um, why is Snow or Drizzle lucky?"

"Because it weakens the power of the God Suzaku, which is affiliated with fire, right?" The prompt response came from the large, close-range avatar standing to Haruyuki's right, Cyan Pile—Takumu.

Followed by Lime Bell—Chiyuri—wearing her pointed yellow-green hat and with a large bell equipped in her left hand. "So then we'd better hurry, huh? We don't know when the Change will come."

Takumu was one thing, but the feeling that he was lagging in understanding even behind Chiyuri, who had only become a Burst Linker two months earlier, was practically tangible in his hands. Haruyuki hurried to open his mouth. "S-so then I should fly us there. Four people's tough, but I could just barely—"

But before he had even gotten to the end of his sentence, Kuroyukihime was shaking her mask lightly. "No. I don't want to be disturbed by any other Burst Linkers who might be around. The possibility of being close to someone who dived at the same time is low, but flying makes us conspicuous. We'll run to the Chiyoda Area."

"Oh. Y-yeah, you're right." He hung his head.

Kuroyukihime took a few steps toward him before adding in a softer tone, "And you're the key player in this strategy. You can't tire out your wings before we get started, not even a tiny bit."

"R-right! Understo..."

*Huh? Me? The key player?*

Freezing halfway through his reply, Haruyuki felt Fuko pat him gently on the back.

"We're counting on you, Corvus. I know you can do it."

"That's right, Haru. No matter who you're up against, you can't be beat when you're in the sky."

"You'll just make it happen, Haru!"

Takumu and Chiyuri added their own encouragement, and everyone except Haruyuki nodded deeply all at once. They walked toward the opening in the exterior wall of the ice tower that had once been his skyscraper condo.

*Key player? What am I supposed to do? It can't be; no way... Maybe I'm charging into the territory of the invincible super Enemy alone or something?*

A cold sweat pouring from every part of his metal body, Haruyuki felt as though something like this had happened before, and he fumbled around in his memory. Six months earlier, a time he would never forget, when they had similarly sallied forth into the Unlimited Neutral Field from his house on the mission to subjugate the Armor of Catastrophe, he had been stunned at abruptly being ordered into an air-raid role.

*It's true I've gotten stronger in my own way since then, but even still, why is it always, always me getting the scary jobs...*He let his thoughts run in negative circles for a few seconds and then came back to himself with a gasp. He hurried to catch up with his companions, who were already jumping one after another from the balcony of ice protruding from the exterior wall of the tower. As he joined the end of that train and headed toward the surface, he tried somehow to psyche himself up.

*I mean, sure, it's a God, but in the end, it's just a bird, right? I just saw a real owl—I mean, horned owl—I mean, snow-faced owl before, didn't I? I was totally fine being in the same hutch as a real bird of prey, so I don't need to be afraid of a virtual Suzaku or sparrow or whatever. And it's not like I'm gonna fight it and try to win or anything. All I have to do is fly full speed, get Shinomiya's avatar, and then get out of there. That's totally a breeze, right?*

"Yeah! I'm gonna do it!" Haruyuki cried in a whisper beneath his helmet as he landed on the ground and started running with the others south through the large, icy valley.

The direct distance between Suginami and Chiyoda Wards was nearly ten kilometers. If they were in their real bodies, it would have been completely impossible to run all the way there at full speed without resting. But their duel avatars had no conception of fatigue, as long as they didn't go beyond a certain limit. The five fell into a wedge formation with Black Lotus at the tip, hovering at high speed, and ran intently on a route through Shinjuku starting at Kannana Street and then along Tokyo Tokorozawa Route 4.

Along the way, the shadows of large Enemies appeared countless times, but they used side roads to avoid them all. Unlike in a Primeval Forest or a Factory, there were almost no obstacles in an Ice stage, so they could use central Tokyo's dense network of roads essentially as is. However, because this also meant that there were few objects that could be destroyed, no breakable lump of ice they set their eyes upon was left unsmashed in the effort to charge up their special-attack gauges.

About forty minutes later, they had just climbed the hill continuing from Yotsuya to Kojimachi on Shinjuku Boulevard when a new scene abruptly spread out before Haruyuki's eyes.

Splendid. Magnificent. Gorgeous. No matter how many adjectives he piled on, it wasn't enough.

Several spires, like the enormous lances used by Beasts, shot up into the sky. Enshrined within, as if protected by these, was the fiercely beautiful Imperial Palace. Thick walls rose up tall all around, and these were further encircled by a deep, broad palisade. All the walls and pillars were made of ice colored a deep indigo; inside, countless red torches flickered. There was no sign of anything moving, but it most certainly wasn't an abandoned building or some kind of ruins. From the depths of the palace came the definite and intense sense of the presence of something, someone.

The Imperial Palace in the Unlimited Neutral Field—

"The Castle," Haruyuki said in a trembling voice, slowing his pace.

Before him, Kuroyukihime slowed similarly and came to a stop, carving out sharp ruts in the ice. "Yes," she replied. "The alien world in the center of the Accelerated World. The impenetrable sanctuary the former Nega Nebulus challenged with its entire force, only to be smashed to pieces in a mere two minutes."

Haruyuki's whole body shuddered at her words as he strained his eyes once more.

The castle walls, around thirty meters high, carved out what was essentially a perfect circle. The layout should have been the same as the Imperial Palace in the real world, so he assumed it was about 1,500 meters in diameter. Shinjuku Boulevard, on which they stood, stretched out ahead, becoming an ice bridge over the infinite palisade encircling the Castle. On the other side of the bridge, thirty or so meters wide and five hundred meters long, stood an imposingly massive south-facing gate, the door closed to repel all comers.

"Master, that's the west gate, corresponding to the Hanzomon Gate in the real world, isn't it?"

Kuroyukihime nodded again in reply to Takumu's question. Chiyuri jumped up onto her tiptoes and, glancing back and forth at the gate area, said doubtfully, "But Kuroyukihime...The Four Gods...That's what they're called, right? There's no huge Enemy anywhere?"

"Bell, here, look over there." Fuko walked up to stand beside Chiyuri and extended her left hand straight ahead. In the plaza beyond her fingertips where the ice bridge and the large gate connected was a slightly raised, perfectly square platform-like object. Pillars decorated each of the four corners, and the platform emanated the somehow severe air of an altar. "The instant anyone steps onto the bridge, the God pops up there. Their territory is the entire bridge, five hundred meters long and thirty meters wide. Incidentally, the palisade areas other than the bridge generate an unsuitable, abnormal gravity, making it impossible to jump over, even with my Gale Thruster. Immediately after flying out over the ravine, you're dragged into the darkness at the bottom and die instantly. In this case, you regenerate on the outside edge."

Forced to imagine falling into an infinite darkness, Haruyuki and his childhood friends were pushed into silence.

"Two and a half years ago," Kuroyukihime began speaking softly, "Raker and I commanded one squad and challenged the God Byakko, who was guarding this west gate. We had previously taken down Legends countless times with essentially the same number of people, so we were ready to fight, inwardly boastful that the super class of Enemy was nothing. But as you know, the result was an atrocity. To be honest, just standing here now and looking at the gate...my knees go weak."

"K-Kuroyukihime..." Her name slipped out of Haruyuki, and the inky black, mirrored goggles shook shortly from side to side.

"I'm sorry. I didn't mean to frighten you. Of course I have no intention of pulling back now. But, well, I want you to etch at least this into your hearts: A God is not something a person can fight. Whatever reason you might have, you absolutely must not attempt to face it. When I give the instruction, or when you personally feel that the situation has taken an unexpected turn, at that moment, use every bit of strength you have and retreat beyond the bridge."

"Th-that's—of course, we'll try to, but..."

As Haruyuki attempted to indicate his compliance, Kuroyukihime met his eyes through his helmet dead-on and said in a much more severe tone, "'Try' is not enough. This is an order. Listen. When I say run, you run. Even if I, or Raker, or even both of us are about to be killed by Suzaku."

"That's...!" Instantly, Haruyuki inhaled sharply and raised his voice. "I'm the one who's supposed to charge the bridge! You and Raker said that before, didn't you?!"

Kuroyukihime and Fuko exchanged glances, then grinned with a deep warmth that could be sensed even through the mechanical masks of their avatars. They began talking at Haruyuki from both sides, switching off with each other.

"Ha-ha! Silly Crow. I would never send you on a solo special attack."

"That's right, Corvus. Bell and Pile would get mad at us if we did."

"We'll keep Suzaku focused on us. We won't let it turn its eyes on you for even a second."

"Please, the only thing you should be thinking about is rescuing Ardor Maiden."

At this unexpected barrage, all Haruyuki could do was stare in turn at the faces of the two older Burst Linkers. The truth was, he wanted to shout, *I'll go by myself!* just like he had worked himself up to do when they left his condo. But at that point, he was utterly convinced that he could never go up against a God alone, an Enemy that made even Kuroyukihime tremble. When it came to battle ability, Haruyuki didn't even measure up to the ankles of these two older Linkers. He could insist on going, but it would be nothing more than empty posturing.

The one thing he could do was fly with all his might. That was the current Haruyuki's actual ability and limit.

Unable to say anything, he hung his head, and Chiyuri, standing to his left, patted his shoulder lightly. "Sister, I'm sorry!" she said brightly at the same time. "I thought we were all just going to cheer Crow on when he charged into Suzaku's nest alone! I wouldn't get mad, no way."

The minute she spoke, Haruyuki's knees buckled. "H-hey!" he said reflexively. "You could at least heal me!"

"Naah, that'd just make the Enemy's Hate grow."

Takumu, Kuroyukihime, and Fuko all burst out laughing.

*Right, there's one other thing I can do, and that's believe. In my friends' abilities, our bonds, and the miracles they make happen.* Murmuring to himself in his heart, Haruyuki clenched both hands tightly.

Kuroyukihime brandished the sword of her left hand in the sky. "Now we'll run for a bit more. The south gate where Suzaku and Ardor Maiden await us is to the right, down Uchibori Street."

After they had run a few minutes more, gazing at the majesty of the Castle on his left and the government district of Kasumigaseki transformed into frozen skyscrapers on his right, the second large bridge that was their destination came into view. It was exactly the same size as the one in the west: five hundred meters long, thirty wide. The perfectly square altar on the other side and the enormous castle gate beyond that were also exactly the same. In the real world, this was called Sakuradamon, the Castle's southern gate. The sacred space protected by one of the Four Gods, the fire bird Suzaku.

They proceeded forward, encountering no obstructions, and when they finally reached the foot of the icy bridge, all five pulled up in an easy stop.

Sakurada Street in the south intersected Uchibori Street stretching out east-west, creating a large junction. On the land immediately to the southwest, a large building with sharp angles soared upward. He was pretty sure that this was the National Police Agency, nicknamed Sakuradamon after the adjacent palace gate. But naturally, there wasn't a single police officer in this version of the building.

Standing in the center of the junction, Kuroyukihime pulled up the system menu from her own health gauge and checked the time. "It's been exactly an hour since we dived. So far, everything's going as planned."

That meant that 3.6 seconds had passed in the Arita living room in the real world. The amount of time it would have taken Utai waiting there without diving to take two breaths or so. But he was sure it felt several times longer than that.

Kuroyukihime whirled around. "All right, then," she said in a clear, echoing voice, looking at each of their faces in turn. "Now we carry out phase two of the Armor of Catastrophe Purification Plan: Rescue Ardor Maiden."

The other four shouted, "Yes!" together.

Nodding once, the Black King continued, radiating a dignity befitting her title. "Let's confirm the details of the plan one last time. The initial positioning is me, Black Lotus, at the very edge of the bridge base. Immediately behind me is Lime Bell. Farther behind, about two hundred meters down Sakurada Street, will be Sky Raker and Silver Crow." She paused to allow everyone to draw out these positions in their minds. "I advance, signaling the start of the operation. I proceed to the center of the bridge and make Suzaku appear. When it does, Raker takes off with Crow on her back, using the Gale Thruster. She flies full speed toward the gate at an altitude of thirty meters. During this time, I hit Suzaku with a long-distance Incarnate attack and make myself its target, then immediately start to retreat. Is everything clear so far?"

"Yes!" the four responded.

Kuroyukihime nodded once more before looking at Fuko and Haruyuki. "Immediately before Raker in flight reaches the space above myself in retreat, Crow disengages. Adding the propulsive power of your own wings, you pass above the advancing Suzaku at full speed, aiming for the south gate. Raker lands in my position and deploys a defensive Incarnate. We retreat together while guarding against Suzaku's fire breath. I intend to keep a minimum distance of a hundred meters from Suzaku's position, so we shouldn't die immediately, but we will likely take a considerable amount of damage. Bell will heal this from behind us on the bridge with her Citron Call Mode One. When Raker and I have retreated to a point near the foot of the bridge, Crow should have reached the altar of the Four Gods directly before the south gate. Ardor Maiden will appear in the center of that, so you pick her up, then a sudden ascent and a reversal of one hundred and eighty degrees. Go south over the bridge again, overtake Suzaku, and escape outside its territory. That's all."

The unfaltering explanation complete, Haruyuki expelled the breath he'd been holding.

This was the optimal solution, after careful consideration of the situation and their fighting abilities. Simple, ingenious. Once the operation began, there was no need for them to check in with one another any further. But there was one step and one factor missing.

The step was how they were going to coordinate Haruyuki's full-speed charge with Utai's dive when she was still in the real world. And the factor was one name that she hadn't mentioned in her instructions.

Having reached these questions, Haruyuki still couldn't bring himself to say anything, but almost as if she had read his mind, Kuroyukihime said, her voice dropping noticeably, "I'm sure you've all already realized this, but for this strategy to work, we need to control Utai's appearance in the Unlimited Neutral Field down to the second. And the only way to do this is for someone to leave the field and tell Utai the timing. For that role...Cyan Pile, I'd like to ask you."

"Understood, Master," Takumu replied promptly. But Haruyuki noticed that this reply was just the tiniest bit delayed compared to his usual swift reaction time.

Takumu's role of messenger to Utai in the real world was an essential element of the operation. But it was undeniable that the person selected for this would be the "last man standing." Clever Takumu must have guessed this long before Haruyuki, probably even before Kuroyukihime had begun to explain. That he alone would not be able to remain on the battlefield where their lives were going to be risked against a God.

Haruyuki wasn't sure if he should say something or not. But he understood that no matter what he said, he would just be hurting Takumu's pride. Chiyuri, who always smoothed things over at times like this, was similarly silent.

"Our opponent this time is a flying type, right?" Takumu broke this momentary quiet with his own words. "I secretly thought this might be a bit tough for me, given that I'm so rigidly a close-range type. I gladly accept the role of messenger. But, Master, when we challenge Genbu or Byakko or some close-range type in the future, please give me a chance to fight, too."

"Yes." Kuroyukihime nodded, calm as usual. "At that time, I'll name you leader of the shock corps, Pile. I'm counting on you. Get strong enough to beat them down."

"Yes, I will. I definitely will," Takumu replied, as if trying to convince himself, and nodded deeply.

Kuroyukihime turned back and took a deep breath. "Now then, any questions? Anything you want to say? Anything is fine. We do have plenty of time. I told Maiden that we'd likely make her wait five minutes at most, so if we felt like it, we could chatter away here for three days."

"What? We can't make Miss Mei wait that long. It's sad, Kuroyukihime!" Chiyuri cried. Apparently, she had settled on that nickname for Utai in the Accelerated World. She would no doubt soon come up with a name full of fondness for real-world use as well.

*Lucky. I wish I could call her a cute nickname instead of Shinomiya. Wonder if she'd get angry if I called her "Ui" like Niko...* These thoughts flitted through his mind, but Haruyuki hurriedly brushed his mental chatter aside.

There was one thing he should probably take this opportunity to say to everyone there. Something that was likely equally, if not more, important than the plan to purify the Armor of Catastrophe. Naturally, this was the matter of the mysterious parasitic object that was quietly spreading throughout the Accelerated World—the ISS kit. However, after struggling with it for a few seconds, he decided not to say anything.

At that moment, they needed to focus solely on rescuing Ardor Maiden and muster up every bit of strength they had to do so. He couldn't bring up something that was not directly connected with her and carve away even the tiniest bit of their concentration.

And he wasn't the only one who had seen the ISS kit close-up. Utai, who had exchanged Incarnate attacks directly with Bush Utan, the owner of a kit, was actually closer to the true nature of that parasitic object than he was. In which case, discussion on this matter should happen after they rescued Utai's avatar and Nega Nebulus was completely restored.

Thinking this way, Haruyuki kept his mouth closed, and Chiyuri, Takumu, and Fuko similarly did not move to speak.

"Good." Kuroyukihime nodded sharply, slowly looking at all of their faces. "It seems that you've all made your mental preparations. Now, before the start of the operation, I have just one instruction for Lime Bell. If some unexpected situation should occur and everyone on the bridge is defeated by Suzaku, you absolutely must not try to save us. You have to return to the real world via the nearest portal and pull out the cable connecting Crow's Neurolinker and his home server. Understood?"

A possibly cruel order. If they were forced to rely on this final safety, that would mean that not only Utai, but also Kuroyukihime, Fuko, and even Haruyuki had fallen into a state of unlimited EK.

But Chiyuri lifted the brim of her pointed hat resolutely and nodded firmly. "I understand, Kuroyukihime."

"We're counting on you. All right, then, shall we get started?" Kuroyukihime said casually, as if they were about to dive into the weekly battles to protect their territory.

She then turned to Takumu. "Now, Pile, there's a portal immediately after the main gate of the police station there," she instructed smoothly. "As the starting gun for the start of the operation, shoot off one blast of your Lightning Cyan Spike toward the sky before leaving for the real world. On the signal of your awakening, Utai will immediately dive. This relay will take approximately a second of real time, so the calculation is that sixteen minutes and forty seconds will pass here. During that time, Crow and Raker will drop back two hundred meters south on Sakurada Street and prepare for takeoff. A minute before Utai's appearance, I will enter the bridge. When you see Suzaku appear, Raker, take off. From there, we proceed as planned."

"Understood, Master. Okay, Raker, Bell, Crow. It's up to you now."

Instead of replying, Haruyuki thrust his right fist into the air, and Takumu met it with his left before whirling around. The blue avatar ran off without looking back and disappeared through the gates of the police station.

A few seconds later, a single bolt of lightning rose up toward the sky heavy with snow-filled clouds. Beyond the station was the Ministry of Internal Affairs and Communications, and beyond that, a forest of large buildings and the Tokyo High Court, so this light shouldn't have been visible from any position other than that of Haruyuki and his companions.

With that, in sixteen minutes and forty seconds, Utai Shinomiya—Ardor Maiden—would appear on the other side of the large bridge. Whatever happened, Haruyuki had to grab her and escape to this side of the bridge.

"Well, Crow. Shall we get moving? Bell, Lotus, good luck," Fuko said, and patted Haruyuki's shoulder.

"R-right! Kuroyukihime, um, uhh, I'm gonna do everything I can." He managed to push these few words out of a throat tight with nerves, and Kuroyukihime stared at him with violet-blue eyes.

"I know you will," she replied briefly.

The following fifteen minutes felt almost infinite and yet incredibly fast, like a raging river.

Standing next to Sky Raker equipped with her Gale Thruster, Haruyuki intently tried to focus his mind, but he couldn't even tell if he was succeeding in that or simply drowning in the random noise of his brain. Snowflakes danced down in the now-silent Unlimited Neutral Field; time itself seemed to have frozen.

Even at this distance, the massive castle gate to the north of Sakurada Street, enshrined another seven hundred meters beyond the length of the bridge, had lost almost none of its imposing presence. It obstructed Haruyuki's view almost as if it locked away the world itself.

"Two and a half years ago, you tried to break that gate down," he muttered, almost unconsciously, and Fuko immediately next to him let slip a faint smile.

"Not just the gate. We tried to attack the castle on the other side."

"Oh, r-right."

There was no doubt that the first Nega Nebulus had been a

much more fearsome group than it was now. Haruyuki sighed at the thought and then gave voice to the question that abruptly popped up in his mind.

"But during the fight then, why did you decide to take on all four of the Gods? I know Kuroyukihime said yesterday that the Four Gods are four parts of one body, but there are four gates, so wouldn't it have been better for the entire Legion to attack one of them?"

"That's exactly what some people thought a long time ago, and so they tried it. And what they learned was that the Four Gods are linked to one another. Whenever one of them alone is attacked, the other three send healing spells and it ends up being quite the battle. But today, we're not trying to defeat it, so that doesn't matter right now."

"Oh, th-that makes sense."

Thinking about it, if Haruyuki could come up with that idea, then it was only natural that it had already been tested. Bobbing his head up and down, he continued. "Right. There must be a ton of Legions who've challenged the palace. And not just the Castle. They dug around in unexplored areas; they came up with all kinds of battle techniques. They're lucky. If I had become a Burst Linker sooner—"

"Hee-hee-hee, what are you talking about, Corvus?" Fuko cut him off with a smile and words like a sigh, and suddenly hugged Haruyuki tightly. He froze, while a somehow playful whisper reached his ear. "It starts now. Your Brain Burst—all of it starts now, Corvus. For me and Lotus as well. The road we thought was ending really goes on and on. It spreads out infinitely. And you're the one who made me realize this."

The hands circling around his back held him even more tightly. The voice that rose up in his ear also was tinged with a warmth to melt the chill of the Ice stage. "In your silver wings is the power to open the world, Corvus. Your future spreads out in every direction. I want to see where those wings take you. I'm sure Lotus and Maiden feel the same way. Now then, shall we go rescue her? It's time." Gently, she released him from her embrace.

At some point, Haruyuki's mind had become completely clear, filled with a single, firm purpose.

Fly. He would simply fly. That ability was the reason for the existence of Silver Crow, this avatar that Haruyuki's heart had given birth to.

"Yes!" Haruyuki assented firmly.

Sky Raker kneeled down, back turned to him. He set his knee down in the center of the two rocket boosters of her Enhanced Armament Gale Thruster, and grabbed tightly onto her shoulders.

"I'm ready."

Fuko nodded and stared intently at the large bridge before them.

There were two small shadows at the foot of it: Black Lotus and Lime Bell. Ten seconds later, Lotus brandished high the sword of her right hand and brought it down sharply.

# 11

The Black King advanced, a single soldier.

She stepped onto the bridge stretching out five hundred meters from the Castle's south gate. She spread both arms out diagonally to her rear and, in a form that had her body pitched forward as far as it could go, she charged, carving deep ruts in the ice at her feet.

*Bomf!* Beyond her, in the center of the square altar that lay on the other side of the bridge, a bright red flame appeared. Swirling, vortex-like, the flames grew in intensity before Haruyuki's eyes. Soon, the entire twenty meters of one side of the altar was transformed into a sea of fire. In the center of that, something—a terrifyingly enormous *something*—was beginning to materialize.

"Here we go!" Fuko shouted back to Haruyuki, the instant they saw it.

The Gale Thruster howled beneath him. Its pale flames shot out and illuminated their surroundings, instantly vaporizing the ice on the road. The incredible thrust shot the two duel avatars off the ground like a catapult.

Air howled in his ears; to resist the roaring wind pressure, Haruyuki pressed himself as close as he could to Fuko's back. The details of the buildings on both sides melted into flowing lines of pale blue. The sound of the Thruster grew louder and louder and louder.

Their two-hundred-meter runway was very rapidly approaching

its end. In the blink of an eye, they had flown by Lime Bell, the bell of her left hand readied, in the center of the large intersection. The pair charged on, into the sky over the bridge, racing forward at maximum speed and an altitude of thirty meters.

Ahead of them, the something that was born from the sea of flames was taking on a clear shape.

First, two massive wings spread out to both sides, scattering glittering droplets like molten metal. Their span was essentially the width of the bridge; each and every feather, a devil's flaming sword. Snowflakes dancing in the atmosphere evaporated long before they touched those wings.

Between the outstretched appendages, sturdy shoulders appeared next, followed by a long, arched neck jerking upward, and then a head began to materialize. Decorative feathers extending sharply like a dragon's horns. Long, pointed beak. And even more dazzling than the flames, glittering more redly than rubies: two eyes.

The massive bird shrouded in flames—guardian of the Castle, super-level Enemy, the God Suzaku—turned its open beak toward the heavens and released a tremendous roar.

The moment this war cry and the infinite rumbling of piercing thunder coiled around it shook the world, Haruyuki saw it. The thick clouds blanketing the sky rippled and shuddered and briefly ripped outward in circular waves.

What was this thing?

What. Was. It? An Enemy? A soulless monster moved by the Brain Burst program?

No. That...that bird was alive. Angry at having its slumber disturbed, it rampaged to burn up the intruders. It seemed to be made of nothing but rejection and the intention to attack, the very concept of an unbelievable titan...

It was a pure aggregate of the will to destroy.

The moment he realized this, Haruyuki was aware of his own resolve to fly wavering inside himself.

He cowered. This presence in the Accelerated World he had once wanted to see, this manifestation of absolute power that eclipsed even the Seven Kings of Pure Color, who Haruyuki had found so overwhelming only a few days earlier, burned into all the channels of his five senses, and his breathing stopped.

...*We can't. That's...I can't go near that thing*...The thought pierced the center of his numbed consciousness.

But Sky Raker's flight did not stop. On the contrary, the noise from the Gale Thruster grew louder and louder, and the flames jetting out seemed to stretch on forever. The enormous flame bird in the distance flapped its wings and began to move forward from the altar. Even with the sensation of acceleration pressing down on him, the distance between them and it decreased with terrifying speed.

Haruyuki's hands shook and unconsciously, he began to pull his fingertips from Raker's shoulders.

Instantly.

Black Lotus, standing less than a hundred meters below him up ahead, abruptly began to gush dazzling rays of light from her entire body—the overlay of her Incarnate. The color was a pure red, rivaling that of the flames enshrouding the massive bird.

"Aaaaaaaaah!!" Kuroyukihime's fierce battle cry ripped open the heavens. The ghostly light of her Incarnate doubled in intensity. From her avatar, starlike in its brilliance, a crisp voice was released: "Overdrive!! Mode Red!!"

It was a command Haruyuki didn't know. And the phenomenon that it brought about was also unknown to him.

Vivid red lines popped up on Black Lotus's jet-black armor. At the same time, the design of the sword of her right hand changed. It grew 50 percent longer, the tip constricting into a diamond shape. It was no longer a sword; it was a lance.

Kuroyukihime forcefully pulled that arm back and made a cross with the sword of her left hand, readied horizontally. The overlay pouring out of every crevice of her body at once gathered in her right arm, to concentrate in a single point at the tip.

This force, focused to such an extreme that it threatened to carve a hole in anything it even touched, was released at the charging God Suzaku as she shouted the technique name.

"Vorpal Strike!!"

A roar like a jet engine, loud enough to drown out the howls of the massive bird, accompanied the enormous crimson lance as it shot over a hundred meters in an instant to land squarely in the center of Suzaku's thick chest. The flames enshrouding the Enemy scattered into space like blood.

And then Haruyuki was sure he saw it. Suzaku's HP gauge—so vast, it was stacked up in five layers—sliced away, albeit just the tiniest bit.

*Kuroyukihime. Kuroyukihime. You, why...How did you get so strong...*

The thought that flashed through the back of his mind was rejected by another emotion that came welling up from the bottom of his stomach.

*Her, strong? No. I already know that's not it. She's simply* trying *to be strong. For her own sake. For someone's sake. For that something important shining in her heart. And I am, too. Right now, I don't have enough power or brains or anything, but I can move forward. And that is real strength, the kind that anyone has right from the start. Move forward, breathe, throw your chest out. Okay, howl it!!*

"Hnngaaaaaah!!"

"Fly!!" Fuko responded.

"Here I go!!"

*Shhp!* He spread the wings on his back; he beat the ten metal fins with every ounce of his strength—Haruyuki flew.

The air howled in his ears, compressed, became a wall. He broke through with the glittering of the Incarnate lodged in fingertips stretched out before him. *Fmp!* The pressure was broken. Haruyuki became a single beam of silver light and plunged forward.

Ahead and slightly below, the enormous body of Suzaku drew nearer with every breath. Blazing heat, as though burning the air itself, beat at his avatar. But he no longer felt any fear. Because Haruyuki wasn't alone. Kuroyukihime, Fuko, Chiyuri, Takumu—they were all holding him up.

And that younger girl, too, who was, at that precise moment, landing in the Unlimited Neutral Field for the first time in two and a half years.

He had only met her two days earlier, but Utai Shinomiya was already a firm presence in Haruyuki's heart. And not because she was going to purify the Armor of Catastrophe. Not because she would strengthen the Legion's fighting ability. He wanted her to join the new Nega Nebulus as a new friend.

That was what he was flying for now. Without fear, without flinching: simply moving forward. Ever forward.

Silver Crow, a silver arrow racing along at an altitude of thirty meters, and Suzaku, charging ahead on the bridge with a roar, crossed paths, sending several sparks flying.

Suzaku kept on, rushing toward Kuroyukihime behind him and Fuko, who should have landed beside their fallen comrade by now. All that was left was for the two of them to lure the Enemy far back, onto the bridge. All he had to do was believe in them and let them handle it.

Ahead of him as he charged forward, in the center of the altar from which scattered flames still rose, *fmp!*—a scarlet flickering.

She was here. Utai, Ardor Maiden. Perfect timing. Takumu had pulled off his role as messenger flawlessly. The shrine maiden avatar clad in white and red materialized before his eyes. He wasn't even a hundred meters away now. To pick Utai up, Haruyuki went to drop altitude.

At that moment—

"Haruyuki!!"

A shriek colored with shock and terror and despair.

The shout of his real name, a fundamental taboo in the Accelerated World, was followed from behind by "Run!! You have to get away now!!"

"......?!" Unable to comprehend the situation, Haruyuki glanced back over his shoulder.

And then he saw it.

The God Suzaku tilting those wings and pulling into a turn to the left. Its long neck carved out an arc, and the deep red eyes were focused straight ahead on this side of the bridge—on Haruyuki.

Its target had most definitely changed. But why? He could see the lingering damage effects of Kuroyukihime's Vorpal Sword in Suzaku's chest. Haruyuki, on the other hand, hadn't even touched his Enemy. It didn't make sense for it to come after him. As these confused thoughts flashed through his mind, he felt like he heard a voice.

The anger, the disdain of the Enemy, supposedly nothing more than a moving object without a will of its own.

*Small one. Accept the reward for the folly of penetrating Our domain. The flame of Our breath…*

*Become ash.*

The enormous beak opened wide.

Flames flickered in the depths of a throat filled with darkness. The breath attack. If he got hit with that, there was no doubt he would die instantly.

*Run, Haruyuki!!*

He heard Kuroyukihime shrieking again.

For an extremely tiny unit of time, so short that the word *instant* was even too long, Haruyuki hesitated.

If he rapidly ascended right then, he could probably evade the breath. If he kept going all the way up to Silver Crow's maximum altitude of fifteen hundred meters, Suzaku probably wouldn't come after him. But…

Aah, but

Haruyuki gritted his teeth below his silver mask so hard, they threatened to crumble.

And then he made his decision.

He wouldn't pull back. He couldn't run away here. If he ran now, Utai Shinomiya, waiting for him just a dozen or so meters ahead, would be attacked by Suzaku and die. And if that were to happen, she wouldn't reproach Haruyuki returning to the real world. She would probably tell him in her usual high-speed typing, YOU HAD NO OTHER CHOICE.

But the truth was, he did have a choice. Because in that moment, Haruyuki could choose what he was going to do. Because he had been given these wings to keep flying toward her as long as there was the tiniest possibility that he could rescue Utai.

"Unh…Aaah…" Returning his gaze once more to the altar, he pushed his voice out from the depths of his stomach.

"Aaaaaaaaaaaah!!"

With this battle cry, Haruyuki mustered up every ounce of his focus, so much so that he almost burnt out the synapses in his brain, and made his wings flutter. The light housed in the tips of his two hands, thrust out straight ahead, spread out over his entire body. Wrapped in the same silver overlay as when he used his sole Incarnate attack Laser Sword, Haruyuki plunged forward.

Behind him, he sensed an incredible energy being generated. A vortex of flame to instantly vaporize all things was released from Suzaku's maw, and coming at him, dyeing the world crimson.

*Haruyuki!!*

*Corvus!!*

*Haruuuuuuu!!*

The three screams barely touched his awareness. But he shook free of even that, became a single ray of light, and flew.

*Kuroyukihime. I know I promised to run when you said to run. I'm sorry. I'll apologize loads and loads later. But in order for me to keep being me, I have to do this now.*

This fleeting thought became a white spark, bounced off, and disappeared, and then there was nothing left in him but the will to keep pushing ahead.

He was getting closer to the altar with each thought of a breath. Ardor Maiden, who had appeared in its center, was simply standing there, as though she couldn't understand what was going on.

Haruyuki stared at the small shrine maiden and shouted in a voice that was not a voice, *Your hand!!*

Like a switch had been flipped, Ardor Maiden raised her slender hands.

Dropping down to a meter above the bridge, Haruyuki stretched out his own arms. Their hands touched, and they grabbed tightly on to each other—Haruyuki yanked Utai's avatar up with all his might and held her to his chest.

*Hold on!!* he shouted again, and Utai's arms were no sooner around his neck than he was climbing once more. He would do a 180-degree loop, turn around, and escape—

Abruptly, the world around him changed color.

Flickering with a wavelength from orange to crimson. Red. The color of fire.

His avatar's entire body sang out. Suzaku's flame breath had caught up with them. Despite the fact that the flames themselves couldn't be touching them yet, the HP gauge in the top left of his vision was decreasing with terrifying force.

It was impossible. He couldn't ascend. The instant he dropped his speed by even the tiniest amount, they would be swallowed in the flames and melt. He had no choice but to keep going straight. But not far ahead of them, the rock of the castle gate was blocking the way.

For his self-respect, at least, perhaps the only thing to do was end this by crashing into the gate. But no—he hadn't come that far to commit suicide. He was going to live. He was going to survive with Utai. He would do it.

"Open!!" Haruyuki shouted, the surface of his avatar crackling and burning.

At the same time, Utai in his arms raised her own voice. "You must open!!"

But the thick, ice-covered indigo castle gates stayed firmly, tightly closed, as if mocking them.

*No.*

A light…

In the center of the doors standing tall, he could see a mere sliver of white light, like a thread.

# 12

Quiet.

Cold. And hard.

He was lying with his right side on a crisply chill, level surface. Almost as if his entire body had been frozen solid. He couldn't move his limbs at all.

But he felt a mysterious warmth in his arms. *Throb. Throb.* An indistinct vibration. It was…

Suddenly, he heard a voice. "This is a little uncomfortable."

Haruyuki's eyes flew open with a gasp. He saw round, cute scarlet eye lenses before him. "Ah!" he said, and worked his frozen arms to loosen his hold. The adorable face mask receded slightly.

"Sh-Shino—I mean, Mei?" he murmured in a shaky voice, and her mask moved up and down.

A pure, quiet voice reached his ears. "That's right. You saved me, C."

Those words sent a jolt through him.

He couldn't really remember what had happened. He had picked up Ardor Maiden standing on the altar…run from Suzaku's flame breath…plunged straight into the closed castle gates…

What had happened after that? Were they actually dead? Was this the ghost state?

No, if it was, everything in his field of view would have changed to a single shade. But at that moment, he could clearly see that Utai's eye lenses were glittering like rubies.

Still unable to believe that they had managed to flee from that terrifying vortex of flame, Haruyuki asked in a hoarse voice, "Um, are we maybe alive...?"

Utai nodded firmly once more. "We are alive. But...aah, but..." The end of her sentence was husky, and it shivered and melted into the chill air before disappearing.

Ardor Maiden shifted her gaze to the cold gloom of the space around them. In an extremely, terribly faint whisper, she announced to Haruyuki, "Here...This place is inside the Castle."

**To be continued.**

# AFTERWORD

Reki Kawahara here, bringing you *Accel World 6: Shrine Maiden of the Sacred Fire*. This is probably the book that's taken the longest to write out of the series so far. But I do hope you enjoyed it…?

Now then, there are many, many things that I lack as a novelist (patience, ambition, the ability to work at home…), but the one I am most lacking that I am aware of is the ability to bring a story to a neat end.

To be honest, although I've created a variety of stories for more than eight years now, including when I was writing web novels, not a single one of them had a proper ending! In my maiden long-form work, *Sword Art Online*, right up into my first published work, *Accel World*, I end with "Our fight starts now!" and all. (I break out into a cold sweat now, wondering at the fact that I even won that award.)

It's not as though I'll be completing it any time soon, but having written this much of *Accel World*, I have been sort of wondering exactly how I'm going to end this story. I have absolutely no clue, by the way (lol). I can imagine all sorts of ways to expand it, and yet no ideas to wrap it all up come to mind; I can't help but feel this is not great for a novelist.

That said, as a reader, I actually love stories that end in this open manner. Of course, it's wonderful when the story ends with a detailed explanation of the rest of the main character's life chronology-style, but I suppose I'd have to say that I want that feeling of "their story continues into the future as well." In RPGs, too, I totally love the world after you beat the game (lol). If I ever get the chance to make a game, I want to make one that has a bonus scenario that's three times as long as the game itself that starts playing once the end credits are done! Or rather, someone, please make this game!

But I digress. All of this is to say, I have the keen feeling that this *Accel World*, too, in the ending that will likely come someday, will find some footing along the likes of "our fight...," so let me apologize for that now. I'm sorry!

I got a little carried away with the previous volume, which set me behind on my schedule, but despite this very great inconvenience, the illustrator HIMA was kind enough to draw a cover so wonderful it took my breath away. And my editor, Miki, who made no fuss about lending me three hundred yen when sad little me forgot my wallet. Once again, I am in your debt! And everyone who has read with me so far, my apologies for ending with a "to be continued" again! I'll give this a proper conclusion in the next book probably! Taku will probably be part of the action, even!

Reki Kawahara
On a certain day in August 2010

# THE CHART-TOPPING SERIES THAT SPAWNED THE EXPLOSIVELY POPULAR ANIME ADAPTATIONS!

**SWORD ART ONLINE, VOL. 1-4**
**LIGHT NOVEL SERIES**
SWORD ART ONLINE © Reki Kawahara
KADOKAWA CORPORATION ASCII MEDIA WORKS

**SWORD ART ONLINE, PROGRESSIVE 1**
**LIGHT NOVEL SERIES**
SWORD ART ONLINE: PROGRESSIVE © Reki Kawahara
KADOKAWA CORPORATION ASCII MEDIA WORKS

**SWORD ART ONLINE, PROGRESSIVE 1**
**MANGA SERIES**
Sword Art Online: Progressive
© REKI KAWAHARA / KISEKI HIMURA
KADOKAWA CORPORATION ASCII MEDIA WORKS

**SWORD ART ONLINE, VOL. 1-4**
**MANGA SERIES**
SWORD ART ONLINE: Aincrad
© Reki Kawahara / Tamako Nakamura /
KADOKAWA CORPORATION ASCII MEDIA WORKS

**SWORD ART ONLINE, GIRLS' OPS, VOL. 1**
**MANGA SERIES**
Sword Art Online: Girls' Ops © REKI KAWAHARA /
NEKO NEKOBYOU
KADOKAWA CORPORATION ASCII MEDIA WORKS

**VISIT YENPRESS.COM**
**TO CHECK OUT ALL THESE TITLES AND MORE!**

www.YenPress.com

ACCEL WORLD, Volume 6
REKI KAWAHARA

Translation by Jocelyne Alen


Edited by ASCII MEDIA WORKS
First published in Japan in 2010 by KADOKAWA CORPORATION, Tokyo.
English translation rights arranged with KADOKAWA CORPORATION, Tokyo,
through Tuttle-Mori Agency, Inc., Tokyo.



Yen On
Hachette Book Group
1290 Avenue of the Americas
New York, NY 10104
www.hachettebookgroup.com
www.yenpress.com

Yen On is an imprint of Hachette Book Group, Inc.
The Yen On name and logo are trademarks of Hachette Book Group, Inc.

First Yen On edition: March 2016

Library of Congress Cataloging-in-Publication Data

Names: Kawahara, Reki, author. | HIMA (Comic book artist) illustrator.
Title: Shrine maiden of the sacred fire / Reki Kawahara ; illustrations, HIMA ; design, beepee.
Other titles: Jōka no Miko. English
Description: New York, NY : Yen On, 2016. | Series: Accel world ; 6 |
Summary: During the battle with the Acceleration Research Society, Haruyuki sustained corrosion damage from the revived Chrome Disaster and now he must undergo a grueling purification process, or risk being cast out of the Accelerated World.
Identifiers: LCCN 2015049264 | ISBN 9780316296403 (paperback)
Subjects: | CYAC: Science fiction. | Virtual reality—Fiction. | Fantasy. |
BISAC: FICTION / Science Fiction / General.
Classification: LCC PZ7.K1755 Sh 2016 | DDC [Fic] —dc23 LC record available at http://lccn.loc.gov/2015049264

10 9 8 7 6 5 4 3 2 1

RRD-C

Printed in the United States of America